Meet Me at Willoughby Close

Meet Me at Willoughby Close

A Willoughby Close Romance

KATE HEWITT

TULE
PUBLISHING

Chapter One

I T WAS RAINING in the Cotswolds. Icy, sleeting drizzle that slicked the roads and froze to the windscreen. Wasn't it supposed to be sunny here? Ellie Matthews craned her neck, her fingers clenched the steering wheel, as she peered through the iced-over windscreen. Night had fallen hours ago and her daughter Abby had stopped with her heavy, theatrical sighs awhile back, which was a bad sign. It meant she'd given up, and that made Ellie feel like giving up as well.

It wasn't supposed to be like this. It was supposed to be sunny, first of all, even if it was six o'clock on a January evening, which meant, in any part of England, unending darkness. But in Ellie's mind it had been sunny and stupidly, it had also been spring. There might have been a few rainbows and unicorns in her blissed-out fantasy of their new start in life. Wychwood-on-Lea *might* have looked the tiniest bit like the set of a musical, with people singing and dancing in the streets. But whatever. It wasn't supposed to be bloody raining.

In the back of her beat-up estate that had seen better days ten years and a hundred and fifty thousand miles ago, Marmite gave a doleful *woof.*

"Sorry, buddy," Ellie called back. "We'll be there soon." Her poor dog hadn't had a wee since Birmingham, which should have only been an hour ago, but with the state of the roads and the fact that her sat nav seemed intent on putting Wychwood-on-Lea in deepest Shropshire, it had been a lot longer than that.

In the passenger seat next to her Abby stirred, blowing a strand of hair from her eyes and refolding her arms in a way Ellie knew well. Her daughter was not happy. But then, her daughter was rarely happy, and Ellie couldn't blame her. Things were going to be different here in Oxfordshire. She'd promised both Abby and herself that they would be. They needed to be. But first it had to stop raining.

"I think we're almost there," she said to Abby, who exhaled loudly.

"How on earth would you know?"

She wouldn't. "I have a feeling," Ellie answered. "A good one." She'd abandoned the sat nav several miles back, when it had tetchily informed her, the computerized voice seeming to get stroppier by the second, that she needed to make an immediate U-turn and get back on the M6. No, she did not.

"I know we're close," Ellie persisted. "We drove through Chipping Norton and that's only a few miles from Wychwood-on-Lea. It's somewhere around here…" She leaned forward again, squinting to peer through the windscreen. The car's laboring defrost wasn't up to melting the ice that stuck to the glass in a bobbly pattern, presenting her with a distinctly warped view of the world. Not that there was much to see. West Oxfordshire's county council didn't seem to splash out on much street lighting in between its picturesque hamlets.

"Mum." Abby grabbed her arm, making Ellie let out a little shriek as the tires skidded across the wet road and Marmite whined from the back. "It's there. Turn right. *Turn right!"*

Ellie had a glimpse of a miniscule sign pointing towards an alarmingly narrow road before she jerked the car to the right, tires squealing, sending them careening towards a prickly hedge, visions of ambulances and A&E dancing through Ellie's stunned brain before she managed to even the car out. She pressed the brakes, her heart thudding, as she pulled over. Sweat prickled between her shoulder blades and she let out a shuddering breath.

"Goodness, that was close."

"It certainly was. You almost missed the turn." Abby gave her the glimmer of a smile, sunlight breaking through the scowl, and Ellie smiled back. It wasn't her daughter's fault that life had been such hard going. But things really were going to be different here. Maybe there wouldn't be rainbows or unicorns or people singing on street corners, but Ellie hoped more than anything that her daughter could find a friend.

"Okay." She took another deep breath and then glanced at the narrow road they'd just turned down, hemmed in by hawthorn hedge on either side, the stark branches gleaming darkly in the rain. "So. This is the way to Wychwood-on-Lea. Good eye, Abby."

"Thanks."

Taking another big breath, Ellie glanced behind her at the dark, rainy road before indicating and then pulling back on. "We're almost there. Really, I mean."

"What, you were lying before?"

"I was being optimistic."

She'd been trying to stay optimistic for the last month, or really forever, but especially since she'd bagged a job as administrative assistant for the history faculty at the University of Oxford. Considering her only job experience was ten years of working in a GP's office in suburban Manchester, it seemed incredible—a true miracle on par with statues crying real tears—that she'd been hired. She'd only applied for the job on a whim, if you could call desperation a whim. With Nathan announcing a sudden, open-ended trip to Australia and the mean girls of Year Six finding fresh ways to make Abby's life even more of a misery, not to mention her parents' suffocating concern coupled with more than a dash of condescension, a new start for them both had started to seem imperative.

And she liked the sound of Oxford, had imagined working in a medieval building with all those dusty books and dreaming spires. She'd pictured herself cycling down some narrow, cobbled street, or sipping espresso and talking about modern art in some bohemian café.

Of course it wouldn't be like that—she didn't know the first thing about modern art—but she'd needed to hold on to that rose-tinted image to keep her nerve. After ten years spent more or less in a rut the big, wide world was a little frightening.

Her mother's skepticism and her sister's disbelief had fueled her determination to prove them—and her own secret fears—wrong, and when she'd found a rental cottage in a village only half an hour from Oxford, it had felt like another miracle—as well as some much-needed validation. She'd rented it over the phone, without even coming down to take a look, trusting that the photos were accurate and the estate agent was honest. This was going to work. She'd make sure of it.

"So this is Wychwood-on-Lea," Ellie murmured as a few buildings came into view. She drove at a crawling pace down the village's high street, first past a dark expanse of village green and then on to a narrow street with terraced houses and shops on either side. And... that was it. Wychwood-on-Lea was in the blink-and-you'd-miss-it category, but that was okay.

She'd been tired of city living. Endless noise, all that pollution, and it wasn't as if she ever took advantage of any culture. The cinema once a month for the latest fantasy film—Abby's choice—was about as far as she got. Abby had been a bit nonplussed to discover the cinema nearest to their new home was fifteen miles away. Her daughter wasn't as convinced about the benefits of moving to Oxfordshire as Ellie was. Yet.

"Now we need to find Willoughby Close." The cottage she'd rented was part of the converted stables of a manor house, and it had looked incredibly charming on the website, four lovely little houses of golden Cotswold stone, with oak doors and mullioned windows, all of them sharing a cute, cobbled courtyard. Ellie had imagined chatting with her neighbors over coffee, children running in and out of houses. They'd be like a family, only better, because they wouldn't sigh and shake their heads and wonder where she'd gone wrong.

"Willoughby Close is near Willoughby Manor, isn't it?" Abby asked and Ellie put on the brakes. Gently.

"Yes, why?"

"Because there's a sign that way." She pointed to a little brown sign that aimed at a single-track lane off the high street.

"Great," Ellie said, injecting a double shot of enthusiasm into her voice. "This is it."

Two minutes later she was maneuvering the car through a pair of imposing wrought iron gates, and then turning off the sweeping drive onto a decidedly rutted track, hemmed in on either side by cedar trees. It looked rather dark and foreboding, and Abby had folded her arms again, which was even more ominous.

Ellie drove around a curve and then they were there, the cottages of Willoughby Close just as they'd looked on the website. Well, mostly. Sort of. They were swathed in darkness, not a single light on, and no cars or bikes or signs of any life at all. The whole place looked kind of… empty.

"Everyone must be out," Ellie said uncertainly. She hadn't been expecting a welcoming committee, but it would have been nice to see a few lighted windows, a friendly neighbor poking her head out the door and exclaiming, *"Oh, you must be Ellie and Abby. We've been waiting for you."* Okay, yes. A welcoming committee. Seriously, what was she like? It was as if no one but her had ever moved house before.

"Come on," Ellie said as she pulled in front of Number One and turned off the car. "Marmite needs a wee."

She got out of the car, icy rain needling her in the face as she opened the boot and Marmite lumbered out with a sigh and a fart. Lovely. Her giant, hairy beast of a dog, half Golden Retriever and half Rottweiler, began to sniff around. Abby climbed out of the passenger side, arms still folded, and glanced dubiously at their new home.

"This is it?"

"Yes, isn't it lovely?" Ellie held onto her cheer with effort. She knew Abby wasn't thrilled with the move, but the

cottage *was* pretty. The little cobbled courtyard was sur-
rounded on three sides by friendly-looking cottages, even if
they were empty and lightless at the moment, and in the
distance Ellie could see the dark towers of the manor house
thrusting against a darker sky. "Come on, let's have a look."

"What about our stuff?"

"We'll unload later." They'd only brought boxes of
clothes, books, dishes, and linens from Manchester. The
tatty, secondhand furniture Ellie had had for her entire adult
life she'd consigned to the skip. New start, new furniture.
She'd had two beds and a kitchen table delivered to the
cottage already, and the caretaker, Jace Tucker, had emailed
her yesterday to say they'd arrived and were safely inside.
The rest they could pick up in bits and pieces, poking
through charming charity shops in quaint villages on sunny
Saturday afternoons. That was part of the ever-increasing
fantasy too. It was all, Ellie told herself yet again as she
unlocked the front door, going to be fabulous.

The door creaked open and the smell of fresh paint, plaster, and unused appliances hit her. Ellie fumbled for the
lights as Abby squeezed past her and Marmite butted into
her legs, making her nearly fall over.

"Here." Abby flipped the switch on the other side of the
door, bathing the room in a bright, electric glow. Ellie gazed
around, blinking. It was very empty. Not, of course, that that
should be a surprise, but somehow she'd been expecting…
what? House fairies to have magically furnished her new

home?

"Is that our beds?" Abby nudged a cardboard box that did not look big enough to hold two beds. Some assembly required was, Ellie suspected, going to be a massive understatement. "What about the mattresses?"

Mattresses. Ellie stared at her daughter, her smile finally starting to slip. She'd bloody forgotten to buy mattresses. "Sorry, Abby," she said, and her daughter shrugged, scuffing one foot along the floor, before turning away.

"It's okay."

Of course it was. Abby could huff and sigh with the best of them, but ultimately she stuck by her mother. The two of them against the world for what felt like forever, battling a deadbeat dad and mean girls and condescending if well-intentioned relatives, but here they were finally going to find some allies. Some friends.

"I'll go online tonight," Ellie promised. "And do expedited delivery so we'll have them tomorrow."

"We don't have Wi-Fi, Mum," Abby said. She sounded like a mother reminding a child of the house rules.

"I'll sort that out too." Ellie knuckled her forehead, wondering if it would be wrong to dig out the bottle of wine she'd stuck in their start-up box of emergency provisions—tea, kettle, mugs, bowls, cereal, bread, and of course chocolate spread. And wine. "At least we have a few days to sort ourselves out." It was Thursday, and Abby wasn't starting school until Monday. Ellie had arranged to start her job on

Tuesday, to make sure she could take Abby to school for that first all-important day.

"Right."

"It is a nice place, though, don't you think?" Ellie walked around the downstairs of the cottage, which was one large open-plan living area. The kitchen was tucked in a corner, all granite counters and stainless steel appliances, neither of which had featured in their boxy two up-two down back in Manchester. A woodstove beckoned invitingly, empty and cold as it was currently, in another corner, and a pair of French windows overlooked a garden now cloaked in impenetrable darkness, but Ellie was sure it would look pretty in the morning.

"Shall we look at the upstairs?" she asked, and Abby nodded.

Up a steep staircase was a tiny hall landing, two bed-rooms, both with built-in cupboards, and a bathroom that had a gorgeous claw-footed tub and a glassed-in shower, both which made Ellie want to strip off and immerse herself in hot water immediately.

"Nice bathroom," Abby said grudgingly, and Ellie grinned.

"I'll say. You can have dibs on the tub."

"I'll take the shower."

"Perfect. Now." She clapped her hands before heading downstairs again. "We need to sort out supper and Marmite and sleep, in that order."

"Okay." This counted for enthusiasm from her daughter, and with a bounce in her step, Ellie headed back outside. The rain had tapered off and clouds parted to reveal a sliver of moon that bathed the little courtyard in silver. Never mind rainbows, this was perfect. It would be perfect. Ellie took a deep breath of fresh, cold air, letting it fill her lungs and buoy her soul. Here was their new start, at last.

They started hauling boxes from the back of the car, dishes rattling around and Marmite sniffing hopefully at an open sack of dog food. Ellie had just put down a rather heavy box of Abby's fantasy books when she felt her phone buzz in her pocket. Repeatedly.

"That must be Gran," she said as she slid her phone from the pocket and swiped the screen with her thumb. Seven missed calls and four new voicemails. That seemed excessive even for her parents.

Frowning, Ellie thumbed a few buttons. She hadn't heard her phone ring, but reception had been patchy on the narrow roads between here and the M6. Patchier, it seemed, than she'd realized.

The first message was, predictably, from her mum. After living two streets away from her parents since she was nineteen, and seeming to disappoint them at every turn, they were understandably worried by Ellie moving two hundred and fifty miles south.

"Just wanted to make sure you arrived all right, darling… it is raining an awful lot, but perhaps not down in Oxford…

but the roads are tricky and you've never had the best sense of direction, have you? I'm really not sure about all this, Ellie... I still don't understand why you had to traipse off to Oxford of all places..." Her mother let out an all too familiar, weary sigh. "Please do ring... I know you're busy but I'll feel better when I know you're safe. Nathan phoned, by the way," she added, her voice brightening. "He arrived in Australia safely. Just wanted to let us know. Wasn't that kind of him? All right, then." Of course Nathan would phone her mum, and not his own daughter. Her ex-husband had a bad case of Peter Pan syndrome, and her mum couldn't help but play Wendy. Sighing, Ellie deleted the message.

She listened to the next message, this one from her sister Diane.

"Just checking you arrived in one piece. And I cleaned your flat for you, since I'm not sure you remembered that and I think you might want your deposit back. The toilet was disgusting, by the way." Diane sounded both brisk and self-righteous, which was not surprising since it tended to be her default setting, although she always meant well. She was protective of Ellie to the point of deep irritation, although Ellie tried not to mind too much because even though they were as different as they could possibly be—Diane having married, had three children at neat two-year intervals and now working part-time as a physiotherapist while Ellie had bumbled and scraped her way through an unplanned pregnancy, school dropout, and a marriage that never should

have happened—her sister had been there for her. Repeatedly, and at the most crucial time. Still, her bossy older sister rants got a little old, as did the assumption that Ellie was essentially hopeless, shared by their parents, even though she'd held down a steady job for a decade, raised her daughter essentially on her own, and still managed to stay sane. She loved Diane, but she wouldn't mind living a little bit farther away from her, as well as her mum and dad. Three people who loved her to bits but were constantly acting as if she couldn't find her head if it wasn't screwed on. She needed the distance to remind herself that she was a capable, organized, confident person. At least, she was trying to be.

Third message. "I'm trying to reach Eleanor Matthews." The male voice and cut-glass syllables were both unrecognizable. "She was due to start work as my personal assistant today, and I've been trying to reach her for several hours. If this is Miss Matthews, could she please ring me, Dr. Oliver Venables, as soon as possible? Thank you." The sudden, loud click of the phone being hung up hurt Ellie's ear.

Her stomach plunged unpleasantly as she tried to process the message. She wasn't due to start at the history faculty until Tuesday, and she didn't even know who this Dr. Oliver Venables was. She was a general administrative assistant, i.e., dogsbody, to the faculty, not someone's personal secretary. She was tempted to ignore the call, but she had a feeling that would be a bad idea. He'd sounded important and worse, irritated.

"Mum?"

Ellie looked up to see Abby standing in the kitchen area, a half-unpacked box of food around her feet. "What about tea?"

"Right." Ellie hurried over and banged a pot of water on the stove, thankful the gas and electric were both switched on. "Pasta tonight, all right? We've got a packet of spaghetti somewhere, and some sauce…"

"Okay." Abby's hands were lost in the sleeves of her oversized black hoodie and standing amidst the boxes, her thin shoulders hunched, she looked younger than her eleven years and entirely vulnerable. Ellie couldn't resist giving her a quick sideways hug, even though her daughter didn't do hugs and predictably squirmed away.

"Can you keep an eye on that water, Abs? I just need to make a call."

Ellie went upstairs to her bedroom, her heart thudding and her palms turning slick, which was stupid, because she knew she was in the right here. Wasn't she? Quickly she scrolled through her emails, but she didn't see anything from Dr. Ven-whatever. She checked her spam folder, and then her heart did an unpleasant somersault. There was a message from the history faculty, and the subject heading was 'Urgent-Early Start'. Damn it.

The phone rang four times before it was picked up, and Ellie listened to the cut-glass tones she recognized from the message with a wince. "Oliver Venables, may I help?"

"Yes." She cleared her throat, wincing again at how loud it sounded. "This is Eleanor Matthews…"

"Miss Matthews." Oliver Venables' voice was caught between relief and definite irritation. "You were due to start this morning. May I ask what has happened?"

"I'm sorry, uh, Dr. Venables, but I wasn't expecting to start until Tuesday." Ellie closed her eyes and crossed her fingers, half-waiting for the blast of aristocratic outrage coming her way. All she got was taut silence. "Also," she ventured to add, "I don't think I'm actually your personal assistant?" For some reason she made this sound like a question even though she hadn't meant it to be one. "I'm the general administrative assistant for the history faculty…"

"Yes, and you have been lent to me for the next term," Dr. Venables cut across her in a tone of barely-concealed impatience. "The deputy head of administration sent you an email about it several days ago."

"Right." She wasn't going to mention the email in her spam folder. They should have *rung,* for heaven's sake. "I'm sorry," she added, because she didn't want to mess this job up.

"Never mind all that," Dr. Venables cut her off. "We'll just have to start now as we mean to go on. Please report to my office in the history department tomorrow at nine."

"Tomorrow? But I've only just…"

"Term starts Monday, and your contract starts tomorrow," Oliver cut across her. "I looked at it this morning."

Did it? The agreement to start on Tuesday had only been verbal, but... "If I could just..." Ellie began only to have Oliver interrupt her yet again.

"I shall see you tomorrow, Miss Matthews." And without waiting for her to reply, Dr. Oliver Venables hung up the phone, leaving Ellie with her mouth gaping, her mind spinning, and a definite sinking sensation in her stomach.

Chapter Two

S HE WAS LATE. Twenty-four hours and eight minutes late, to be exact. Oliver Venables glanced at his watch for the third time in two minutes, suppressing a sigh of irritation.

Normally he wouldn't be that bothered; Hilary term, as well as his first lecture, didn't start until Monday. But when his own PA had quit so suddenly, and he'd been off work for six weeks to help Jemima, setting him back over a month with his book deadline, every day counted. Every minute counted, and Eleanor Matthews was now nine minutes late.

A sudden clattering of the door to the history department's administrative office had him lifting his head. A flurry of voices, a sudden trill of laughter, and he glanced at his watch again. Ten minutes.

Then he heard the rich, comfortable tones of the deputy head of administration, Jeannie Walters. "I'll just take you through. Dr. Venables is waiting."

The click of heels, a perfunctory knock, and then Jeannie opened the door to his office. Oliver instinctively stood up and straightened his tie. Jeannie stepped aside and a woman walked through, making him blink. He didn't think he'd formed a mental picture of Eleanor Matthews, but even so this was not it.

A tumbling frizz of dirty-blonde hair, eyes the color of aquamarines, a slightly crooked nose and a too-wide smile that slipped off her face before Oliver could manage a tight-lipped smile back.

"Hello. I'm sorry I'm late."

"Ten minutes late or twenty-four hours late?" Oliver returned crisply, with a pointed look at his watch. Good grief, he sounded like a pompous ass. But he always reverted to form when he was nervous, and something about this woman inexplicably made him... not nervous, no, but unsettled. Wrong-footed. He'd been thinking she would be older, a granny type like his former PA. Why he should have thought that, he had no idea, since he'd seen from her CV that she was in her late twenties. Still he hadn't connected the dots to form this picture.

"I'll just leave you to it then, Dr. Venables?" Jeannie asked, and he nodded. She closed the door, leaving him alone with his new assistant.

"Sorry," Miss Matthews murmured. Her cheeks were flushed and she bit her lip. "I wasn't expecting to be coming in today. I had a verbal agreement to start on Tuesday."

"One I was not aware of." Oliver took a steadying breath. He was not making the start, or the impression, that he'd hoped for. "Never mind it all now. We should just get on."

"All right." She looked at him uncertainly, her eyes seem-ing huge in her face as she clutched a battered bag to her chest. Why had Edith Ampleforth had to quit so suddenly, just because her sister had had a stroke? She'd been sixty-two years old, a comfortable battle-axe with a typing speed that made his head spin and a decided skill in brewing tea just as he'd liked it. Strong, with only a drip of milk. Eleanor Matthews didn't seem likely to possess any of those qualities.

"You might as well take off your things," Oliver said, gesturing to her bright pink duffle coat, bobble-knit hat and rainbow-colored scarf. She looked like she'd had a torrid affair with a knitting shop.

"Okay, thanks." Her fingers shook as she unwound her scarf, making Oliver feel guilty. He wasn't being particularly friendly, or really at all, but then he'd never been known for his friendliness. He was an academic for a reason. People tended to be difficult, and he never seemed to have the right words to say, so why bother trying?

He sat back down and then stood up again, having the grudging need to make her feel at least a little bit more welcome. "Would you like a cup of tea?"

Eleanor's eyes widened in surprise at that unexpected offer and she stilled in the process of unwinding what appeared to be several miles of rather hideous scarf. "Oh yes, please."

Oliver looked around his office, as if a kettle would suddenly make itself known, or fly through the door on metal wings. He'd never actually made his own tea before, because he'd never had to.

"I'm happy to fetch you a cuppa as well," Eleanor suggested. She had a strong Northern accent that wasn't unpleasant, just... different. He didn't hear it much in Oxford.

"Well, all right then, yes, why don't you?" Oliver said. "If you know where the cups and things are..." Because obviously he didn't. He half-regretted his meant-to-be-friendly offer of tea; it would undoubtedly take ages for her to manage it, and mean another delay to the start of proper work.

"I think I saw a little kitchen on the way in," she said. "Won't be a tick." She hurried back out to the hallway, leaving Oliver feeling impatient and disgruntled and still unsettled in a way he couldn't explain. Eleanor Matthews was as far from Edith Ampleforth as seemed possible. She was so... *young,* and strangely vibrant too, and he didn't think it was just down to her psychedelic scarf and hat. No, something about the woman herself seemed... bright. He couldn't make sense of it.

A surprisingly short while later Eleanor returned, bearing a tray with two mugs, milk and sugar, and a plate with two rich tea biscuits. "There we are," she said briskly. "Milk, no sugar, am I right?" She glanced up at him, a smile glinting in her jewel-like eyes that for some reason made Oliver answer

with rather prissy tightness,

"Yes. Thank you."

The smile faltered for a second and then Eleanor straightened, taking her own cup.

Oliver gestured to the chair in front of his desk. "If you could take a seat? I'll show you your desk in a moment, but it's urgent that we begin as quickly as we can."

Eleanor's gaze flicked around the book-lined walls of his office, mullioned windows overlooking George Street, the framed certificates and air of dusty academia. "Urgent. Yes."

Was she mocking him? Oliver watched her, unable now to gauge her seemingly decorous expression. Admittedly, most people probably wouldn't consider a book on the Victorian perception of childhood to be a matter of urgency. But he wasn't most people, and Eleanor Matthews was being paid to do exactly that. Straightening, he gave her a repressive look and resumed.

ELLIE TRIED NOT to fidget as she listened to Dr. Oliver Venables go on about the book he was writing about Victorians and childhood, or something like that. Apparently it was going to be her job to type up his notes, something that made her wilt a little inside. She'd expected to be in a busy office with other people, chatting as she typed and photocopied and answered phone calls, being efficient and useful and *sociable*. From the way Oliver Venables was talking, it sounded as if she was going to be stuck in a broom cupboard with a bunch of fusty notes all by herself for the next eight weeks.

Well, it could be worse. She was a fast typist and after she finished writing up his book, she would go back to the general administrative assistant job she'd signed up for. She was determined still to look on the bright side and cling to her sense of optimism by her fingernails.

"Any questions?" Oliver asked, his voice ringing out as if he suspected she hadn't been listening. And in truth she hadn't been, at least not as much as she should have. Why was it when she tried to listen hard she found herself focusing on simply *looking* attentive rather than actually hearing the important bits? And why couldn't a man in the twenty-first century write a book on the computer instead of by hand, so someone else had to type it all out? He probably used a quill and a bottle of ink too.

"I don't think so, no," she murmured. Besides having to look super attentive she was also consumed with worry for Abby. She'd hated leaving her at eight o'clock this morning, her daughter looking miserable and mutinous in a house full of nothing but boxes. They'd both spent an uncomfortable night, sleeping on piles of blankets, and she hadn't even had a chance to order the mattresses yet. What was Abby going to do all day in an empty house with no Wi-Fi or TV or any creature comforts at all?

"I'll be fine, Mum," Abby had said with a sigh. "I'll just

read."

Her daughter loved to read, huge, doorstop tomes about dragons and elves and mystical wizards—the kind of books that didn't appeal to Ellie at all, but which Abby gobbled up one after the other, and then went onto online forums to discuss in myopic detail. They also happened to be the kind of books other girls her age thought were weird and well, dorky. Which both Ellie and Abby had learned the hard way.

"Miss Matthews?" Dr. Venables was staring at her, his mouth a thin line, his eyebrows raised in expectation.

"Please, call me Ellie." She had no idea what she'd just missed, but it was obviously something.

"I'll just show you your desk...?"

Ah, so that was it. Ellie rose from her seat in front of Oliver's desk. "Thank you." She followed him out of his office, down the corridor, to a room that really had been a broom cupboard, or so Ellie suspected. It was tiny, barely fitting a desk and a chair, with one miniscule window overlooking the back courtyard. She felt as if she was about to be entombed.

"It is a bit small," Oliver said after a tiny pause where they both stared at the cramped space. "I'm afraid they swapped some offices around at the end of term and I was off for a bit so I wasn't able to keep my PA's office." He gave her a brief, tense, and apologetic smile. "Department politics."

"It's fine." Ellie hung her bag over her chair. Besides the computer there was a phone on the desk. "Will I be taking your calls as well?"

"Yes, I did mention…"

"Sorry, of course." She really should have listened better. At this rate she was going to get fired before she had a chance to prove herself at all. Ellie turned to him with as bright a smile as she could manage. "So, shall I make a start?"

A few minutes later she was seated at the desk with a stack of notes scrawled in a spidery hand. Oliver Venables wrote exactly as she might have expected—in a fountain pen and barely legible. It was going to take her ages to decipher these and transcribe them onto the computer. Ages stuck in this tiny box-like room with no company whatsoever, and a microscopic view of the dust bins. She needed another cup of tea.

Tiptoeing so as not to alert her boss that she was already skiving off, Ellie went over to the kitchenette that served the entire floor and switched on the kettle. The rest of the history faculty was a good-natured flurry of people and voices, with the occasional click of a door or burst of laughter, phones ringing, people chatting, *life* happening. And meanwhile she was reenacting Harry Potter under the stairs. She needed her Hogwarts letter.

Still, there was no point bemoaning the unavoidable. As the lowest admin staff on the totem pole she knew she had to go where she was told, and for the next eight weeks at least it would be Oliver Venables' broom cupboard. Fine. She could deal with it. She had to deal with it. And there would be a bright side eventually. She was still determined about that.

Ellie took her cup of tea back down the hall, unable to resist sneaking a glance through the window of Oliver's office door. He was seated at his desk, one long-fingered hand driven through his hair as he frowned down at yet more notes. This book on Victorian childhood was clearly going to be epic.

He was kind of good-looking, in a fine-boned, scholarly kind of way. Not her type, although she didn't really know what her type was. Besides her on-again, off-again relationship with her ex-husband, she'd only had a handful of mediocre dates, with men her sister had pushed on her— nothing close to resembling a relationship. She'd never had the time or opportunity to discover what her type was, of anything. Since she was seventeen life had been conducted in survival-mode, which didn't give you a lot of scope for experimentation of any kind.

She couldn't imagine what a relationship with Oliver Venables would be like. She could not picture him looking affectionate or relaxed, going in for a kiss or even a hug. The man wasn't just stiff upper lip, he was stiff everything. Not in *that* way, of course. The thought made her giggle and she covered her mouth in case he heard.

She squeezed through the door into her office and sat down at her desk, wondering why on earth she was thinking about Dr. Venables like that. Simply because he was moderately attractive? Gray-green eyes, flyaway chestnut-brown hair, and a very nice cleft chin. Underneath the tweed blazer and button-down shirt he'd looked lean but muscular, not quite the weedy academic one might expect. Good grief, what was *wrong* with her? She was checking out her boss, which was ridiculous for all sorts of reasons. Clearly she needed to date more, or at all. Not that that was likely to happen anytime soon.

Blowing absently on her tea, Ellie fired up her computer and pulled the sheaf of Oliver's notes towards her. "The Victorian Child: Icon, Innocent, or Ignored?" she read aloud, vaguely impressed by the title. "Well, let's find out."

Three and a half hours later Ellie's whole body was cramped from sitting hunched in the chair, and she felt as if she was about to go cross-eyed from trying to decipher Oliver Venables' handwriting, which was a step down from chicken scratching. She stood up and stretched, ready for a much-needed lunch break.

She'd already called Abby twice, wanting to make sure she was okay, and her daughter had sighed heavily and assured her she was, promising yet again not to wander from the house, use anything electric, or turn the gas stove on. So Ellie was a little paranoid. But Abby was only eleven, and she wasn't meant to be a latchkey kid.

Back in Manchester, Abby had often gone to her sister's or her mum's after school while Ellie worked. Leaving that behind had been a tough call, and one she still sometimes doubted the wisdom of. Diane had certainly doubted—in the month since Ellie had gotten the job her sister had lectured her endlessly about the dangers of chasing some foolish dream down south and leaving behind all she, and more importantly, Abby knew.

Never mind that Abby was miserable at school, tormented by cliquey mean girls, and that Nathan had just bought a one-way ticket to Australia without even informing his daughter he was leaving the country. Never mind, either, that her parents' and sister's concern and sympathy had started to feel like a stranglehold, one that was choking Ellie slowly to death. Ellie was, Diane had proclaimed loudly and often, Making A Mistake.

Right now, with a crick in her back and her wrists and eyes both aching, not to mention her daughter spending the day alone, Ellie wondered if she was. She'd spent the morning rushing around, pulling clothes out of boxes, trying to come up with an ensemble that looked vaguely professional but she feared looked as if she was a wannabe flower child who had dressed in the dark. Then she'd broken the speed limit trying to get to the train station on time, bolting down a double espresso from the pop-up café in the car park that had made her stomach churn.

What she'd really wanted was a bacon buttie, greasy and delicious, but the little café didn't sell them; it was wholegrain this and organic that. Not that there was anything wrong with either, but it had just been one more reminder that Ellie was out of her element, a humble Northern fish in swanky Southern waters.

The commuters on the train to Oxford that she'd sat cheek by jowl with, damp coats lightly steaming in the humid press of the train car, had reinforced that fear. Everyone looked so... *privileged.* They were all reading *The Telegraph* and talking in plummy voices about the latest opera or French wine they'd sampled. Didn't anyone here watch *X Factor* or go down to the pub like a normal person?

All right, she was overreacting. She knew that. Part of the reason she'd moved down south was for a different experience, and in any case on the walk from the train station to the history department's building on George Street, she had seen enough loud-mouthed lads to reassure her that she hadn't ended up as an unwanted extra on the set of *Jeeves and Wooster.* But none of those loud-talking, gum-cracking blokes in dirty, baggy jeans and football jerseys was working for the history faculty. Once she'd stepped through the doors of the elegant building she'd immediately started to feel clumsy and gauche. Her Mancunian accent suddenly became as thick as treacle, and she'd noticed Oliver Venables' infinitesimal wince when she'd first spoken. She wasn't from this world. She could never even pretend that she was—and neither could Abby. She hadn't considered how that would feel; it hadn't even been an element in her decision making. She'd wanted a change, had decided that change, any change, would be good. Now she hoped she hadn't made a huge, awful mistake in moving here.

Still, there was nothing she could do about it now but

make the best of it, something Ellie had been doing for most of her life, or at least since her marriage. Get up the duff in sixth form? Make the best of it. Marry someone who was never going to commit to *anything?* Make the best of it. Slap on a smile and act like it was grand, even when it was patently awful.

Grabbing her coat, Ellie decided to head outside for lunch. She'd been so busy navigating the heaving pavements of Oxford that morning that she hadn't taken in her surroundings at all. So much for dreaming spires. Perhaps she'd get a chance to look around now.

Outside the mizzling rain had cleared, and the sky was a fragile, ethereal blue that made Ellie's spirits lift. Nothing could keep her down for too long. She started down the street with a spring in her step, admiring the ancient university buildings with sandwich places and smart coffee shops squeezed in between, the eclectic mix of academics, students, business types and buskers all vying for space on the crowded pavement.

She'd just ducked her head into a busy sandwich shop, intending to buy something for lunch, when she saw Oliver Venables at the front of the queue. Ellie almost ducked back out again, but it was getting late and she was hungry. The place was so crowded he wouldn't even notice her. She couldn't say exactly why, but she didn't relish the prospect of some uncomfortable tête-à-tête with her new boss. What if he grilled her on what she'd typed so far, or something equally awkward? From the back of the queue she had the freedom to study him, or at least the back of him. His hands were dug into the pockets of his coat, a navy blue duffle that somehow made him look younger. Several times he pushed up his glasses with his middle finger, a trait that would have seemed geeky if he wasn't so... wasn't so... what *was* it about him? Why did she keep thinking about him this way—noticing how long his fingers were, how wavy his hair, the dimple that appeared in one lean cheek as he gave a quick, distracted smile at the server? Ellie had sidled sideways to get a better look at him, and had almost lost her place in the queue.

Then Oliver turned around, baguette in hand, and clashed gazes with Ellie, who had unfortunately been staring openly at him. Whoops. She managed to plaster a sunny smile on her face.

"Hello."

"Hello. Are you..." He cleared his throat. "Are you getting on all right?"

"I think so, yes. I've almost finished the introduction and chapter one."

"Excellent. If you could email me the file, I'd greatly appreciate it." So he did use computers. He just didn't type on them, apparently.

"Okay. Will do."

Oliver nodded once, and Ellie found herself nodding back, and the moment stretched on, awkward and endless.

She tried to think of something to say, but came up with nothing. So she smiled again, and Oliver looked surprised by it, and then it was her turn to order and he was walking briskly out of the shop.

Chapter Three

B Y THE TIME Ellie got back to Willoughby Close at half past six she was exhausted. The train from Oxford had been heaving with people who, like her, just wanted to get home, and when she'd finally managed to snag a seat after the Hanborough stop, she'd had to sit next to a man who insisted on eating a chicken balti on his lap. She could still smell curry in her hair.

There had been a few bright moments to what had, overall, felt like an endless day—Jeannie, the head of administration, had brought Ellie a much-needed cup of tea in the middle of the afternoon, and had perched on the corner of her desk to chat for a few minutes. Her dry sense of humor had made Ellie smile, and the offhand comments about Oliver Venables had made her wonder.

"He keeps himself to himself mostly," Jeannie had said. "Although he can be kind when he puts his mind to it. But most of the time his head is up in the clouds—you know the type. Doesn't think about practicalities, and his last PA encouraged it. Half battle axe, half Mary Poppins. I don't think he's ever made himself so much as a cup of tea." Which wasn't that surprising, considering how lost he'd looked when he'd mentioned making one this morning.

Now, as she finally pulled into the empty courtyard of Willoughby Close, she felt a weird mix of discouragement and relief. It was so cute... and so *dark*.

She'd like some neighbors, for Abby's sake as well as her own. She'd hated the thought of her daughter here on her own all day. It would have felt different if there had been a kindly old lady or even a slightly harassed mum popping in to check on her. But she couldn't depend on the kindness of strangers when she'd just moved hundreds of miles away from the choke hold of her family.

"Abby?" Marmite snuffled hopefully at Ellie as she came in the door. Abby had made a start on unpacking, and the kitchen looked lived in, chocolate spread-smeared countertop included.

"Hey, Mum." Abby slunk down the stairs, dressed in her usual black hoodie and holey jeans.

"You survived." Ellie wanted to go in for a hug but decided against it. Her daughter didn't do cuddly.

"Looks like it."

"How was your day?" Ellie bustled over to the kitchen, recapping the jar of chocolate spread and starting to load plates into the dishwasher. Abby hunched her shoulders.

"Sorry for the mess."

"You started unpacking." She gestured to a box of books

that had been emptied, the books stacked in a tottering tower next to it.

"Sort of."

"Sorry I wasn't here all day." Guilt ate at her insides and soured her stomach. She'd had such better plans for today. They were meant to have made this house a home, and explored the village, and gone shopping. Settled in and made friends and in the fantasy that Ellie was ever embroidering, some kind villager would have invited them to an impromptu supper. By bedtime they would have both had best friends.

Sighing gustily, Ellie looked around the living space. Actually, it was rather a mess. Abby hadn't so much as unpacked as merely emptied boxes, leaving the contents scattered across the floor. "So, what shall we do for tea? Takeaway?"

"Can we afford it?"

Cue the guilty cringe. An eleven-year-old should not have to worry about whether they could afford dinner. "I think so."

"Okay." Abby brightened a little, the anxiety that constantly clouded her eyes giving way to a tiny bit of sunshine. More than anything Ellie wanted to see those clouds depart forever. For the last few years of Abby's primary school she'd watched her daughter turn inexorably inwards, trying to make herself more and more invisible so as not to be picked on by the kids in her class who were both cooler and crueler than she was.

Ellie had been party to far too many early morning stomach aches followed by feet-dragging walks into the school yard, seen Abby slump against the wall of the school while children played around her over and over again. She'd had too many pointless conferences with teachers who couldn't make it better or didn't care. No more. That was one thing, the most important thing, she was resolved on.

"So, curry or fish and chips?"

Abby gave her a cheeky grin that made Ellie smile back even as she wanted to cry. She needed to see her daughter smile more. "Do you even need to ask?"

"Fish and chips it is, then."

"Minus the fish."

"Right." She'd seen a chip shop on the high street, and feeling buoyant with hope now that she was home with her daughter, Ellie found the number on her phone and placed the order. "Success," she said with a fist pump, and Abby rolled her eyes.

"Congratulations. You made a phone call."

"It feels epic after the day I've had."

"Why?" Abby scooted up onto the counter top, long, skinny legs dangling. "What was your day like?"

"Nothing terrible," Ellie said quickly. The last thing she wanted was for Abby to worry about, well, anything. "Just a bit dull, if I'm honest. I'm typing a history professor's notes into a book." Actually, the book's subject of the Victorians' view of childhood was rather interesting, even if Oliver Venables' writing style was as dry as day-old toast. "My boss is your typical fussy professor." For some reason that felt unfair to Oliver. "So, chips." She clapped her hands, determined to be upbeat. Maybe a little manic. Abby was giving her that dubious, don't-start face. "And tomorrow we'll go shopping. Mattresses are at the top of the list."

"And some food."

Ellie winced as she realized how depleted her one emergency box of supplies must be. "What did you eat today besides chocolate spread and toast?"

Abby raised her eyebrows innocently. "Chips?"

"I see." Ellie grabbed her coat and reached for Marmite's lead. As usual, her dog's reaction was to spin in circles as if possessed, tail wagging hard and fast—and knocking over the various piles of books, towels, and clothes Abby had left all over the floor.

"We'd better get out of here," Ellie said with a laugh, and clipping on Marmite's lead, she headed outside. Abby followed, and together they stood in the little courtyard and breathed in the fresh, cold air. The sky was a deep, endless black, pinpricked by a thousand stars, so unlike the sodium-yellow glow of streetlights they were both used to back in the city suburbs.

The road leading from Willoughby Close to the main drive was completely dark, and Ellie felt a little bit like Hansel and Gretel wandering in the wood. She ended up using her phone's light as a torch as they picked their way across the ruts, Marmite trotting along happily behind them.

"Perhaps tomorrow we can have a look at the school," Ellie said brightly.

Even in the dark she saw her daughter's grimace. "Let's save it till Monday."

Abby was understandably dreading the start of school; her experience so far had been awful and in any case what kid wanted to start a new school in the middle of Year Six? If Ellie's job had come at a different time, or things hadn't been quite so dire already, she would have waited for Abby to start secondary school in September before making a move. Unfortunately she hadn't had the luxury of such a choice.

"You'll only be there for a few months anyway," she said, still not sure if this was a good thing or not. "What we really ought to do is visit the secondary school where you'll be going next year."

Abby just shrugged, clearly not looking forward to that either. Ellie had already checked—the local secondary was highly rated and only a short bus ride away. It even had a fantasy books club that Ellie had pointed out online. Maybe in a bigger school environment her daughter would have a chance to find a kindred spirit or two.

They finally reached the main road, narrow as it was, and Ellie peered down it towards the high street. There were no pavements and if a car came at a clip they could both be flattened. "We might need to get high-res vests," she said, and Abby gave her one of her looks.

"You are kidding, right?"

"I'm not sure. It's going to be dark when you go to school, Abby, at least at the beginning." She would be dropping her off for breakfast club at eight in the morning, which in January meant pretty much pitch dark.

"Do you want to make me even more of a nerd than I already am?" Abby demanded, and Ellie, as always sprang to her defense.

"You are *not* a nerd."

Abby blew a strand of hair out of her eyes. "Whatever."

They'd had variations of this conversation since Abby was eight, when she'd started to grasp the unfortunate hierarchy at school. She'd come home one day, frowning, and asked Ellie what a nerd was. Ellie had answered firmly, "A person who likes books." Maybe it hadn't been the right response; maybe she should have been honest. But when your kid was picked on pretty relentlessly it was hard not to want to encase them in emotional bubble wrap as often as you could.

At any rate, it hadn't taken Abby that long to figure out what being a nerd really meant. She'd come home a few days later, given Ellie a long, thoughtful look, and said, "I know what a nerd is, Mum." Then she'd gone into her bedroom and shut the door.

But why was she dredging up those awful memories now? Abby didn't have to be the nerd of Lea Primary. She didn't have to be labeled before she'd even begun. And hopefully there wouldn't be a gaggle of mean girls, ponytail girls, Abby called them, who did ballet and tap dance and tossed their heads and giggled behind their hands.

They reached the high street, which was deathly quiet at seven in the evening. The only sound came from the pub on the corner, The Three Pennies, and even that sounded fairly sophisticated—live music and gentle laughter. No one would be tossed out on his ear here, Ellie suspected, for drinking too much or swinging a fist.

They found the chip shop and picked up their order from a bored-looking teen who barely looked up from her phone, and bizarrely this made Ellie feel better. All right, she might have preferred a cozy grandmotherly type to remark that she hadn't seen them in the shop before, and sneak them an extra carton of chips, but at least this felt normal. Spending the day in the rarefied world of academia had made her feel more than a little self-conscious, not just for herself, but for Abby. She wanted to belong here, at least eventually, at least in part. That was the whole reason she'd moved.

Back at the cottage Ellie decided to be proactive and found some sticks of wood lying about that she bundled into the woodstove with some scrunched up newspaper. What should have been a cozy, comfortable blaze ended up being a damp, smoky mess—wood needed to dry out, apparently, before attempting to light it on fire. Who knew? She opened the French windows, blasting them both with freezing air, to clear out the smoke, and they ate their meals on their laps. At least the chips were good.

And tomorrow would be great. Tomorrow they'd start making Wychwood-on-Lea—and Willoughby Close—their home.

The next morning Ellie woke up to a hammering on the front door. She sat up in bed, blinking sleep out of her eyes, the vaporous fragments of a dream involving her new boss disappearing like mist in her head. Oliver Venables had been juggling baguettes and bossily informing her how to do it properly, something that had made a lot of sense in the hazy dreamscape.

"Mum." Abby thrust her head through Ellie's doorway. "Someone's at the door."

"I can hear." Ellie grabbed her ratty dressing gown from the hook on the door and headed downstairs. She had no idea what she looked like, but she could *feel* the frizzy mass of her hair like an electric halo. Her normal morning look, then.

"Hello?" She opened the door, jaw dropping slightly at the sight of the sexy man standing there. He had rumpled dark hair, a five o'clock shadow at nine in the morning, and was wearing a pair of faded, well-worn jeans that molded lovingly to his muscular legs and well, other parts. Ellie yanked her gaze upwards. "May I help you?"

The slow, knowing smile made her toes curl. "I'm Jace

Tucker, the caretaker at Willoughby Manor?" He yanked off one leather work glove and thrust out his hand. "You must be Ellie Matthews."

"Um, yes." Ellie tried to tuck her hair behind her ears but it sprang back out, undeterred. Marmite thrust his head between her legs in an attempt to get a sniff of the stranger, nearly knocking her off balance. She threw out one hand to brace herself against the doorframe. "Sorry, I just woke up. Obviously." She managed a smile.

"I was stopping by to check everything was all right?" Jace arched an eyebrow. "It looked as if there was a lot of smoke coming out of here last night."

"That would be my attempt to start a fire. In the wood-stove, I mean." Ellie grimaced. "Sorry."

"There's plenty of firewood from the estate, if you'd like it."

"Is there?" Ellie brightened at this gesture of neighborly good will. "Thank you…"

"I'm always having to remove dead trees from the grounds. I'll bring some over in my truck later, if you like."

"That would be brilliant." Ellie found she was not immune to Jace's sexy smile, and he had the smug, laughing look of someone who knew it. The last thing she needed in her life was another man who played on his charm. Not that she could compare Jace Tucker to Nathan. Already the caretaker had been more useful than her ex-husband ever had been.

After Jace had left Ellie grabbed a quick shower, determined to make a start on their day. "How about we spend the morning unpacking," she suggested to Abby, "and then head out to buy our mattresses and other bits and bobs?"

"You mean, like a sofa?" Abby stood in front of the fridge, arms crossed. "And chairs? A TV would be nice."

Ellie took a deep breath. It had been a moment of reckless madness to throw all that stuff away, but she'd needed to. She'd needed to excise her past, or at least Nathan's part in it. All the fruitless, wasted years, the cheap veneer of happy family life that had rubbed off at the first opportunity. While Ellie had been trying to make a home, Nathan had sloped in and out, being charming when he felt like it. It had driven Ellie mad, and worse, it had eventually driven her to despair.

"We'll do our best," she said now. She'd put aside some money for new furniture, but it wasn't going to go all that far, and her first paycheck didn't come until the end of month. Once again she wondered what on earth she'd been thinking, uprooting her and her daughter's life, taking away everything they'd known, even the TV. It had been cathartic but costly.

Several hours later the cottage was looking more cozy, with their clothes put away in the built-in cupboards, and their dishes in the kitchen. Jace, true to his word, had stopped by with a truckload of firewood, and Ellie and Abby had helped him stack in the little lean-to next to the front door. His unhurried manner and relaxed friendliness had put them both at ease, and he'd left reassuring them he was available whenever needed.

Abby had raised her eyebrows at this, giving Ellie a knowing smirk and making her blush. *"Abby."*

"What?" Abby's eyebrows went even higher. "I didn't say anything."

"You didn't need to." Jace was undeniably attractive, but he didn't make her heart skip so much as a beat. He was too sexy for his own good—and hers. She'd much rather have someone who was a little homelier, a little more down-to-earth. Not that she'd even thought about dating in just about ever. She had no energy, emotional or otherwise, to put into a relationship. She'd worked way too hard at trying to make her last one work.

After they'd stacked the firewood, they'd headed out in the car, trusting the sat nav to take them to the nearby market town of Witney; fortunately it seemed to know where it was going for once.

Witney was as quaint as Ellie could have wished for, with a pedestrianized shopping area and plenty of charity shops, although the prices even of secondhand items were double what they would have been up north. They spent the afternoon browsing in the various shops, and came away with a secondhand TV, several battered kitchen chairs and a nearly-new sofa that would be delivered tomorrow, as well as two brand-new mattresses that Ellie managed to heave and then scrunch into the back of her car.

A large food shop at Waitrose put them back almost as much as the mattresses, but Ellie couldn't seem to say no to anything, whether it was luridly pink strawberry Pop Tarts or the latest fantasy DVD. Her daughter deserved a few treats.

Back at Willoughby Close they unpacked it all and then Ellie spent the next few hours attempting to assemble their beds, squinting at the instructions that were in tiny print and in every language, it seemed, but English. It was nightfall before she managed to have them assembled, and bewilderingly she had several screws left over when she was finished, but the beds seemed sturdy enough. She hoped, anyway.

"If this collapses beneath me and I break both my legs I know who to sue," Abby warned her, but she was smiling. She'd become more and more optimistic throughout the day, and Ellie had heard her humming under her breath as she'd arranged her books in the built-shelves in her bedroom. That simple, happy sound made her heart feel like a balloon inside her chest, soaring upwards. This was going to work. It was already working.

Downstairs she surveyed the room with satisfaction. Wintry sunlight poured through the windows, and the view of fields and trees from the French doors was a balm to the soul. With a few bits of furniture, some prints on the walls, a bowl of fruit on the table, the house felt much more like a home. Marmite was sprawled by the woodstove, which was burning merrily thanks to the load of logs from Jace. Humming the same tune as her daughter, Ellie went to make tea.

By Sunday afternoon, Abby's mood of cheery optimism had started to flag. As the start of school loomed closer she became increasingly quiet, and Ellie felt the familiar, sour churn of anxiety in the pit of her stomach. They'd been here so many times before. When she suggested Abby lay out her uniform for tomorrow, her daughter shook her head, looking pale and pinched and decidedly miserable.

"Abby." Ellie sat on the edge of her bed, wincing at the audible creak of the frame. She had a feeling she'd needed to use those leftover screws. "Things can be different here, you know. Better. This is a new school, a new start, new people." New friends.

Abby flopped onto her bed and wrapped her arms around her knees tucked up to her chest. "But not a new me," she said quietly.

The ache in Ellie's heart nearly made her breathless. "I don't want a new you. The current you, the real you, is fantastic." It was just those stupid mean girls who didn't realize it. Who stuck notes on Abby's back and stole her lunch and whispered and then laughed as they shot her vicious looks. And that was only what Abby had told her about.

Abby made a face. "You're my mum. You have to say that."

"Not necessarily. No one's paying me to, are they?" Ellie

teased. She was trying to stay light because if she didn't she was afraid she might cry. She'd worried and ached and wanted so much for her daughter. She listened to other parents moan about slumber parties and taking girls to the cinema and felt like shaking them until their teeth rattled, but she supposed that was the plight of the parent of a bullied child.

She wanted Abby to have friends, but even more importantly she wanted Abby to believe in herself. Yet as much as she tried, and heaven knew she had, Ellie couldn't give her daughter that kind of confidence. She knew in her heart that only her daughter could determine what happened tomorrow, whether she went in to school dragging her feet and hanging her head, or whether she genuinely believed it could be a fresh start. "Look, you had a bad deal back in Manchester," Ellie said. "Your teacher even admitted that your class was difficult, and plenty of other teachers and parents agreed. And unfortunately, mega unfortunately, some of the girls got it into their stupid heads that it was fun to tease you, and it went from there." On and on and on, for over three years. Ellie had tried to change schools several times but everywhere decent was oversubscribed.

"And that could happen here." Abby's voice was small, her head lowered, as she picked at her already chewed and ragged nails.

"But it doesn't have to." Ellie took a deep breath. She'd read enough books on bullying and helping your child make friends that she felt she could have a PhD on the subject, and yet every time she had this kind of conversation with Abby she felt as if she was spinning in a void of ignorance.

It was so hard to know what to do or say, and she'd tried every tactic out there, rinse and repeat. Nothing seemed to make a difference to Abby or her situation, and yet here she was, trotting out another pat phrase that she did believe, with her whole heart, even if her daughter didn't. "A confident attitude really can make all the difference. And you have so much to be confident about, Abby. You're bright and funny and most importantly you're kind. Anyone would want to be friends with you."

"Funny, because no one has."

"That's because kids can be stupid."

"Right." Abby heaved a sigh and reached for her book, ever the cue that their heart-to-heart was now over. "It's all about self-confidence. Riiight." She rolled her eyes, making Ellie feel like she'd failed at her pep talk once again. Okay, it wasn't *all* about confidence. Because kids could be stupid and mean, following the crowd of popular kids blindly, whether it was out of foolishness or fear. But Ellie still wished she could convince her daughter that if she believed in herself a little more, then perhaps other people would too. It couldn't hurt, anyway. She feared that after years of playground persecution, Abby had lost that ability, and Ellie couldn't blame her.

"Things are going to be good here, Abby," Ellie said quietly. "We can make them good." Abby made a face, her gaze glued to the pages of her book. With a sigh Ellie rose from the bed. Abby had clearly had enough of her pep talk, and recalling that she had her broom cupboard and stuffy Dr. Venables to face tomorrow, Ellie thought maybe she was the one who needed to hear it anyway.

Chapter Four

"WHAT ON EARTH..." Oliver rose from his seat, astonished at the sight of his new PA bursting into his office. She unsettled him at the best of times, and this was clearly not one of them. "Are you ill?" he asked, flummoxed, because she looked dreadful. Pale, blotchy skin, a wild look in her eyes, her nose running.

"No," Ellie said, and then burst into noisy tears.

Oliver stared at her, bewildered and frankly appalled by this unprecedented outburst. He was absolutely no good with tears. His family had never done them. The one time he'd wept in front of his parents his mother had looked away as if he'd wet himself, and his father had snorted that no son of his should make that kind of emotional display.

Nowadays an ineffectual pat was the best he could do, so much so that Jemima had started making a joke of it. "A pat from you is a bear hug from someone else," she'd said just that weekend, when she'd fallen to pieces yet again and Oliver had stood there, helplessly handing her his handkerchief, wondering how she could cry so much.

"Sorry," Ellie gasped, rubbing the heels of her hands across her streaming eyes. "Sorry, you're probably horrified by this."

He was, but she didn't need to point it out. Was he that obviously out of his emotional depth? Not that it would take all that much, but still. Not knowing what else to do—as usual—he handed her his handkerchief.

Ellie glanced at the square of starched and pressed linen and let out a wobbly laugh. "Of course you have a handkerchief."

Oliver drew himself up. "I'm not sure what that means."

"You're like a modern day Mr. Darcy." She pressed the handkerchief to her eyes. "Except not."

"Are we referring to the novel *Pride and Prejudice?*"

"No, I'm referring to the film with Colin Firth," Ellie said, sniffing. "But never mind." She blew her nose loudly on the handkerchief, making him wince, and then she gave him a wry smile through the last vestiges of her tears. "Don't worry, I'll wash it. And iron it, too. Promise." She stuffed the crumpled handkerchief in her pocket.

"It doesn't matter," Oliver said, although it had been one of his better handkerchiefs, a Christmas present from Tobias, bought by Jemima at Peter Jones. Never mind. "Would you... would you like a cup of tea?"

She eyed him wryly. "Do you actually know where the kitchen is?"

"I'm sure I could find it," Oliver answered with dignity.

Ellie laughed, the sound of genuine warmth and humor improbably making Oliver smile. "I'm sure you could. Eventually. Jeannie told me on Friday that in five years here you have not made yourself a single cup of tea."

"Your predecessor did the job admirably." Oliver heard how tart he sounded, but since when had this become a conversation about his tea-making habits, or lack thereof? In any case, he made plenty of tea. He lived alone, and he brewed himself a cup every morning, as well as a cup of Horlicks before bed, a habit instilled in him by his nanny. He was perfectly adept at managing a kettle, and if Ellie was intimating that he was somehow snobbish about the whole thing, well, that was just wrong.

"I won't be a moment," he said, and she flung out a hand.

"No, sorry, I was only joking. I'll make it." She hurried out of the room before Oliver could protest—not that he'd been going to, precisely.

GOOD GRIEF, WHAT was wrong with her? Ellie squeezed her eyes shut as she waited for the kettle to boil. She had completely lost it in front of her boss. When she'd started crying he'd looked, for a few seconds, as if she'd just been sick on herself. And she had been, emotionally anyway. The memory made a laugh bubble up inside her, despite the sorrow and worry that pressed down on her like a two-ton weight on her chest. Oh, but it had been hard leaving Abby to the mercies of Year Six that morning. So hard.

Her poor daughter had barely been able to choke down a bowl of Shreddies, and then had walked with increasingly slow steps to school while Ellie had done her best to cheerfully chivvy her along. By the time they'd arrived at the gates of Lea Primary, a cozy, Victorian building that had a cluster of 1960s breeze-block extensions, Abby had looked nearly green.

"Can't I be homeschooled?" she'd asked with sudden desperation, turning to Ellie with huge, panic-filled eyes.

Ellie had stared at her helplessly. "Abby…"

"Joking." Abby had held up one hand. *"Joking,* Mum. Obviously." Except Ellie knew she hadn't been joking. And her mind was already racing, wondering if she could manage it. Abby could do an online course, share her broom cupboard… but that was no life for an eleven-year-old girl. Unfortunately this wasn't, either. She wanted so much for Abby than this choking fear and misery, but she felt helpless to provide it. This was meant to be their fresh start, yes, but in that moment Ellie couldn't see a single rainbow or unicorn. Not even close.

With a deep breath, Abby had squared her skinny shoulders and started towards the school gate. "Those who are condemned to die…" she muttered under her breath, and Ellie winced as she watched her daughter slink into school, shoulders now slumped, head bowed before she'd begun.

Abby had written off school without giving it a chance, and already Ellie could see the other kids noticing. A trio of chattering girls shot her curious looks before breezing past her, and a shudder went through Ellie. Sometimes being a kid sucked. And sometimes being a mum did as well. Where was that darned bright side now? Everything felt dark.

She glanced around at the other mums, many of them decked out in spandex and Lycra, ready for the day's work out. One woman wore jodhpurs and riding boots and was talking in a jolly-hockey-sticks type of voice that made Ellie feel like even more of an outsider. She listened to snatches of conversation about dinner parties and spa weekends and pet ponies and after offering a few awkward smiles to no one in particular, she drifted away.

She'd spent the train ride into Oxford battling an increasing feeling of panic, and had ended up emergency-calling her sister as she walked to the history building. Diane could be a bossy pain in the arse but she'd been there for Ellie when she'd desperately needed her to be, something her sister couldn't let her forget, just in case it happened again. Which it wouldn't.

"Tell me I'm not making a mistake," Ellie had blurted after her sister had answered.

Diane let out a huff of disbelieving laughter. "You want *me* to tell you that?"

"I just dropped Abby off at school and she looked like she was going to her execution. Seriously. I could practically hear the death bell tolling. I felt like running into the classroom and dragging her off to safety."

Diane sighed heavily. "She's bound to be a bit nervous, Ellie, considering what she was put through at her last school."

"I know, but…" Tears pricked her eyes and she blinked furiously. Diane would be horrified to realize how emotional she felt. How fragile. If she knew she might come down to Oxford and try to take over her life, and that was something Ellie knew she couldn't stand. She needed to make this work… on her own. "I wanted things to be different here. Better."

"Maybe they will be," Diane allowed. "For your sake I hope they are, because I don't think anyone can cope with another one of your disasters." Ellie swallowed hard. She hadn't needed that reminder. "But that doesn't make the first day any easier," Diane concluded, gentling her tone. "Give it some time," she added, now injecting a note of optimism into her voice that Ellie doubted her sister felt. She certainly didn't, not in this moment at least. "She might come home tonight raving about the place. And if not tonight then tomorrow or the next day or the next week. These things don't happen overnight."

"Why can't they?" Ellie huffed. She wanted instant fixes. Even after all the disappointment and despair she'd been through, she still believed in that elusive happily-ever-after— and she wanted it *right now.*

"I've got to go to my next appointment," Diane said. In the background Ellie heard a door slamming and the electric beep of Diane unlocking her car. "Talk soon, okay? And you got your rental deposit back, if that makes you feel better. And if things get really dire, you can always pack it in and move back up here."

"I don't want to quit, Diane."

"Sometimes you need to know when to quit."

"I just got here," Ellie exclaimed. Did her family really think she was that hopeless, that one day in she should be thinking of heading back?

"Right, well, I'm just saying. If. We're worried about you, Ellie."

"I know." Ellie had often struggled with her family's worry, telling herself it was well-intentioned even if it hadn't felt like it. Condescending and suffocating, was more like it. When advice and sympathy were doled out with despairing looks and a lot of head shaking, not to mention the occasional pointed comment that Diane would never have ended up pregnant at seventeen/divorced/single mum/take your pick, it was hard to accept it gratefully.

Still Diane's call had made her feel marginally better, although not enough to ease the pressure building in her chest, the fear and worry that felt like a howl needing to escape. It had risen and risen and then burst out in the most unfortunate of places, Oliver's office.

Why couldn't she have waited until she was in her cupboard, with only the computer to witness her mini emotional breakdown? Instead she'd fallen apart in front of the one person who was least likely to be sympathetic. Except… he'd been quite thoughtful, in a repressed kind of way.

The kettle switched off and Ellie made the tea, bustling back to the office, determined to feel or at least seem a little bit more composed. She couldn't afford to give into that kind of emotional hysterics, not in front of Oliver, and not in front of anyone. That was why she insisted on always looking on the bright side; the alternative was to dwell in darkness and fear.

The look of relief on Oliver's face when she returned to his office and he saw she was no longer crying was almost comical.

"Sorry about all that," Ellie said as she set a cup of tea in front of him. "I think I just needed to get it out of my system. Now." She pinned a bright smile on her face. "Shall we get on? Do you have the notes for chapter two?"

"Ah, yes." Oliver shuffled through the papers on his desk, his head bent, before handing her the sheaf of papers that compromised his rough draft of the second chapter. "Thank you." He paused, pushing his glasses up on his nose with one finger before continuing cautiously, "Is… is everything all right, then?"

Ellie let out an uncertain laugh followed by a sigh that felt as if it came right down from her toes. "Not really, but it's not awful, either." Not yet, anyway. And she wasn't going to give in to the fear that it *would* be awful, and soon. "I'm just... worried." She paused, debating how much to reveal. How much Oliver really wanted to know. "My daughter started school today."

"Your daughter..." He looked surprised. "I hadn't realized you were... that is that you have children. A child."

"Yes, she's eleven. She had some first day jitters, you know? But it's fine. It's going to be fine. We've only just moved here and things have been difficult for a while, so..." Right, that was enough of that. Oliver was looking distinctly nonplussed by all this information. TMI, clearly, but telling him she had a paper cut seemed as if it would be. "Anyway." Ellie brandished the sheaf of papers he'd given her. "I'll get a start on this."

She spent the morning immersed in the world of Victorian child law; it was fascinating, and rather harrowing, to read about the chimney sweeps who were sent out to work clambering up chimneys as young as five years old, working twelve-hour days. In comparison Abby had nothing to complain about, even if just the thought of her daughter sent another pang of anxiety ricocheting through her. How was her day going? Had she found a kindred spirit?

Late in the morning the phone rang, shocking Ellie. It hadn't rung once since she'd started work, and now she picked it up cautiously.

"Hello?"

"Is Ollie there?" A woman's voice rang out, high and

strained. *Ollie.* That was unexpected.

"This is his assistant. May I take a message?"

"Oh. Yes, I suppose." The woman sounded as if she was on the verge of tears. "This is Jemima. Please tell him Tobias has Scouts tonight. He needs to be here at six."

"Tobias. Scouts. Six." Ellie scrawled on the margin of Oliver's notes, the only paper available. "Got it."

"Good." The woman let out a quavering sigh. "Thank you," she said, and then she hung up without waiting for a reply.

Ellie replaced the receiver thoughtfully back in the cradle. So, who were Jemima and Tobias? A wife and son were the most obvious answers, and yet it made Ellie pause. Why shouldn't Oliver Venables be married? Just because he'd had the emotionally repressed air of a long-confirmed bachelor didn't mean anything. Plenty of British men were the same, and they still put a ring on it. Still, she couldn't help but feel the teensiest bit disappointed, which of course was ridiculous. Oliver Venables was nothing but her boss. She left the message on his desk while he was out, and got on with her work.

At five o'clock Ellie knocked on Oliver's door to say she was going home. She needed to pick up Abby from the after school club by six, which meant leaving the history faculty at five on the dot.

Oliver looked up from his laptop, blinking owlishly. "Is it five already? Goodness..." He looked dazedly around his office as if surprised where he was.

"I've finished chapter two and sent you the file."

"Good." He paused, still blinking. "How… how are you finding it?"

"Your handwriting isn't the neatest, but it's fine." Ellie smiled uncertainly, wondering if she'd been too honest, but then Oliver continued,

"No, I mean… the text. Is it interesting?" He laughed, looking rather adorably embarrassed. His cheeks were pink and his glasses had slid down. He pushed them up with his middle finger. "Sorry, it sounds as if I'm fishing for compliments but I'd genuinely like to know."

"Well…" How honest to be now? "It's quite fascinating, the whole history of how children have been perceived through a certain period in history…" she began carefully.

"Is it?" He leaned forward, his eyes sparkling behind his glasses, one tweed-clad elbow resting on his desk. "I'm passionate about the subject, but of course I have no idea if anyone else will be. It seems as if most of what I'm interested in bores the rest of the world rigid."

For some reason having Oliver say the word *passionate* made Ellie blush. He *looked* passionate, his face alive with interest, his gray-green eyes sparkling, a slight smile curving lips that were quite mobile and well, lush. Was he passionate with Jemima?

Thinking of Jemima reminded her of the message she'd left on his desk several hours ago. "Did you get the message from Jemima?" she asked, because it was after five and she knew Scouts started at six.

Oliver blinked. "Message...?"

"I left it on your desk..." Right on top of all his papers, but everything was a mess and Oliver didn't seem like the type to think of checking for messages. "Tobias has Scouts at six tonight," Ellie explained, "and Jemima would like you to be there. Sorry. I should have checked you'd received it..." She stopped, feeling guilty, because Oliver was already rising from his seat, stuffing his papers and laptop into his battered leather messenger bag as he glanced at his watch. "I can get there if I leave now."

Which made Ellie feel even worse. "I'm so sorry, I should have double-checked..."

He shrugged her words aside. "My fault, and I should have remembered anyway. Jemima only told me about twenty times." The smile he gave her was rueful, a sparkle still visible in his eyes. "Are you taking the train? We can walk together."

Chapter Five

THE TRAIN STATION was heaving with cranky commuters as Oliver navigated the turnstile and then hurried towards the platform, Ellie matching his brisk stride. They hadn't had a chance to talk on the narrow pavements on the way to the station, with so many people jostling by, but he rather hoped they could have a few minutes' chat on the train. She'd told him she was travelling to Charlbury, which was one stop before his. He'd like to hear her opinion on his book. He had a feeling Ellie would give him an honest answer, rather than the ego-stroking nonsense most of his colleagues would offer. He lived in a world where everyone's back needed to be patted, and often.

Amazingly, he found them both seats, and he slid in first, tensing slightly when Ellie joined him in the narrow seat, her leg brushing his. He could smell her perfume, something flowery and light that reminded him of spring rain. She gave him a quick, apologetic smile and moved so their legs were no longer touching.

Even so their bodies seemed rather close to one another.

He hadn't realized quite how small the seats on a train were. Unless he angled himself away in an obvious manner, his shoulder brushed hers. When she moved to put her bag on the rack above them, her breast brushed his arm and Oliver felt himself react. Good grief, he was hardly some randy boy to be affected by such a small touch. What on earth would she think? He inched closer to the window.

"So." She gave him a quick grin. "This is cozy."

"Quite." He could feel himself reverting to standoffish form. Typical. The trouble was, small talk had always eluded him. Perhaps it came from a childhood where the adage 'children should be seen and not heard' was taken to its extreme; his father would have preferred they weren't seen, either. Perhaps it came from years at boarding school, trying to make himself invisible, or from an adulthood spent in libraries and classrooms, hiding behind books, immersing himself in research. In any case, he couldn't think of what to say now. He'd wanted to talk about his book, but it seemed arrogant and impolite to ask for her opinion now, as if he was merely looking for flattery.

To his relief, Ellie mentioned it first. Perhaps she found small talk as onerous as he did, although upon reflection that seemed unlikely. She never seemed to be at a loss for words. "I think you have a very interesting subject matter," she said, twisting in her seat so she could appraise him frankly. This close her eyes looked extraordinary, a deep sea-green, and as clear as Venetian glass. "But your tone is academic and well,

I'm sorry to say it, but rather dry."

"Dry?" For a second he'd lost himself in her eyes, noticing the golden glints in the irises. Had he been staring? He cleared his throat. "What do you mean?"

"I mean... dry." She shrugged, smiling no doubt to soften the blow. "You make even interesting things sound rather dull."

Ouch. Oliver blinked, trying to arrange his features in an expression of kindly interest rather than... well, hurt. It was stupid to feel offended by her words. She was only offering him the opinion he'd asked for, and he had a feeling she was right. He didn't put emotion into his writing. He didn't put it into his *life.*

"The thing is," Ellie continued earnestly, leaning forward so a strand of her curly, crazy hair swung down and brushed his cheek for a stunned second, "there's so much humanity in these stories, isn't there? The chimney sweeps who are barely more than babies... when I read it, I don't care about the facts—what percentage of six-year-olds were in school, for example. I want to hear about Charlie Smith who swept chimneys in Mayfair to help buy medicine for his consumptive mother." She looked starry-eyed, her cheeks flushed, her lips slightly parted. Oliver stared at her for several seconds before he managed to find the sense to string some words together.

"Who's Charlie Smith?"

Ellie refocused on him, laughing lightly. "I don't know. I

made him up. I just mean personal examples rather than dry statistics."

"Hmm." Oliver leaned back a little; Ellie's hair had come undone from its messy topknot and the ends were brushing his shoulders every time she moved. He didn't think she realized and he had the sudden, outrageous urge to wrap a finger around one of those crazy curls and pull. His head needed examining. She had a *daughter*. She might be married. She probably was. "I shall certainly think about that."

"I'm probably not the right person to ask," Ellie told him as she made a face. "My usual reading is a bit... lighter. The last thing I read was the latest Jilly Cooper. You probably haven't even heard of her."

"I know Jilly Cooper." She looked astonished and he rushed to clarify, "I don't *know* her, know her, of course. But I remember sneaking looks at my mother's copy of *Riders* when I was a boy." Why on earth he'd mentioned that, he had no idea. Now she'd think he was some creepy pervert. He felt heat crawling up his face and he tried for a light laugh. "I remember a certain salacious scene involving nettles." Wonderful, that made him sound even more perverted. He needed to stop talking now.

Ellie laughed, a sound of genuine humor that was as clear as a bell and had several people nearby looking round and smiling as if they wanted to share the joke. "Oh, I remember that scene. Billy and Janey and a well-placed dock leaf." She giggled, and Oliver saw she was blushing now, and the moment felt awkward in an entirely different way. It was almost… almost as if they were flirting.

"Well, anyway." Oliver resisted the urge to tug at his collar. "I'm no Jilly Cooper obviously, but my publisher wants this book to have mass appeal, so I shall take your advice on board as best as I can."

"Okay." Ellie's eyes were sparkling and Oliver had the feeling she was laughing at him, in a nice way. He smiled back weakly, and then as the train started to slow she rose from her seat. "This is Charlbury." Oliver started to rise as well, simply as a matter of politeness, only to nearly bang his head on the coat rack above them. He stood there, crouching slightly underneath the rack, feeling undeniably awkward, and Ellie's mouth curved into a teasing smile. "See you tomorrow," she said, and then she was gone.

WHAT HAD THAT been about? Ellie let out a laugh of sheer disbelief that she'd been talking Jilly Cooper sex scenes with Oliver Venables. Admittedly, that scene with the nettles had been quite something. Ellie could remember reading it goggle-eyed with the other Year Eights, devouring every delicious detail of Billy Lloyd-Foxe's sexy moves.

As Oliver had apparently. She pictured him as a bookish boy, clever and a little bit scrawny, sneaking peeks at the racy book with his mother in the next room and she giggled out loud. It made her boss seem more real, more likable.

She'd been surprised when he'd suggested they walk to the train station together, and even more so when he'd snagged them both seats. She'd smelled his aftershave as he moved, something plain and old-fashioned, bay rum perhaps, and her gaze had been drawn to silly things—the stretch of his shoulders as he put away his bag, the humor glinting in his gray-green eyes—humor she hadn't expected, because she'd sort of assumed Oliver was as boring as his book. But underneath the dry exterior, just like with his writing, there was a real human story to be told.

And she'd leave it at that, rather than start dwelling on the sexy cleft in his chin or the way his sudden, shy smile had made her insides flutter a little, because it seemed all too likely that Oliver Venables was married. Besides, she needed to think about Abby now.

All thoughts of Oliver, sexy and otherwise, evaporated as Ellie drove to school to pick Abby up. She had no idea whether her daughter had spent the last ten hours in hell, heaven, or primary school purgatory. The front door of the school had been propped open for parents, the reception area empty, and so Ellie wandered down a few corridors and into a few classrooms before she finally came upon the abject few condemned to stay until the bitter end of after school club. A pair of girls were giggling over something on a mobile phone, and a couple of boys were playing a game that involved swapping cards with pictures of football players. And then there was Abby.

Ellie caught sight of her daughter hunched in the corner, a book held up to her face, and felt a lump form in her throat.

"Hey, Abby." She tried to smile, but it felt wobbly. Abby didn't look as if she'd had the day Ellie had hoped she had. Her daughter didn't respond, just closed her book and rose from her seat. Ellie exchanged stiff pleasantries with the supervisor while Abby gathered up her stuff, and then they were heading outside into the frosty darkness.

"So," Ellie said the second they were both in the car with the doors closed, because she really could not wait any longer. "How was it?"

Abby shrugged. "Fine."

"Fine? That's it?" Ellie tried to sound light. "How about some deets?"

Abby pretended to shudder. "Please do not ever use the word 'deets' again. You're not capable of it."

"Then tell me something that happened today. Something good."

Silence. "They had chocolate cake for pudding at lunch."

"Okay." That was something, at least. Sort of. "Anything else?"

Abby folded her arms and stared out the window. "Not really."

Ellie never knew how to handle these conversations. Whether to push or back off, go for a pep talk or simple, heartfelt commiseration. Every option felt fraught, a virtual minefield of emotional bombs just waiting to detonate in both of their faces. "So do the other kids seem nice?" Ellie finally asked as they turned into the drive for Willoughby Manor. The manor house was cloaked in darkness, and briefly Ellen wondered about the woman who lived there. Jace had told her it was an old lady whose only relative was a nephew who lived in London. Ellie wondered what she thought of her new neighbors.

"They're okay," Abby said after a pause, her tone repressive.

They got out of the car and Ellie unlocked the front door, bracing herself for Marmite's ambush. Her dog did not like being stuck at home all day, and the ripped-up paper towel littering the entire downstairs was evidence of his displeasure, or at least his boredom.

Ellie side-stepped Marmite's front-paws attack and went to the kitchen. She wasn't going to press Abby for more details. She certainly wasn't going to nag.

"What does 'okay' mean, exactly?" she asked as she opened the fridge. So much for that well-intentioned resolution. She had very little self-control when it came to these things.

"It means *okay.*" Abby had buried her face in Marmite's scruffy fur, but at Ellie's question she lifted her head and started walking towards the stairs. "They didn't talk to me and I didn't talk to them. So it's all good." Before Ellie could reply to that statement Abby had disappeared, slamming her bedroom door and making the rafters shake. Well.

She'd just leave it, Ellie told herself as she made sausages and mash for dinner, Marmite sniffing hopefully for dropped bits. She wouldn't ask Abby if there looked like anyone she might like to talk to, if she wanted to join a club, if she wanted to *try*. She wouldn't, because she knew how that went. Her daughter closed right up and Ellie was left feeling as if home was as much of a battlefield as school was, and that wasn't good for either of them.

She fed Marmite and then called Abby down for dinner; her daughter slunk down the stairs and threw herself into a chair.

"There's no one I feel like being friends with, before you ask."

A reluctant smile twitched at Ellie's lips. "I wasn't going to ask." At least, she'd been going to try not to.

"Yeah, right."

"No one?" Ellie asked after a moment, trying not to let her heart start a relentless freefall. A new start was going to be challenging under these circumstances, and yet she still hoped. Still fought for that happy ending she felt deep in her bones that Abby deserved.

Abby pushed her sausages around on her plate with her fork. "No one. But at least there's no one making my life miserable, either. So that's a plus."

It was so much less than what Ellie wanted for her daughter, but she remembered what Diane had counseled about giving it time and she decided to let it go for now.

"Oh, and there's this," Abby said, rising from the table to dig a crumpled paper out of her school bag. "An information evening this Friday at the comprehensive. Woo-hoo." She rolled her eyes as Ellie scanned the paper. It was an evening for parents and pupils, with presentations from various teachers and current students. Maybe, just maybe, there would be someone promising there. Someone Abby might actually like.

Later, after Abby had helped her clear up the dishes and slouched back upstairs to do her homework, Ellie decided to take poor Marmite for a walk. He didn't like being cooped up indoors, and she always felt guilty because of it. She'd never actually wanted a dog, because what full-time working single parent did? It had been one of Nathan's impulsive ideas; he'd brought the puppy during one of his visits when Abby had been seven and her daughter had fallen in love. There was no way Ellie could have refused to keep him.

"Abby?" she called upstairs. "Do you want to come with me to take Marmite for a walk?"

"I'm good here."

Sighing, Ellie reached for Marmite's lead while her dog began to run in crazy circles of canine anticipation.

Jace had assured her she was free to roam anywhere on the estate except the manor's formal gardens. Since there were acres of woods to explore, Ellie didn't think she'd have a problem keeping away from a few box hedges. She hadn't counted on her dog going into a frenzy of excitement at being released into the wild, however, and the moment she stepped into the woods off the main drive, Marmite let out a woof of joy and then wriggled through some dense undergrowth, disappearing into the darkness of a forest that now resembled something out of Brothers Grimm.

"Marmite…!" Ellie's voice echoed through the forest, followed by an excited and alarmingly distant woof. After a lifetime of walks in city parks, Marmite was clearly reveling in his freedom, and Ellie couldn't blame him.

Still, she had no idea how to find him. The woods stretched endlessly in every direction, dark and dense and rather unwelcoming at seven o'clock on a winter's night. Ellie shivered in the chill air, a hint of dampness on the breeze that whispered through the stark branches of the trees overhead.

She scrunched through wet, mulchy leaves for a few minutes, dodging branches that loomed suddenly out of the darkness, threatening to stab her in the eye, and calling Marmite's name half-heartedly because it was clear he'd done a runner. Her only hope was that he'd find his way back eventually, because she had no idea how to find him.

What if there were traps in the woods, for foxes or something? What if Marmite broke a leg or for that matter, what if she did?

The flipside of being a determined optimist was feeling constantly terrified that everything was about to go horribly wrong. It was this secret dark side that kept Ellie awake at night, staring at the ceiling until her eyeballs ached, imagining worst-case scenarios that left her dry-mouthed but determined to find a way through. Optimism was her choice, but fear was her secret default, and in moments like these she couldn't suppress it.

"Marmite," Ellie called a bit louder. *"Marmite!"*

She froze as she heard Marmite's exuberant woof, sounding closer than before. The sound was coming from behind a prickly hedge... a box hedge.

"I have a bad feeling about this," Ellie muttered as she squeezed through the hedge to emerge suddenly and alarmingly into the manicured gardens of Willoughby Manor.

"Oh. Oh, no." Ellie's gaze zeroed on her huge dog who was racing around a lawn that looked as if it had been trimmed exactingly with nail scissors, his huge, muddy paws turning up great, big clumps of pristine turf. This wasn't good.

An outdoor light snapped on, flooding the lawn with brightness. It was worse than she'd thought. Marmite had made a complete and utter *mess* of the once-perfect lawn, and was still joyfully doing so. Even worse, an elderly woman in tartan and tweed and black rubber boots stood on the terrace above, glaring down at him. Ellie half-expected her to be holding a shotgun, but thankfully she was unarmed. This had to be the lone resident of Willoughby Manor, and the owner of Willoughby Close.

"I'm so sorry…" Ellie called up, her voice faltering as she lunged for Marmite's collar. Her dog danced away from her easily. "He's not used to…" Obeying. She lunged again and Marmite evaded her, clearly seeing this as a game. If dogs could smile, then he was giving her a pie-eating grin.

"This lawn was my father's pride and joy." The woman's voice quivered as it carried on the still, frosty air. "We played croquet on it every summer."

"I really am so sorry," Ellie said again, helplessly. What else could she say? What could she *do*? Not catch her dog, obviously. She tried again and Marmite danced away, practically laughing. Damned dog. Damned everything. At that moment it felt as if the whole world was going wrong.

"Marmite," Ellie said, her voice pitched somewhere between stern and utterly desperate. Unfortunately her dog knew the difference. "Stop this right now."

With a joyful woof he dodged past her and raced up to the terrace where the elderly lady was still staring at them both in outraged affront. She backed up as Marmite came towards her, all muddy paws and a hundred pounds of damp, smelly dog. Ellie froze, knowing she was unable to stop whatever happened next. What if Marmite jumped up on her, knocked her down? What if he *killed* her? This was getting more horrific by the minute.

"Sit down," the woman suddenly thundered, making Ellie, as well as Marmite, freeze in shock. Then, to Ellie's relief, her dog parked his large bottom and gazed obediently up at the woman who had issued such a stentorian command.

"Thank you," Ellie said breathlessly. She ran up and looped Marmite's lead around his head, holding on tight. "I really am so, so sorry." She glanced back at the lawn, cringing at the muddy sight. It was completely wrecked. "I'll…" She swallowed past the tightness in her chest and forced herself to say, "pay for it, of course. To be repaired. If you just give me a name of someone to call…" Would Jace do it? For cheap?

The woman gave her a considering look. "You are my new tenant, I presume?"

Ellie cringed inwardly. Her new tenant who was about to be evicted, perhaps. "Yes… I'm Ellie Matthews. I live in the first cottage with my daughter Abby."

"I am Lady Stokeley." The woman drew herself up; she barely topped five feet but she had more presence in her little finger than Ellie could hope to have in her entire body, ever. She was positively regal. She fixed Ellie with an imperious look, her eyes bright blue in a mass of wrinkles, before nodding towards the muddy remnants of her lawn.

"Never mind all that. I haven't played croquet in thirty years, more's the pity. I was rather good. But," she finished, eyeing Ellie sternly, "control your dog."

Chapter Six

THE SPORTS HALL of the local comprehensive was heaving with parents who veered between looking maniacally jolly and simply exhausted, and their rather morose children as Ellie edged into the room with a reluctant Abby by her side. It was Friday, the day of the parents' evening at Lea Comprehensive, and the end of her first full week of work at the history department.

It had been a long, tiring week, and tonight Ellie would have much rather put her feet up with a large glass of wine and a DVD box set. Abby would have preferred to stay home as well, and had, over dinner, claimed that these types of evenings 'weren't that important' and that 'no one really went', but Ellie had been adamant. They were going. And they were going to find some kindred spirits even if it killed her.

Abby's week had continued as it had started, as far as Ellie could tell. Abby hadn't spoken to anyone at school beyond the basics of asking for the pencil sharpener to be passed, and no one had spoken to her. It was more than a little heartbreaking, but Ellie tried not to show it. She got that her daughter was too weary and heart-sore to make an effort, she did. Sometimes, when she let herself, she felt the same. Starting over was hard, especially when you already felt battered and bruised by life.

But at some point, Abby needed to get back into the ring and put up her dukes. Come out swinging and fighting for her own happiness. The trouble was, Ellie had no idea how to help her do that.

As for work… that had continued apace too. The academic term—called Hilary term for some reason Ellie didn't yet understand—had started, and Oliver had been away from his office for hours at a time, taking lectures or tutorials or whatever it was university professors actually did. Apparently he had another office at Balliol College, and he did some open hours there for students to drop in and ask questions. Ellie had found she missed his presence, which was ridiculous since she'd hardly seen him.

Fortunately the monotonous hours of typing were broken up by regular phone calls—Jemima called several times a day, usually for no real reason that Ellie could make out, and a lot of other people rang too. Professors and students and once the BBC, wanting an expert opinion on a documentary they were filming. Oliver Venables was, it seemed, a bit of a big deal.

She'd also been dragged out of her broom cupboard by Jeannie, who claimed a person would go mad spending all their time typing, and insisted she have her tea breaks with the other support staff in the main office. Ellie had to confess that after several hours of deciphering Oliver's scrawled handwriting and immersing herself in the intricacies of Victorian labor laws, she was starting to go more than a little cross-eyed. She enjoyed chatting with the other assistants, listening as they swapped joking horror stories about the peculiarities of the academics they worked for. They all seemed to have a healthy if slightly laughing respect for Oliver, and no one told a horror story about him, which Ellie counted as a win.

She was looking forward to the weekend, pottering around the house and hopefully going for a walk with Abby and Marmite. Normal life stuff that still felt precious. But first they had to get through this evening.

"So." Ellie looked around for a familiar face, but of course there weren't any. There were hundreds of parents and pupils, a sea of strangers, and she and Abby were bobbing there, adrift and alone. "Why don't we..." Her gaze snagged on a table of budget nibbles—crisps and digestives and a few plastic pitchers of watery-looking orange squash. "Get something to eat?" Abby shrugged in response and Ellie started to shoulder her way through the crowd.

They stood there for a few awkward minutes nibbling stale crisps. Ellie tried to catch someone's eye, hoping for a friendly smile, but everyone seemed to be having a joyful reunion with a dear friend they hadn't seen in ages.

"I wonder when the presentation will start," she said and Abby just rolled her eyes. So this was fun.

Then, through the press of mopey kids and over-bright parents, she saw a familiar figure. Tall, lean, the lights glinting off his glasses. What on earth was Oliver doing here?

"I know someone," Ellie said excitedly, and without thinking too much about what she was doing or what she would say when she saw him, she started pushing her way through the crowds, Abby trailing behind.

"Mum," her daughter hissed. *"Mum.* What are you doing?"

"I want you to meet my boss," Ellie explained breathlessly, and then came to a halt in front of Oliver, who was standing a bit away from the crowd, a dark-haired, sulky-looking boy by his side. This, Ellie supposed, was Tobias.

"Ellie?" He looked startled, and Ellie smiled widely. Too widely, perhaps.

"Hi!" Her voice rang out, a little too loud. But it was so nice to see someone she knew. "This must be Tobias." Tobias, understandably, looked fairly freaked out to have a strange woman knowing who he was. And then, to make it creepier, Ellie asked him, "How was Scouts?"

Abby had inched away from her, as if she could distance herself from Ellie's over-friendliness, or even pretend that they weren't here together. Tobias was staring at Ellie blankly. And then Oliver came to the rescue.

"Ellie is my personal assistant," he explained to Tobias.

"She took a call from your mum about Scouts."

"Oh. Okay."

Cue even more awkwardness. Ellie turned to Oliver, determined to rescue the conversation. "So Tobias is going to Lea Comprehensive?" Duh. Obviously. "I didn't realize you lived so nearby." Although perhaps she should have, considering he'd said his stop was one after hers on the train.

"I don't," Oliver answered. "I live in Oxford, but Tobias and his mother live in Kingham."

So, did that mean he and Jemima were divorced? Separated? Ellie sought for something neutral to say. "Well, it seems like a good school." Oliver nodded distractedly and Tobias gave her the death stare only a preteen was capable of, a mix of contempt, disbelief, and bored indifference. Excellent.

"So this is Abby," she said, patting Abby's arm. Her daughter gave Oliver and Tobias a stretching of her lips that Ellie supposed was meant to be a smile and did not make eye contact.

"Pleased to meet you," Oliver murmured. Tobias nodded. Sort of.

Fortunately Ellie was saved from having to extend the painful conversation by a woman coming to the front of the hall. She cleared her throat loudly into the microphone before speaking, making everybody wince. "If everyone could take their seats…"

The mass of people shuffled towards rows of folding

chairs, and Ellie followed Oliver and Tobias. She was not going to lose the only people she knew in this crowd. Abby grabbed her arm.

"Mum, what are you doing?" she hissed.

"Trying to make a friend," Ellie returned. "That's my boss, Abby, and his son."

"I know, but we don't actually know them and you're acting like…"

"Like what?"

Abby shook her head, falling silent as they took their seats next to Oliver and Tobias. She was so clearly not happy with this arrangement.

Ellie turned to Oliver, whose knees were pressed up against the chair in front of him, his elbows balanced awkwardly on his thighs. "So where does Tobias go to primary?"

"A private school outside Cheltenham," Oliver answered, lowering his voice a little so Tobias, who was expending all his energy on looking bored while sneaking looks at Abby, wouldn't hear. "But he hasn't enjoyed it that much, so…"

"I understand." It sounded like maybe, just maybe, Tobias had had a similar experience to Abby. And, Ellie noticed with a leap of hope, he was wearing a Lord of the Rings hoodie while Abby had on her elven leaf necklace. Soul mates, then, or at least possibly, *please,* friends. One friend. That's all she wanted for her daughter. Well, it wasn't all she wanted, but it was a start. She didn't think it was too much to ask or aim for.

The presentation began and Ellie listened to the head teacher drone on about subject choices, adjustment to secondary, and lunch and bus options, with the expected encouragement to 'make a worthwhile contribution to the life of the school'. Several presentations by students and other teachers followed, and by the end everyone was squirming in their seats, eyeing the table with the crisps and squash.

Ellie turned to Oliver as the last speaker finished and murmured conversations erupted all around them.

"So…"

"Tobias," Oliver said, "why don't you get Abby a glass of squash?"

Tobias looked startled by this sudden command and then with a wordless nod he slid from his seat. Abby followed him, both of them trying to look nonchalant.

"That was subtle," Ellie teased, and Oliver looked confused.

"I just want him to be a gentleman."

Bless. "How come he hasn't enjoyed his school?"

Oliver gave a troubled sigh. "His parents separated last year and then… well, it's been difficult."

"I'm so sorry…" Ellie murmured, saddened for the sulky-looking boy even as she was processing the salient information that from the sounds of it, unless Oliver talked about himself in the third person, which was not an impossibility, he could not be Tobias's father.

"It's been a very tough time for Jemima," Oliver continued. "My sister. She hasn't been coping well, and I try to do
what I can. But I'm no substitute, I'm quite sure."

"That's very kind of you, though." Ellie was now struggling with a mix of conflicting emotions—sorrow for
Oliver's nephew, and an unsettling relief that her boss was
single, or at least unmarried. Although she didn't actually
know that he was single. He could be married to someone
else, just not Jemima. Or he could have a girlfriend, some
uber-intelligent professor-type who made glasses and tweed
seem sexy. In any case she shouldn't care whether he was
taken or not.

"They seem to be getting along," she said, with a nod
towards Abby and Tobias. They were standing by the drinks
table, holding plastic cups of squash and talking in what
looked like sporadic bursts. Ellie had no idea what they were
saying but just the fact that her daughter was engaging with
someone her age was practically enough to have her fist-
pumping the air.

"You mentioned your daughter has had a tough time as
well?" Oliver said, and she turned back to look at him.

"Yes, she hasn't had a great time at school for the last few
years." Out of protectiveness of Abby Ellie decided not to go
into too many details. Abby wouldn't like her over-sharing
with Oliver, or with anyone, for that matter. "I took this job
so we could both have a new start." And so far that wasn't
working out all too well for Abby, but maybe this was the

beginning of something better. Ellie was already starting to feel more optimistic. There was a rainbow around here somewhere, she was sure of it.

"It's a hard age," Oliver said quietly. "Regardless."

"Yes, it is, isn't? I wouldn't be eleven again, even if you paid me." Ellie thought of the mean notes sent in classes, girls who were your best friend one day and your arch enemy the next, and you had no idea why or how it had happened. She'd survived by making friends with boys instead, but that hadn't worked out too well either, in the end.

"I wouldn't, either," Oliver agreed, his voice heartfelt enough to make Ellie wonder what kind of tough time he might have had. She didn't have the chance to ask anything more, though, because Abby and Tobias were drifting back to them and people were starting to leave the hall, heading out into the dark, wet night.

"So you guys will be in the same year," Ellie said, and Tobias and Abby just stared at her. She was, of course, stating the obvious. "Maybe even the same set." More staring. It was time to go. "See you on Monday," she said to Oliver, and then they headed out into the night with everybody else.

"So Tobias seems cool," Ellie remarked casually as she unlocked the car. "I saw he was wearing a Lord of the Rings hoodie."

"Mum, that was Game of Thrones."

Same difference as far as Ellie was concerned, but she

went with it. "So you guys have some similar interests?"

"Yeah, he's into fantasy," Abby said, and now she sounded as casual as Ellie, both of them trying to act like none of this really mattered. "He told me about this middle earth website that sounds pretty cool."

"Brilliant." She sounded so light, Ellie marveled, as if she didn't care, as if she wasn't hanging all her hopes and her whole heart on this one tiny exchange. "Maybe you'll see him again in school next year."

Abby let out a snort. "As if. Lea Comprehensive has five hundred kids in each year group. Besides, he won't remember me by then."

Ellie begged to differ, but she knew better than to do that now. Still, she wondered if there was a way she could get Tobias and Abby together before secondary school started, even if it was just for another quick chat about middle earth.

The rest of the weekend passed by pleasantly and all too quickly; Ellie caught up on shopping and housework and then had the promised wine and boxed set on Saturday night. On Sunday she and Abby took a long, rambling walk by the river Lea, keeping well away from Willoughby Manor's manicured gardens.

The day was cold and clear, their breath creating frosty puffs of air, and as they came across a wooden footbridge to the top of the high street, Ellie paused for a second to savor the scene. The narrow street with its jumble of shops led down to the village green and then a patchwork of sheep pasture and farm fields that stretched to the horizon. It was all so perfectly pastoral and peaceful that Ellie couldn't imagine them *not* both finding happiness here.

Surely it was better than the cramped house they'd had in Manchester, with sirens wailing at night and rubbish blowing up against their legs as they walked to school. When Abby had been three she'd once peeled a used condom from where it had stuck to her ankle and asked, in a loud, piping voice, if it was a balloon.

"Isn't this lovely?" she said to Abby, heartened to see a faint smile on her daughter's face.

"Yeah, I s'pose…" But then Abby tensed, a guarded look coming over her face before she turned to avidly study the notices stuck in the window of a charity shop.

Ellie followed her daughter's covert glance to see a girl about her age walking with her mother. The girl had her blond hair in a high ponytail, her eyes narrowed, her nose in the air. The mother looked a bit more approachable, with her wavy, dark hair pulled into a messy topknot, her clothes expensive but looking carelessly thrown on, skinny jeans, leather knee-high boots, and a cashmere poncho thing that Ellie had seen a lot of mums around here wear. It seemed like the yummy mummy uniform, and Ellie could not see herself rocking one.

Both mother and daughter had an air about them, one of privilege and wealth that Ellie had never so much as sniffed.

"Who is that?" she whispered and Abby just shook her

head. Ellie waited until they had passed, disappearing into the post office shop, before she asked again. "Abby…?"

"Mallory Lang," Abby said on a sigh. "She's in my year."

Mallory Lang. Even her name sounded popular. "Is she… nice?" Ellie asked, and Abby gave her a look.

"Oh, she's *so* nice. Always shooting me looks and then giggling and whispering to her friends." Abby hunched her shoulders. "Come on, let's go home."

"But…" The pit of Ellie's stomach felt icy and unpleasant. "You said things were fine at school." Ellie had thought she knew how low her daughter's expectations for her social life were, but this was worse than she'd feared, which was saying something. "Abby, is this Mallory girl bullying you?" Because if she was, Ellie was going to be hard-pressed not to go into school fists flying, guns blazing. No one was going to bully her daughter. Not again.

"It's fine, Mum. Just leave it." Abby subjected Ellie to a fierce glare. *"Don't* go into school and have a talk with the teacher, okay?"

"I won't." Yet. Admittedly Ellie understood Abby's reluctance. She'd gone in to school in Year Four it had been an unmitigated disaster. The teacher had sat everyone down on the classroom rug during circle time and lectured them about being nice to 'poor Abby'. The bullying had gotten a million times worse. Ellie struggled with how to know how to handle bullying, but even she knew that was not the right way.

They walked in silence down the high street, passing a

variety of shops that Ellie would have liked to have had a poke through—she spotted a secondhand shop with a homely cluster of dusty, willow-pattern teapots in the window, a knitting shop with baskets of rainbow-colored wool, and a tearoom, all of them looking quaint without being twee. Abby, however, wasn't breaking her stride for anything, and neither of them spoke all the way back to Willoughby Close.

A truck was parked in the courtyard, and Ellie's heart leapt when she saw a man with a tool belt slung round his waist coming out of Number Four.

"Is someone moving in?" she asked hopefully and he shook his head in regret.

"Sorry, not that I know of. I was just finishing caulking the bath." He smiled, his eyes crinkling at the corners. "Colin Heath. I renovated the cottages."

"Ellie Matthews, resident. They're lovely." She nodded towards Abby. "And this is my daughter, Abby."

They chatted for a few minutes, and Colin promised to have them over for dinner when his girlfriend Anna arrived from America. "She's coming next month. I can't wait." His grin was so goofily endearing that Ellie couldn't even summon a twinge of envy for how loved-up he obviously was.

She unlocked Number One and paused at the sight of an envelope had been pushed under the front door, the address, in crabbed, elderly handwriting, made out to 'The Residents of Number One, Willoughby Close.'

"It's an invitation to tea with Lady Stokeley," Abby said after she'd ripped open the envelope. "Up at the manor. I didn't even know she knew about us."

"Ah, yes, well. I ran into her the other day." Ellie hadn't revealed the terrible turf episode to Abby.

"Well, that should be cool," Abby said without a huge amount of enthusiasm. She was still smarting, Ellie suspected, from the near run-in with Mallory Lang. "It's for next Saturday."

"I don't think we have any plans." Which was obvious. They didn't have any plans for anything, except Colin Heath's vague dinner invitation next month.

Marmite flopped in front of the woodstove with a loud, comfortable fart, and Abby headed upstairs.

"Abby…" Ellie began, although she didn't know what she was going to say. She wanted to say something about their non-interaction with Mallory Lang, and the whole school thing that felt as if it was pressing down on her, an oppressive weight she longed to be free of, but the words stayed lodged in her throat, a lump of fear and hope she couldn't begin to verbalize.

"I need to do homework," Abby called, and the next sound Ellie heard was her daughter flopping onto her bed— and then a muffled scream as the frame collapsed underneath her. She really should have used those extra screws.

Chapter Seven

ELLIE PAUSED ON the curve of the sweeping drive, Abby next to her, Willoughby Manor standing in all its imposing grandeur before them. It was the following Saturday, and she and Abby were due at Lady Stokeley's for tea.

It had been a long and tiring week, with the slog to and from Oxford and the days spent cooped up with a laptop and pages of Oliver's illegible handwriting—but there had been some little joys along the way. Ellie was starting to get to know, and enjoy, Jeannie Walters' dry sense of humor, and things with Oliver had reached a pleasant stasis that Ellie couldn't exactly call friendship, but he at least felt a little more approachable and plain old nice than the dry and officious boss he'd been at the start. Ellie was enjoying parts of the book too, although Oliver's writing style was still dusty and academic, at least to her. She'd take a good, old-fashioned bodice ripper any day.

She'd made other inroads, small as they were, into life in Wychwood-on-Lea—after Abby had collapsed dramatically on her bed, thankfully not breaking any bones or calling

Childline, Ellie had rung Jace and he'd come by and fixed it, taking her handful of loose screws and fitting them all in with ease. Ellie had perched by the bed to keep Jace company, but also to discreetly ogle his bum. The man wore a pair of faded jeans to perfection. She didn't think she'd been all that discreet, though, or maybe Jace was just well used to lascivious looks. He'd straightened up and given her a slow, knowing smile that had made Ellie blush. She wouldn't touch Jace in a million years—he was far too sexy, too self-assured, too smug. She preferred Oliver's wry awkwardness to anything Jace had to offer—not that she was thinking about her boss that way, of course.

"So how are you finding it?" Jace had asked after he'd finished repairing the bed and was putting away his tools.

"It?" Ellie didn't know whether he meant the bed or something bigger.

"The house, the village, the Cotswolds." He gave her another grin. "Take your pick."

"Oh, well." Ellie wondered how honest to be. In truth she wasn't sure she knew the answer to his question. At times she loved living here—when she drove to the train station and frost glittered on the village green, the sunlight warming the lovely golden stone of the houses on the high street—but other times she felt a misfit. But maybe that was less to do with the Cotswolds and more to do with her. She hadn't felt as if she fit in in Manchester, either, always too busy to make friends, too self-conscious of her state as a single mum, protective of Abby with a deadbeat dad, feeling like the loser of the family who hadn't been able to hold it together.

"It wasn't meant to be a complicated question."

"It takes time to adjust, I suppose." She was conscious of Abby waiting downstairs. Her daughter would feel aggrieved and far worse betrayed if she overheard Ellie talking about her school woes. "Make friends, settle in, all that."

"Yep." He nodded slowly, his eyes crinkling at the corners, and somehow Ellie had the feeling he understood.

"Are you from around here?"

"Me? Nope. I'm Northern, like you. Newcastle."

"Really? You've lost the accent."

He winked, managing to carry it off without seeming cheesy. "That was a must."

"You don't find it too... snobbish here?" Ellie asked cautiously. "It's just, everyone's kind of richer than I realized."

"Not everybody. Just the people who like to show it. Walk down the village past the school and you'll see a sight fewer Land Rovers and Agas." His grin was teasingly wolfish. "The yummy mummies are only a little bit tasty there."

Ellie imagined he'd had more than a taste. "Hmm." She hadn't made any friends at the school gate yet, yummy mummies or not, but that was in big part because she dropped Abby off early and picked her up late. The few mums she had seen had swished around in expensive exercise gear, checking their Apple watches strapped to their skinny wrists with harried compulsiveness. Ellie hadn't had the courage to offer them more than a cautious smile, and she hadn't always gotten one back.

To her surprise Jace placed a hand on her arm, a touch that was entirely friendly, without any flirt. "Give it time," he said. "It'll come."

"Thanks." She appreciated his encouragement even as she struggled to take it to heart. "Any chance of us getting some neighbors, at least?"

"Someone visited Number Two for a little look round," Jace said. "But we'll see."

"Someone with a family?" Number Two in the close looked to be the biggest cottage, with at least three bedrooms.

"Yes, but I can't say more than that. I'm not sure if they want anyone to know they're looking."

Which was kind of intriguing. "I hope they decide to rent," Ellie said. "It gets a little lonely here on our own."

"You can always stop by mine." Jace lived in the gatekeeper's cottage, tucked away from the main drive and looking like something out of a fairy tale. A man like him shouldn't live in a house with that much decorative stonework.

"Thanks. I might take you up on that offer."

"So are we going in?" Abby asked now, nodding towards Willoughby Manor.

"I guess so." Ellie had no idea what to expect. Afternoon tea in a manor house was way behind her life experience.

She'd debated whether to dress up, and had ended up wearing a corduroy skirt and knee-high boots paired with her only cashmere sweater. She'd bought a tin of fancy macaroons from the tearoom in the village, having a nice chat with Olivia, the thirty-something owner who ran the shop with her mum, although now Ellie half-wondered if she should have baked something herself. Considering the level of her skill in that area, probably not.

The front door of the manor was huge and ancient-looking, with a large lion-shaped brass knocker. Ellie lifted it, the metallic thud seeming to reverberate through the whole house as she dropped it. She exchanged a nervous smile with Abby and waited for Lady Stokeley—or perhaps one of her servants—to open it.

It seemed to take an age but Lady Stokeley finally answered the door, her twin set and tweed skirt incongruously matched with a fleece gillet and a pair of Uggs.

"You'll excuse my appearance," she said in her frosty, imperious way. "It's rather cold inside the house."

Ellie realized what an understatement that was when she stepped inside the soaring foyer. It was bloody freezing. She and Abby both shivered despite their own boots and coats, and Lady Stokeley nodded grimly.

"Keep your coats on."

"It must be difficult to heat such a large home," Ellie ventured, and the older woman let out a rasp of a laugh.

"Difficult and expensive," she said, and led them to a

small drawing room at the back of the house. It was a little warmer in there, with a cheerful blaze taking up a tenth of the enormous fireplace and putting out a paltry but much-needed heat. The room was stuffed with furniture, from a pair of Victorian horsehair sofas that looked as if they suffering from mange to an enormous Welsh dresser of darkest mahogany, and heavy-handed oil paintings of unsmiling ancestors covering nearly every inch of the dam-ask-papered walls. A silver tea set that looked as if it might have once served a czar or two was resting on a marble-topped table in front of the fire.

"Please sit down wherever you like," Lady Stokeley said. "I apologize, it's a bit crowded in here."

"You have so many lovely keepsakes," Ellie said diplo-matically. The room, and maybe the whole house, was a study in shabby elegance. Very shabby, she reflected as a cloud of dust rose from the moth-eaten sofa when she sat down.

"They're not mine to keep," Lady Stokeley replied as she poured. "Everything in the house is entailed."

"Entailed…?" Ellie thought she'd heard the word on *Downton Abbey*, and she sort of knew what it meant. Very sort of.

"Not strictly entailed," Lady Stokeley explained as she handed them cups of fragrant tea. "That law was abolished before I was born. No, it's an equitable settlement, but the result is the same." Her smile was both wintry and pragmatic. "Everything in this house belongs to my nephew, Henry Trent."

Ellie wasn't sure what to say to that. "Does he live nearby?" she asked after a moment.

"No, he works in finance in London, and he's far too busy to visit me." She sighed and took a sip of tea. "Not that I blame him. What young man—well, youngish—wants to spend his weekends moldering away in the country with his widowed aunt?"

"Oh, but..." Ellie was again at a loss for words. She felt a sudden, deep sympathy for Lady Stokeley. Her life sounded terribly lonely.

"Never mind all that," Lady Stokeley announced with a wave of one arthritic hand. "You don't want to hear about me."

"Actually we do," Abby said, surprising Ellie as well as Lady Stokeley. She leaned forward, her face alight with interest. "You must have had such a fascinating life."

"Had?" Lady Stokeley's lips twitched. "I am not dead yet, you do realize."

"Oh, I didn't mean..." Abby gaped, clearly horrified, and Lady Stokeley chuckled, the dry, rasping sound reminded Ellie of dead leaves or paper rustling.

"I know you didn't. And the truth is I did have a fascinating life, but sadly it is no longer nearly as thrilling as it once was. The parties we once had, back in the sixties..." She sighed and then shook her head, eyeing Ellie shrewdly.

"The most exciting thing that has happened to me recently is seeing a dog tear up the lawn."

Abby frowned in confusion. "A dog…" She shot Ellie a questioning glance, and Ellie made an apologetic grimace.

"I really am so sorry about that…"

"No need, my dear. It was quite amusing. And it isn't as if I'm going to play croquet anytime soon, is it?" Lady Stokeley leaned back in her seat. "But enough about me. Why did the two of you move to Wychwood-on-Lea?"

"Well…" Ellie glanced again at Abby, as ever wondering how much to say. "I got a job at Oxford University."

"And I hated school," Abby said with surprising frankness. "Not that it's that much better here."

Shock nearly had Ellie's jaw hitting the floor. Her daughter never spoke like that, to anyone. School was a no-go zone conversation-wise, and Ellie's peacekeeping attempts were firmly rebuffed.

Lady Stokeley nodded in understanding. "I always found school to be rather a nightmare. The teachers were almost as horrid as the other girls."

"My teacher's actually okay," Abby said. "And the other girls aren't terrible."

"Death by a thousand paper cuts," Lady Stokeley remarked sagely, and Abby nodded in fervent agreement.

"Yeah, it's pretty much like that."

Lady Stokeley leaned forward and patted Abby's hand. "Patience, my dear. Girls who peak in primary school tend to live rather disappointing lives. Far better to be interesting from the start."

Abby grinned and Ellie sat there silently, soaking in every word of the conversation. Her daughter hadn't told her anything about school, beyond the fact that it was 'fine'—and Mallory Lang was a mean girl. On the occasions when she'd asked, Abby had given her the Glare of Silence. Ellie was well-used to that glare.

"I don't know why children have to be so terrible to each other," Lady Stokeley mused. "But then when does one learn to be civilized? I am acquainted with a great number of adults who behave in the same manner, only with a touch more subtlety." She gave Abby a smile of genuine sympathy. "You must come up here if ever you feel the need for a kindred spirit."

"Thanks," Abby said, looking pleased, and as if she might do such a thing.

Ellie's mind was still reeling as they headed back down to Willoughby Close an hour later. "You and Lady Stokeley seemed to get along." At the end of their afternoon, Lady Stokeley had insisted Abby call her Dorothy, but Ellie wasn't sure that invitation had extended to her. She'd been mostly silent, listening to Abby and Lady Stokeley talk about school and books and art. Her daughter had become more and more animated, making Ellie feel both grateful and the teeny, tiniest bit jealous. What about all *her* efforts? Lady Stokeley wasn't even that friendly. She'd turned her nose up at Ellie's macaroons. "I'm sorry, my dear," she'd said. "I detest shop-bought biscuits."

"She's cool," Abby answered with a shrug. "And she's seen so much. Did you hear her talk about the sixties? She almost sounds like she was a—what is it called? A swinger?"

The thought of Lady Stokeley as a swinger made Ellie suppress a shudder. "She's lived a long time," she said diplomatically.

"Yeah, and you've got to respect that. She has so much experience."

Which was an extraordinarily mature statement, coming from an eleven-year-old. Her daughter, Ellie realized with a pang, had made her first friend in the village.

Over the next couple of weeks it occurred to Ellie that maybe *she* needed to make a friend. Besides her occasional chats with Jeannie and the other assistants and her work-related conversations with Oliver, she barely spoke to anyone except Abby and occasionally Jace. And Abby had started spending more and more time up at Willoughby Manor.

"I'm helping Dorothy go through her stuff," Abby explained one Wednesday evening as Ellie took a package of mince from the fridge that was two days past its sell-by date. She hadn't had time to get to the Waitrose in Witney and their fridge was looking depressingly bare. Marmite snuffled hopefully at her legs, as he always did when the fridge door opened. But then even he turned away from the old mince, and with a sigh Ellie lobbed it in the bin.

"How about takeaway? And I do want to hear about Lady Stokeley's stuff."

"She's got the most amazing clothes. All this vintage stuff… real fur, and some wild outfits from the sixties. And the photo albums! It's incredible. There are pictures of Willoughby Manor from the 1970s that are hysterical. You should have seen the hairstyles." Ellie just nodded and Abby propped her elbows on the counter. "You seem tired, Mum."

"A bit." Tired and dispirited for a reason she couldn't quite identify. Her sister had texted with her half-term plans—a week in Orlando, something Ellie would never be able to afford. Diana had offered to help with the airline tickets but Ellie didn't think she could get time off then and she knew the trip would have stretched her sister's family budget to the max.

Besides, Abby didn't even get along with her cousins all that well—three sporty, rough-and-tumble boys to one bookish girl made for awkward family gatherings. Still, she'd have liked to go somewhere nice with Abby, even if it was just for a day or two. Maybe she could at Easter.

It was mid-February now, and winter still held Wychwood-on-Lea in its icy hold. Beautiful as it was, Ellie was ready to see more flowers than clumps of chilled-looking snowdrops. She was tired of scraping the frost off her windscreen and dodging icy mud puddles on the narrow pavements of Oxford. She was also tired of leaving for work at the crack of dawn and getting home when it was dark.

She'd wanted more from her life when she'd decided to move—but what?

"I think you need to meet people," Abby said frankly.

"What?" Ellie had been more or less thinking the same thing herself but she was still surprised to hear it coming from her daughter. "What do you mean?"

"You don't have any friends, Mum. And before you say I don't either—"

"I would never say that," Ellie fired back with fierce loyalty.

"All right, but you'd think it." Ellie sighed and stayed silent. "You need friends, Mum. You've always been so busy with work and me that you've never had time for yourself."

"I don't mind, Abby—"

"No, seriously." Abby folded her arms. "You need to get a life."

Ouch. Ellie grimaced even as she acknowledged that her daughter had a tiny point. She'd moved to Wychwood-on-Lea full of hope, painting her future with rainbows and unicorns and yes, friends. A month in and she was already feeling beaten down by the drudgery and—fine, she'd admit it—the loneliness.

"Okay," she said on a sigh. "I'll try to make a friend." She didn't know how, but hopefully her agreement would satisfy her daughter.

"There's a bake sale at school next week," Abby persisted. "Why don't you volunteer for it? I know you'd have to take some time off work, but it might be worth it. A bunch of other mums will be there."

Taking precious time off to volunteer for a bake sale? Ellie would rather go to the dentist for a root canal. All those manicured mummy-types bustling around, bragging about their organic tray bakes, turning their noses up at Ellie's offering, which admittedly would probably be pathetic and messy. Baking had never been her thing, even though she'd gamely baked a birthday cake for Abby every year. Last year Abby had asked for a shop-bought cake, and Ellie hadn't blamed her. She'd never gotten the trick of royal icing and her cakes often looked like they'd been decorated by a toddler.

"A bake sale?" Ellie said doubtfully. "I don't know, Abby."

"You've got to do something, Mum."

Ellie glanced at her daughter, a mixture of hope and determination in her eyes. She seemed fixated on this bake sale idea, which made Ellie wonder if Abby wanted her to volunteer for her own sake. Maybe if Ellie showed up a bit more, tried with the other mothers, Abby would start to fit in as well. "Fine," she said. If I volunteer for a bake sale, then you need to do something too."

Abby immediately turned wary. "Like what?"

Ellie hesitated. She was glad her daughter was spending time up at Willoughby Manor, and that she seemed to have a genuine friendship with Lady Stokeley, but... she wanted her daughter to have friends her own age. Friends at school, girls who would invite her for sleepovers and days out. She wanted Abby to have a normal childhood experience, one that involved giggling and linking arms and just having fun. She wanted to see her smile and laugh without the clouded eyes, the hunched shoulders. Didn't any mother want that for her child? She didn't, however, feel like she could say that now. She felt like she could never say it.

"Well?" Abby asked, arms now ominously folded.

"I know," Ellie said. "How about you make an effort with Tobias?"

"Tobias?" Abby looked even warier. "I don't even see him. We go to different schools." Ellie knew Abby had gotten on some middle earth website that Tobias was on, but whether that constituted a friendship or not she had no idea. Still, Tobias seemed a likelier friend than anyone else Ellie had come across, and she didn't have a way to help Abby make friends at the village school yet.

"What if I invite Oliver and Tobias over for dinner?" The possibility made her heart give a funny little leap. "So we can both have friends."

Abby's eyes narrowed, and Ellie knew she was considering whether this invitation was for her benefit—or her mother's. The answer was obvious. It was for Abby's, of course.

"Fine," she said. "But please, *don't* be awkward about it."

"Awkward?" Ellie stiffened in semi-mock outrage. "Since

when am I awkward about anything?" Abby's eloquent answer was the predictable eye roll. "Okay," Ellie relented, reaching for the takeaway menus tacked to the fridge with a magnet. "I promise not to be awkward. Now on to the more important question. Should we have Chinese or fish and chips?"

Chapter Eight

"DINNER?" OLIVER STARED at Ellie blankly, the rushed and semi-garbled sentence she'd just thrown at him not quite computing. "You want me to go to dinner?"

"You and Tobias," Ellie clarified quickly. "I thought he and Abby hit it off at the school evening, and it might be nice for them to spend some time together." Ellie's cheeks were bright red and she was twisting her hands together, knuckles knotted. She was nervous, Oliver realized. And she was asking him out to dinner. He didn't know how he felt about any of it. Bewildered, perhaps.

"I'll have to ask Jemima…"

"Oh, of course." Oliver hadn't thought it was humanly possible but Ellie's cheeks got brighter. "She's invited too, naturally…"

"She doesn't really go out much at the moment," Oliver said, which was a massive understatement. I'm sure she'll be fine with Tobias attending, though." He reached for his diary. "Do you have a date in mind?"

"Um… this Friday?"

Oliver glanced down at his diary and saw he had drinks with a couple of colleagues penciled in. Without any hesitation, or really knowing why, he struck a line through it. "Friday it is," he said, and then he looked up and smiled.

After Ellie had retreated back to her broom cupboard, Oliver was left musing on the invitation. He hadn't noticed that Abby and Tobias had particularly clicked, but he was not the most socially observant of men and Tobias didn't talk to him much about anything. For the last year, and in particular the last two months, Oliver had done his best to act in a fatherly, or at least an uncle-y, way to his nephew, but he suspected he was something of a dismal failure. Maybe this dinner would be some sort of stepping stone to a better, deeper relationship with the boy.

And as for Ellie... his stomach dipped in a way that was not unpleasant. Strange, perhaps, because he wasn't all that used to feeling... what? Excitement? Interest? He didn't know what to think about Ellie. She might have a husband, or at least a boyfriend. She'd never mentioned such a man, but who knew? Oliver might have missed the cues. It certainly wasn't a date, which was just as well because he was terrible at dating and in any case, he certainly couldn't date his personal assistant, which Ellie was for another four weeks.

Still he found he was rather looking forward to the evening, and Tobias hadn't objected to going when Oliver had broached it to him. He'd taken to stopping by Jemima's a couple of times a week, even though it was over an hour round trip from his flat in Oxford.

"So who is this Ellie?" Jemima asked without much interest when Oliver stopped by mid-week with several bags of groceries and a couple of pizzas for dinner. He'd started the habit of stocking her fridge, since all that was usually in there was a near-empty bottle of Pinot Grigio and if Tobias was lucky, some milk.

"She's my personal assistant, at least for the next few months. She's typing up the book I'm working on."

"Hmm." Jemima twirled a lank piece of hair around one finger, her gaze as vacant as ever. Oliver's heart felt as if it was both twisting and sinking. He hated seeing his sister like this. "Jemima, I really think you ought to get some help."

Her blue eyes widened and she slid off the bar stool she'd been slumped on. "I'm fine, Oliver."

"You're not fine—"

"If you're just going to lecture and nag me," Jemima said, a familiar shrill note entering her voice, "then you might as well not bother coming round."

Oliver sighed and stayed silent. This was how it always went with Jemima. She didn't want to talk about it—not her husband's death, not her obvious lack of coping. Most days, he feared, she stayed in the same stained designer pajamas. Most days he didn't know what to do with her—they'd never been close, and his enforced presence in her life felt oppressive, he suspected, to both of them. His parents, naturally, didn't want to know anything about it.

"I'll pick Tobias up at six on Friday," he said tiredly. "Okay?"

Jemima just nodded, not meeting his eyes, and with a murmured farewell Oliver left.

"MUM, STOP FREAKING out."

"I am not freaking out," Ellie retorted as she spritzed the kitchen counters with cleaning spray for the second time. "I just want things to be tidy."

The downstairs of the cottage looked, she hoped, fairly welcoming. The furniture might be secondhand and a bit on the shabby side, but she'd put up a bunch of pictures and family photos, and she'd bought fresh flowers from the covered market in Oxford that morning. The smell of the lasagna bubbling in the oven was appealing. Marmite had retreated to his basket by the woodstove, looking alarmed by the way Ellie was wielding spray and broom.

Abby, she noticed, had made an effort without appearing as if she had. She wore a pair of jeans that didn't have holes, a hoodie that wasn't black, and the elven leaf necklace she'd had on for the school evening. Pink color brightened her cheeks, and Ellie thought she detected the faint, candy-pink sheen of lip gloss, an unheard-of first.

"They are tidy," Abby said. "And you don't want to look as if you're trying too hard."

Just as her daughter didn't. Ellie put down the spray.

"Tidying up for guests is not trying too hard. Redecorating would be." She'd thought about splashing out on a new sofa, but she couldn't afford it. Anyway, Oliver wasn't the kind of man who would notice a sofa, was he? Outside of academia, he didn't seem like a man who noticed much.

A knock sounded on the door, and Ellie and Abby exchanged a split-second panicked glance as Marmite lumbered to his feet and rushed for the entrance with an exuberant *woof*.

"Okay." Ellie took a deep breath, tucking her hair behind her ears. As usual it sprang back out again. "Here we go," she muttered, and dodging her dog, opened the front door.

"Good evening—" Oliver began, only to be nearly bowled over by Marmite.

"Marmite, down," Ellie said desperately, wishing yet again that she could control her dog. Marmite had decided he liked Oliver, and had planted two enormous paws on his chest. Oliver blinked down at him, clearly nonplussed by the situation.

"I'm so sorry," Ellie said as she tugged on the dog's collar. "He doesn't do that with everyone."

"I'm honored. I think."

Fortunately Ellie managed to get Marmite back with four feet on the floor; unfortunately he let out a fart as she did so.

"Sorry, sorry," Ellie gabbled, mortified by this entirely expected chain of events. "That was Marmite," she added, just in case Oliver might have thought it was her.

"Yes," he said, his mouth twitching in a tiny smile, "I do realize."

"Mum," Abby hissed, caught between humiliation and humor, just as Ellie was. Because really, it was funny. At least, it would be later. Hopefully.

"Come on through," she said now that Marmite was under control, and Oliver came into the cottage, followed by a sullen-looking Tobias. Taking in the boy's hunched shoulders and ducked head, hands shoved into the pockets of his jeans, Ellie wondered if this evening was going to be a disaster. What if Abby and Tobias didn't get along? What if they didn't say anything, and she and Oliver had nothing to talk about, and they all endured an awful hour or two of awkward stops and starts, or worse, total, frozen silence?

Well, then, so be it. There were worse things than a bit of awkwardness. "Would you like a drink?" she asked Oliver, brandishing a bottle of red that cost twice as much as she'd usually spend.

"Oh no, thank you. I'm driving."

"Right." She put the bottle down with a clank and rallied once more. "Squash, then? Or juice? Water?"

"Water would be lovely."

"And Tobias?"

"I'll have squash, please," he half-mumbled. Ellie served them both drinks. Five minutes in and she already struggling with what to say.

"Are you looking forward to starting at Lea Comp?" she asked Tobias in that too-bright tone adults often took with children they didn't know. He gave her the typical dead-eyed stare back.

"Yeah. S'pose."

"It will be a big change." This merited no response. She was desperate, and it was showing. Unable to keep the conversation going, and with no help whatsoever from Oliver, she turned to Abby, who was giving her a don't-you-dare look. "Abby, why don't you show Tobias..." Ellie cast around for something suitable. "Your fantasy books?"

Abby's eyes narrowed and Ellie tried to communicate her apology by telepath. She knew it was awkward, but what else could she do? She needed some traction here. A little bit of give and take.

"Fine," Abby muttered, and turned to go upstairs without waiting for Tobias. After what felt like an endless few seconds, he trudged up after her.

Alone with Oliver, Ellie didn't know whether to relax or feel more tense. She felt both at the same time, weirdly. Oliver gave her a rather adorably wry smile. "Sorry, I'm not very good at this."

Ellie arched an eyebrow. "Good at what, exactly?"

His smile deepened, revealing a tantalizing dimple in one lean cheek. "Socializing."

No kidding. "You don't do it very often?"

"Outside of academia, no. If we were going to talk about

the Victorian period, I could chat all evening. But somehow I think the last thing you want to talk about is my book."

"Maybe not the last thing," Ellie teased. It felt a little bit like flirting. A very little bit. "I can think of a few things I'd like to talk about less. Like infectious diseases. Or Marmite's flatulence."

Oliver laughed, a sound of such genuine humor and warmth that Ellie felt a silly grin spreading over her face like butter on toast. This was getting easier, and definitely more fun. "Okay, but my book is definitely in the top ten. Or should I say, the least ten?"

"Yes, definitely in the least ten." They smiled at each other, and the moment stretched out and started to spin into something else. Sort of. Was she imagining the beginnings of the chemistry she felt between them? Fantasizing? And *why?*

"So, no talking about academia," she said after another taut moment. Her head felt fuzzy and in an effort to distract herself from her cartwheeling thoughts, she opened the oven door to check on the lasagna.

"That smells good," Oliver said as she shut the door and turned to face him. "Thank you for cooking."

"It was no trouble." Okay, someone needed to take the conversational lead, otherwise they'd stay mired in chitchat and a lot of pointless nodding. "So why history? And why a book about Victorian childhood?"

"I thought you didn't want to talk about my book."

"Yes, but I've realized I'm on chapter eight and I haven't

actually asked you that yet. It seems like something I should know." And heaven help her, but she couldn't think of anything else to talk about. Just looking at Oliver, having him in her house, was sending her into a right tizzy. And he looked very good tonight—dark brown cords, a crisp blue button-down shirt, and a battered corduroy blazer, the picture of relaxed intelligentsia. His eyes sparkled behind his glasses and she could see strands of gold in his chestnut hair that she hadn't noticed before. Plus that cleft chin was still very sexy.

"Well..." Oliver drew out the word, his gaze becoming distant and unfocused. "I was always something of a history buff, even as a child."

"How come?"

He looked startled, his gaze snapping back to hers, before he answered slowly, "I'm not exactly sure. Perhaps because in history, you get to know the ending."

Which made it sound as if he'd some uncertain endings in his own life, maybe even some unhappy ones. It occurred to Ellie then how little she knew about him beyond how he took his tea and what his research interest was.

"So where did you grow up?" she asked. "What was your childhood like?"

Another smile twitched at his lips. "Now you're sound-ing like Freud."

"Am I?" She wouldn't know. "Sorry, I'm just curious."

"There's not much to tell, really. Fairly standard childhood, fairly boring." He let out a little laugh. "Stiff upper lip and all that, a few fairly horrendous years at boarding school, you know."

Actually, she didn't. From that alone it sounded as if his childhood had resembled Lady Stokeley's more than it had hers. "My childhood was different," she said with a small smile.

"And better for it, I'm sure."

She was curious now about all he wasn't saying. "I'm not sure. It was fairly average, no boarding school, horrendous or otherwise."

"We're both sounding completely dull," Oliver answered with a laugh. "I told you I wasn't good at socializing."

"You just need practice." The oven timer dinged and Ellie grabbed a pair of oven mitts. "Time to eat."

By the time she had the food on the table and everyone seated around in the mismatched chairs from the charity shop, Ellie was feeling more optimistic about the evening. Abby and Tobias seemed to be getting along; Ellie had overheard them discussing some fantasy book as they came down the stairs, although they both immediately sank into silence when confronted with adults.

Oliver's rueful acknowledgement of his own social limitations was, she acknowledged, both endearing and just a little bit sexy. Why it should be so, she wasn't quite sure, but she liked him better for it. It made his sudden smiles, the genuine laughter that welled up, more precious. When she made him smile she felt like she'd scored a goal. *Win.*

They managed to have some semblance of a conversation over the course of the meal, with Tobias informing Abby where the best attractions in the area were, from cinema to bowling to paintball, which Ellie could see her daughter enjoying. By dessert things started to feel—dare she think it—relaxed, and as Oliver helped clear up Abby and Tobias started to set up a board game—one with complex rules and lots of pieces that Ellie had never really got the hang of—and were intent on playing by the time Ellie had made her and Oliver both coffees.

"That's nice to see," she murmured with a nod towards the pair of them sitting cross-legged on either side of the coffee table.

"It is, isn't it?" Oliver agreed. "It was a good idea you had, bringing those two together."

Just then Marmite let out a groan accompanied by his predictably loud expulsion of gas, and Ellie grimaced. "Sorry, he's suffering a bit after dinner. I usually take him for a walk around now."

"Why don't we both go?" Oliver suggested. "I'm sure Abby and Tobias will be fine on their own for a bit."

There was no reason for her heart to give a little skip, Ellie told herself as she got on her coat and boots. No reason to feel quite so excited. Yet she couldn't deny that, as she stepped out into the cold, starry evening with Oliver at her side, that was exactly how she felt.

Chapter Nine

THEY WALKED IN silence for a few moments, the only sound the crunching of gravel under their boots. Ellie breathed in several lungfuls of cold, sharp air while Marmite raced ahead, joyful in his liberation.

"He's quite a beast," Oliver said with a nod at the dog's fast-disappearing form.

"He is, at that," Ellie agreed.

"Why the name?"

"Marmite?" She laughed. "Because you either love him or hate him, just like the spread. And when I was first landed with him, I wasn't sure which I felt."

"Landed...? Sounds like a story there."

Ellie dug her hands deeper into the pockets of her coat. She wasn't sure how deep into her relationship with Nathan and all its accompanying disappointments she wanted to get—and yet somehow it was easier to talk to Oliver in the dark, with both of them walking.

"My ex-husband gave him to Abby when she was seven," she said. "She fell in love on the spot and I didn't feel I could be the meanest mum on earth and refuse. But it was difficult, and it's continued to be difficult. We lived in a tiny terraced house back in Manchester, and I worked all day. Not ideal conditions for a dog."

Oliver nodded towards the darkened path through the woods that Marmite had disappeared down. "He seems to be doing all right, flatulence aside."

Ellie laughed. "Yes, that is a problem, and one I don't think I can fix. Do you have any pets?"

"Not so much as a gold fish, I'm afraid."

She felt shy as she said, "I really don't know anything about you."

"I think I'm what it says on the tin," Oliver answered wryly. "Not many hidden layers."

"I'm not sure about that." Were they flirting? It was hard to tell. "Are you close to your sister?"

"Jemima?" He sounded surprised. "No, actually, we've never been close. She was always the party-going socialite, and I was... well, me." He gave a small laugh. "I'd like to think we've got closer since all this happened, but I'm not sure that's even true."

Ellie hesitated, desperately curious now to know more yet also not wanting to pry. "All this...?" she finally prompted gently and Oliver let out a big sigh.

"She and her husband Eric separated last year. He was a high flyer, City type, big in finance and all that. I'm not sure why they separated, but two months ago Eric killed himself."

Ellie let out a soft, sorrowful gasp. "I'm so sorry."

Oliver nodded grimly. "It was a huge shock, and Jemima basically fell apart. I took six weeks off work to look after her, but she needs the kind of help I can't provide. She's determined not to seek it though, and I don't know what else I can do." He slid her a sideways glance. "Sorry, I don't mean to offload on you." He gave her a small smile. "Maybe we should talk about my book after all."

"How is Tobias taking it?" Ellie asked. Her heart ached in a whole new way for the boy, as well as for the unknown Jemima and Oliver himself. It sounded like a heart-wrenching situation.

"He wasn't particularly close to his father, but of course it's still a huge loss." Oliver gave a resigned shrug. "I don't know what he's feeling, to be honest. He doesn't open up to me, and I can't say I blame him. I'm rather useless at all that kind of emotional talk. No one ever talked about feelings when I was a child. It was all 'children should be seen and not heard.'"

"That stiff upper lip you mentioned?"

"Right." They walked on in silence, Marmite barking happily ahead of them. Ellie had chosen a route well away from the manor house and its tempting lawn, so she wasn't too worried about what her dog might get up to.

"What about Abby?" Oliver asked. "You mentioned she's had a difficult time?"

"Yes, she has." Considering all Oliver had shared, Ellie

felt it was only fair to tell some of her story. And actually, she wanted to tell it, wanted someone to listen and hopefully understand. "She's been bullied at school for a while now," Ellie said slowly. "Since Year Two or Three. It's hard to know, because she never likes to tell me anything, but I figured it out eventually, and I tried to intervene, but it's so *hard.*" She felt a lump forming in her throat and she did her best to swallow it down. She didn't think Oliver could take her bursting into tears again, and in any case, she didn't want to give into that kind of emotion now. "I want someone to tell me what the right way to handle it is, and I'd do it, whatever it took, you know? But nobody tells you."

"Life doesn't come with a how-to book, much as we all could use one." His words would have seemed light if Ellie hadn't sensed so much heartfelt sincerity behind them. "It is hard," he continued quietly. "Especially when you feel so helpless. I'm sorry." Ellie couldn't remember the last time someone had spoken to her with such kindness. Diane's skepticism and her parents' hand-wringing worry felt like something else entirely, concern mixed with despair and doubt.

"Have you talked to her teachers?" Oliver asked after they'd walked on for a few minutes. They were deep in the woods now, the only light coming from a nearly full moon that bathed the bare branches of the trees in silver. In the distance an owl hooted, the sound both peaceful and melancholy.

"Yes, on various occasions. It never seems to work. Either the teacher comes down too hard and tells the other kids to be nice, which is awful, or they shrug and say children need to sort themselves out. And I can't blame them," Ellie added frankly. "Girls bully in such subtle ways. A pointed remark, a giggle behind a hand, a shared eye roll… little things you might not even notice but which can cut deep."

"I probably wouldn't notice," Oliver answered with a wry laugh. "Back in my day bullying was a bit more obvious. Sticking someone's head down the toilet or locking them in the games cupboard for an hour."

He spoke lightly, yet Ellie sensed a deep, painful current underneath the words. "You sound as if you speak from experience," she said quietly.

"Unfortunately. I was bulled at boarding school up until about age fourteen, when I had a growth spurt and joined the rowing team. But before then…" He shook his head. "Hopeless. I was easy prey, sadly. Glasses, bookish, socially awkward, the works." He gave her a little smile. "Not much has changed, eh?"

"I wouldn't say that." Ellie imagined a young, bookish Oliver being locked in a dark, cobwebby cupboard and felt a rush of sympathy for him. It sounded awful, worse than anything Abby had endured, although in truth she didn't know how much Abby *had* endured, because her daughter didn't like to tell her.

"And did your parents do anything about it?" she asked.

"Oh, no. I never dreamed of telling them. My father would have been horrified, no son of his should be bullied, and so on. And my mother… well, I don't think she would have particularly cared." He grimaced. "Sorry, that sounds as if they were completely heartless but I don't think that was really the case. It was just how things were in those days. And they had their own issues to deal with."

"Kind of like how in Victorian times no one minded about sending a five-year-old up a chimney?"

Oliver laughed, his teeth gleaming in the darkness. "Yes, I suppose. Thank goodness we've moved on a bit, as a society."

"Yes, thank goodness," she murmured. Her heart still ached for the boy Oliver had been, and what he'd had to suffer through. Sometimes being a kid truly sucked.

Ellie had been so wrapped up in their conversation that it took her a moment to realize she hadn't seen or heard Marmite in a while. "Uh oh," she said, and Oliver shot her a questioning glance.

"What is it?"

"I think Marmite's gone AWOL. The first time I took him in the woods he did a runner and ended up tearing up Lady Stokeley's lawn up at the manor." Ellie gave a not-so-mock shudder. "She was actually quite a good sport about it, but I'm not sure she would be a second time."

"Let's call him."

"Mar-mite!" Ellie bellowed, her voice ringing through

the still and frosty woods. "Marmite, come back, boy!" The only thing she got back, predictably, was silence.

Then Oliver tried, his voice lower and louder than hers, a masculine roar. Still nothing.

"I have a very bad feeling about this," Ellie said, just as Marmite came hurtling out of the woods and straight at her, plowing into her legs and sending her near-flying until Oliver steadied her, his hands coming up to grasp her shoulders as her body collided in several key points with his.

The first thing Ellie became aware of was how well-muscled Oliver's chest felt when hers was crushed against it. His thighs felt muscular too, and he smelled delicious. Her brain seemed to have short-circuited because she didn't jerk away, no, she didn't do what any sane, self-respecting woman would do, and right herself as quickly as possible.

No, she moved *towards* him, pressing against him like a cat in heat, her hips rocking into his, until Oliver jerked his hands from her shoulders and he took a step away.

"Sorry about that." His voice sounded hoarse. "Are you okay?"

"Um. Yes." Ellie was glad the darkness hid the scorching blush she could feel rising to her face. Why on earth had she pressed herself against him like that? Had he noticed? Briefly she closed her eyes. The prospect was mortifying. She'd been shameless, and she hadn't even *meant* to. It was as if her body had overtaken her brain. "We should probably get back." Her voice sounded strangled. She crouched down to put on Marmite's lead, letting her hair swing forward to hide her face just in case Oliver could see her flush in the moonlight. She didn't think she'd ever been so embarrassed. Obviously, she needed to get out more. Date more. She hadn't had a date in… years, at least. Diane had insisted on setting her up with a couple of acquaintances after the divorce but they'd never gone anywhere. In fact they'd been fairly atrocious.

"Come on, Marmite." There, at least that sounded semi-normal. She started walking briskly back to Willoughby Close, trusting that Oliver would keep up. She couldn't look at him, not even in the dark. Neither of them spoke, which seemed to confirm her suspicions that he'd felt the way she'd reacted, and was understandably horrified. Was this going to ruin everything—their friendship, Tobias and Abby's friendship, her job? She was so *stupid*.

Abby and Tobias were just finishing up their game as Ellie entered with an over-cheery hello, Oliver following behind. She took off her coat and boots, chatting almost manically about how beautiful it had been outside until she realized both tweens were looking at her strangely. She was making an awkward situation even worse.

"So." Hands on hips and megawatt smile. Jeez, couldn't she ever stop? "Who won the game?"

"I did," Abby said with a touch of pride. "And I hardly ever play, because you don't understand the rules."

"I know, I'm hopeless." Abby had tried explaining the

concept of the game to her more than once, and Ellie had been bewildered by the descriptions of settlements and civilization scores and trade points. "A bit too much for me," she said with a smile aimed at Tobias. He gave her the tiniest smile back.

All in all a success, she decided as Oliver and Tobias made their goodbyes, at least for the younger two. She wasn't even going to think about her and Oliver. She couldn't go there, not even in her head.

There was a little awkwardness at the doorway, and Oliver ended up shaking her hand as if they'd just agreed on a business deal. When the door closed behind them Ellie heaved a great big sigh. "I think that went well."

"Why were you acting so weird?" Abby asked. "What happened out on the walk?"

"Nothing," Ellie practically yelped. "Abby, what are you like? Honestly." She shook her head, deliberately avoiding Abby's suggestive smirk as she bustled around, switching on the dishwasher and wiping down counters.

"He is kind of cute," Abby persisted. "For an old guy."

"Abby." Ellie felt herself start to blush again. It was as if her daughter had x-ray vision and had seen that near-clinch in the woods. Not that it had been remotely close to a clinch. It had been... an unfortunate accident. Yes.

"What?" Abby demanded. "It's obvious you like him. What's the big deal? You should go on a real date."

"I don't want to go on a real date," Ellie said, and even to her own ears she didn't sound particularly convincing. She chose to bristle instead. 'What do you mean, *obvious?*'

"I wouldn't mind, you know," Abby said quietly. "Because of Dad, I mean."

Ellie turned to look at her daughter; Abby looked so small and vulnerable in her over-sized hoodie, her cloud of dark hair, just like Nathan's, surrounding her pale, set face.

"It's not like he's in our lives anymore, is it?" she continued, lifting her chin.

"He's in Australia, Abby."

"Yeah. Exactly."

Ellie remained silent, torn between wanting to protect Abby's tenuous relationship with her father—even now—and being honest. Nathan's sudden extended trip to Australia had been, as all his decisions seemed to be, impulsive and thoughtless. He'd met a backpacker in a bar and decided to accept her casual invitation to visit indefinitely. Ellie supposed it helped she was stacked and blonde.

Sighing, she tossed the sponge in the sink where it landed with a wet thud. "I'm sorry your dad has let you down, Abby. But he does love you." Even if he hadn't sent so much as an email since he'd boarded the plane.

"Yeah, from a distance." Abby shrugged. "Look, I'm over it, okay? But I think you should be over it, too."

Ellie doubted her daughter was over her father's virtual abandonment, but she wasn't about to argue the point. As for her... "What do you mean, I need to be over it?"

"Exactly that. Why haven't you dated in, like, ever?"

"For a lot of reasons," Ellie answered. "I've been busy, and there haven't been a lot of men beating down my door, just in case that escaped your notice."

"You could have gone on one of those online dating sites."

"Seriously? You're telling me that?" Ellie shook her head, her hands on her hips. "I didn't realize you were so eager for me to date."

"I want you to get a life."

Ouch. "I have a life, Abby—"

"No, a real life," Abby cut her off, sounding surprisingly fierce. "So I can have a life too."

Ellie jerked back, trying not to show how surprised and yes, hurt she was by that statement. "What do you mean? Am I cramping your style or something?"

Abby blew out a breath, the strands of her silky fringe flying in the air. "No, of course not. It's just... you're kind of... worried all the time. If you had a life of your own to think about, you might not obsess over mine so much."

Double ouch. Ellie blinked, absorbing that statement. She decided to back away from it, because she didn't want to show how hurt she was, and give Abby an inadvertent guilt trip. "I don't think Oliver Venables is interested in me."

"Are you interested in him?"

Ellie opened her mouth to say no, of course not, because that was the sensible answer. The safe answer. But considering how her body had betrayed her earlier, hips nudging his—dear Lord, would she ever forget that moment—she couldn't quite get the words out with the force she knew she needed.

"I *knew* it," Abby crowed.

"No, it's not like that," Ellie said way too late. "Honestly…" She trailed off, blushing. Great.

"Why are you fighting it, Mum?" Abby asked, and Ellie wondered when and how her eleven-year-old had gained so much worldly wisdom. "Just go with it. He's obviously into you."

"*Into* me?" Ellie thought of the way Oliver had jerked back when she'd been pressed against him. "I don't know where you get that idea, Abby."

Abby shrugged. "He came to dinner, didn't he?"

"Yes, but…" Ellie fell silent, not wanting to admit that Oliver had come to dinner because she'd said it would be good for Abby and Tobias.

"And I could just tell. He kept looking at you, you know, when you weren't looking at him."

"Did he?" Too late Ellie realized how young and giggly she sounded. "No, he didn't," she said quickly, and Abby laughed.

"Whatever, Mum."

"All right, then," Ellie dared to tease. "What about you and Tobias?"

Abby's eyes rounded. *"Mum!"*

"Well, if you're going to tease me about Oliver, I get to tease you about Tobias."

"We're just *friends,*" Abby huffed. "Besides, I'm only eleven."

"I know, I know." Ellie held up a placating hand. "You're not actually allowed to date for at least five years. But since we're talking about him, did you guys get along? As friends, I mean?"

Abby shrugged, her gaze sliding away from Ellie's. "Yeah, I s'pose."

"Okay." She would *not* press. Ellie nodded slowly. "Good." And for once, she left it at that.

Later, as she was lying in bed and having an aggravating amount of difficulty getting to sleep, she let herself relive the highlights of the evening. Chatting with Oliver. Having him seem so interested and genuine. When had someone last listened to her for that long? It had been a balm to her dispirited soul.

And then of course she had to replay that agonizing moment when she'd fallen into Oliver's arms and then pressed herself up against him. Even in the privacy and darkness of her own bedroom, Ellie's cheeks grew warm. And other parts too, because no matter how Oliver had jerked back—and he had—in that split second he'd felt very nice. Far more muscular than she would have expected. It made her wonder what he looked like beneath his battered blazer and button-down shirt. What he would feel like if she touched him.

And that was a fantasy she had no intention of indulging in. There was no point, because no matter what Abby had said, Ellie didn't think Oliver was interested in her. And even if he was…

Well, there was no point even wondering, was there? They were different people, from different worlds. And in any case Ellie had already had one bad experience, trying too hard—over and over again—with a man who wasn't going to change. Did she really want to attempt something similar? Oliver wasn't right for her, and she wasn't right for him, end of story.

Even so it took Ellie a long time to go to sleep.

Chapter Ten

ELLIE SURVEYED THE primary-aged scrum in the school hall and squared her shoulders.

"Once more into the breech," she muttered, and stepped inside the large hall. When she'd asked Oliver if she could have the morning off to help with the school bake sale, he'd been more than amenable. Their evening together had lent a new familiarity to their relationship that felt comfortable and yet also a little bit weird. This was *Oliver Venables,* Oxford don, and he was asking her how Abby was getting on at school. Fortunately they'd both decided to pretend, by mutual, silent agreement, that the moment in the woods have never happened.

Ellie navigated the sweaty press of eager schoolchildren as she skirted the table nearly bowed under the weight of homemade fairy cakes and cookies. Three harried-looking mothers were manning the sale, and one of them was obviously in charge. Ellie approached her, pasting on a smile that felt false as she tapped her on the shoulder.

"Excuse me—"

"Yes?" The woman turned around, brushing a strand of wavy, dark hair from her eyes as she gazed at Ellie with friendly impatience.

With a start Ellie recognized her—this was Mallory Lang's mother, whom she'd seen on the high street. Of course she was running the bake sale.

"I'm here to help." Ellie held out her hands, palms up, although she wasn't quite sure why. "You can put me to work."

"Oh, right, brilliant." The woman nodded towards an empty space behind one of the tables. "Why don't you take that spot? Just serve the cakes and collect money—it's pretty simple. Everything costs twenty pence."

Just because something was simple, Ellie soon realized, didn't mean it was easy. The children were eager and impatient and had no idea how to form an orderly queue. They pressed against the table, causing it to rock back on its legs, hands clutching sweaty fifty-pence pieces that they thrust into Ellie's face, whingy voices demanding this cookie or that cake, and heaven help her if she picked the wrong one by accident.

She tried to keep her smile bright, her voice cheerful, as she navigated the anxious press of children, sharing a few complicit smiles with the other mums that gladdened her heart. They might be wearing designer jeans and own Apple watches but in this, at least, they were just like her.

And then disaster struck.

Losing track of who was in the semblance of the queue, Ellie served one young girl who hadn't been waiting as long as the boy next to her, and a wail rose up among the children, indignant accusations of injustice that made the other mums give her questioning looks.

"Sorry, sorry," Ellie muttered breathlessly. "Here, have an extra cake." She put two brownies in a plastic bag and handed it to the boy who had been waiting longer, only to realize a split second later what a terrible decision that had been. Another wail rose up, this time a clutch of Year Threes demanding that they get free cakes, as well.

She was so not good at this.

One of the mums shot her a sympathetic look that was tinged with a better-you-than-me smirk, and, looking distinctly hassled now, Mallory Lang's mother waded into the fray to see what was going on.

"She gave Jack Bell a free cake," one girl declared in a piercingly loud voice, and Mallory Lang's mother's mouth tightened. *What mother did something so stupid?* Her look seemed to be demanding. Ellie wanted to crawl under the table. Or preferably kick it over. Stupid bake sales. She'd never liked them, anyway. Who knew how many sticky fingers had tasted the dough? Someone might have spit in the batter.

Somehow Mallory Lang's mother, who seemed like one of those frighteningly capable women who most likely color-coded everything in her house, sorted the mess out and the children subsided, momentarily satisfied. They struck Ellie as a pack of wolves that had been tossed a morsel of raw meat but would soon be demanding more. Mallory Lang's mother turned to Ellie with a strained smile.

"Would you mind getting us some teas?"

So now she'd been downgraded to waitress? "Okay," Ellie said as graciously as she could manage, and headed towards the kitchen to beg one of the dinner ladies use of the kettle.

As she stood waiting for the enormous kettle to boil she watched the other mother bustle about the table, smiling at children, handing out change, and looking as if they knew exactly what they were doing. They also, she noticed, all looked as if they were best friends, joking with each other, giving good-natured eye rolls and winks. She'd almost been part of that, for a few minutes, but then she'd done something stupid and now she felt left out. In that moment she thought she knew a little of what Abby felt like on a day-to-day basis.

She made the teas and as she brought them back to the table, the Year Fives and Sixes filed in. Ellie tried to be surreptitious about it but she kept an eye on Abby, who was studying the cakes at the other end by herself. Of course. How did her daughter manage to look lonely in a crowd of children? Although perhaps that was when she looked the loneliest.

"Thanks for this," Mallory Lang's mum said, hoisting the

plastic cup of tea. "I think the rush has died down so if you want to sit down for a moment before it ends and we all clean up…"

So she'd been fired from helping with the bake sale. Fine. With a small smile Ellie retreated to the window and leaned against the sill, sipping her milky tea and watching as the mothers worked the stall, the plastic platters of cakes and cookies slowly becoming depleted.

By the time the sale ended, the other mums were exclaiming how well it had gone and how tired they were and Ellie was feeling bored and frustrated. She'd essentially taken half a day's holiday so she could sit and watch a bake sale, and she couldn't blame Mallory Lang's mum for keeping her away. She'd been rubbish at it.

As the last children left the hall, the boy who'd bagged the free brownie giving her a smirk, Ellie went forward to help with the clean-up.

"I don't think we've actually met," Mallory Lang's mother said as she stuck out a hand. "I'm Harriet Lang, mum to Mallory in Year Six, William in Year Four, and Chloe in Year One." She said this with the pat confidence of someone who had long ago become accustomed to introducing herself in such a way.

"I'm Ellie Matthews, mum to Abby also in Year Six," Ellie said as she took her hand. "We've just moved to the area."

"Oh, have you? Mallory hasn't said anything about a new

girl in the class."

Ellie's smile stiffened but stayed put. "No?" she inquired politely. What else could she say? *No, your daughter wouldn't mention the girl she teases, would she?*

"Well, you know how these tweens are," Harriet continued, brushing her hair from her eyes. "Getting them to tell you anything is like pulling teeth."

"Right." Which was true for her and Abby, but it didn't particularly endear her to Harriet or her daughter. Nothing much would at this point.

"Welcome to Wychwood-on-Lea, anyway," she continued. "Do you and your husband live in the village?"

And so it got worse. "Yes, I live in the village, but there's no husband." Harriet blinked, and Ellie wished she hadn't sounded quite so... well, bitchy might be a bit extreme, but definitely not friendly.

She wasn't like these women. She would never be like these women. And she felt it most acutely when she was standing right next to them.

"Right, of course," Harriet said with an awkward laugh. "Sorry, I shouldn't have assumed."

"Easily done." Ellie gestured to the crumb-scattered trays. "Shall I start washing up?"

No one talked to her while they washed up, but then Ellie suspected she was giving off distinctly unfriendly vibes. She was feeling fed up by the whole morning, and frustrated that she did. She'd wanted this to work. She needed a friend.

She overheard the other mums talking about going out to some organic farm shop café for lattes afterwards, and Ellie headed off the lack of invitation by announcing brightly that she had to go work. She walked out of the school without looking back.

On the train to Oxford she gave herself a talking-to. She could have made more of an effort with Harriet Lang or the others, trading in on those complicit smiles and sympathetic looks. She could have joked about the mishap with the free brownie; she could have joined in with the good-natured complaining about school runs and checking homework and the rest. She was a mum. She was part of *that* group, at least, even if she hadn't felt like it.

Sighing, Ellie leaned her head against the train window and watched muddy fields slide by. She'd botched that up good and proper. Moving here had opened up an insecurity inside herself that she hadn't even realized she'd had.

Oliver was out delivering a lecture when Ellie arrived, but he'd left a print-out of the latest chapter she'd typed, much of it marked in red, with great slashing lines through some of the text, and asterisks with wavy lines leading to cramped writing in the margins. It was going to take ages to decipher it. He'd left a note on top, in his usual scrawl: *Took your advice and am adding personal stories. Sorry for the mess! – O.*

For some reason that made Ellie smile, and her heart gave a little lift as she sat down to work. Five hours later she had a crick in her neck and cramp in her shoulders, but she felt a little more optimistic about life. Oliver had included some heart-rending stories in his revised chapter, and it had been fascinating and emotional to read it.

She was just packing up when a knock sounded on her door and then Oliver poked his head in. His hair was rumpled, his glasses askew, and he sounded breathless, all rather unusual for a man who tended to be orderly to an exacting fault.

"I'm glad I caught you. I wanted to invite you to a party tomorrow night."

Ellie goggled. *Oliver* wanted to invite her to a *party?* All of Abby's advice and observation whirled around in her head as she wondered, with a little thrill, if he was interested in her after all.

"It's a cocktail party for the history faculty," he continued. "And all the admin staff are invited. I didn't want you to miss out." He smiled as he raised his eyebrows. "Think you'll be able to make it?"

So, not a date then. She'd been an absolute idiot to think for a moment, a *millisecond,* that it might be. "I'm not sure," she hedged. A cocktail party with a bunch of academics sounded both dull and a bit frightening. Besides, she didn't have a babysitter for Abby or something suitable to wear.

"I know it probably sounds about as fun as watching paint dry, but it's usually a fairly good 'do. It's at the Eagle and Child, the pub where C.S. Lewis and Tolkien used to meet?"

The uplift to his voice suggested he thought she'd be familiar with it, and of course she wasn't. "Sounds amazing. I'll see what I can do."

"Text me if you do decide to go," Oliver said. He was smiling, his gaze intent, and Ellie's body responded with a treacherous, tingling warmth. It wasn't fair that she was attracted to him when he obviously didn't experience the same kind of reaction. "Do you have my number?"

"Um…" She should have his number, considering she was his PA, but she didn't. She'd always simply put his messages on his desk.

"I'll give it to you now."

Ellie duly took out her phone and typed in the number as he dictated it to her. "Thanks, I'll let you know," she murmured, making no promises.

By the time Ellie arrived home two hours later, having waged war with the rush of weekend commuters and won a seat on the train, then picked up Abby at after school club and stopped by the post office shop to buy a packet of pasta and a wedge of cheese for a last-minute tea, she was exhausted and looking forward to an entire weekend spent at home, and preferably in bed with a good book and a hot water bottle.

"So how was the bake sale?" Abby asked as she tossed her backpack by the kitchen counter and turned to Ellie with her arms folded, eyebrows raised. "Did you make friends?"

"Oh yes, we're all besties now," Ellie returned sarcastically, only to wince at the look on Abby's face. She was so not setting a good example. "Sorry, I didn't mean that. Truthfully it was a little bit dire. But I did try." Sort of, not really.

"Hmm, because you looked like you were trying when I came in," Abby returned. "You were sitting by the window on your own."

"I'd been blacklisted from the bake sale table," Ellie returned as she got out pots and pans to make macaroni and cheese. "I committed the unforgivable sin of giving a kid a free cake."

"Oh, Mum." Abby rolled her eyes. "Don't you know better than that?"

"Apparently not." Ellie banged a pot of water on the stove, feeling distinctly disgruntled.

"It's okay," Abby said in a placating tone. "Better luck next time."

"Right." If Ellie had anything to do with it, there wouldn't be a next time. Helping at a bake sale was not going to make her or Abby any friends. "Why didn't you talk to me?" she asked Abby. "I saw you in the hall."

"I didn't want to cramp your style."

"You wouldn't have, trust me." Ellie smiled, deciding she needed stop taking it all so much to heart. So she'd messed up at a bake sale. This could be something she would laugh about, if she chose to. Something she and Abby could laugh about together. "Anyway, the day wasn't a complete fail. I got invited to a party this weekend."

"A party?" Abby's eyes rounded. "By one of the mums?"

Her daughter didn't have to sound quite so incredulous, Ellie thought, even as she acknowledged what a laughable idea that was. "Nope, by Oliver. History faculty thing."

"Wow." Abby looked impressed. "So is this a date?"

"No, not even close, and in any case, I'm not going." She hadn't been planning on going, and yet stating it so definitively made her feel a little twist of disappointment inside.

"What?" Abby cried. "Not going? You so are."

"I can't, Abby. I have nothing to wear and in any case, you need a sitter."

"I don't need a sitter. I'm—"

"Eleven years old and I am not leaving you alone all night."

"It wouldn't be all night, would it? Or would it?" Abby retorted with a smirk and Ellie shot her a warning look. "Anyway you left me alone all day already."

"That was an emergency measure, and just no," Ellie stated. The water had started boiling and she dumped the packet of macaroni into it, trying to signal an end to the conversation.

"Why don't you want to go?" Abby persisted. Her daughter was annoyingly stubborn sometimes.

"Because I just don't."

"But that's not a real reason."

"Hey." Ellie turned around, blowing a strand of hair

from her eyes. "Who's the child and who's the adult here?"

"You tell me." Abby smirked again and Ellie almost laughed, because really, she *was* acting like a little kid. A stubborn, spoiled little kid about to have a tantrum. She needed to get over herself, and fast.

"I don't know exactly why I don't want to go," she admitted on a sigh. "I think it might be a bit awkward."

Abby propped her elbows on the kitchen counter, her head cocked to one side. "Awkward how?"

"Just awkward." She didn't want to burden Abby with all her own insecurities, some newly discovered, some all too familiar. "Plus, like I said, I don't have a sitter—and that *is* non-negotiable, by the way—or a nice dress. So." She reached for the cheese grater. "Now how about you set the table?"

Ellie thought she'd settled the matter since Abby dropped the subject, focusing instead on whether Ellie would take her to the cinema in Witney at some point over the weekend. Then she offered to walk Marmite after dinner, which seemed above and beyond her usual level of helpfulness, but Ellie didn't question it. She flopped on the sofa, the remote control in one hand, and told herself she was going to have a lovely, long relationship with the TV.

"So it's all sorted," Abby announced an hour later when she breezed in with a happy Marmite and a gust of cold air.

"What's sorted?" Ellie was still slouched on the sofa, a half-empty bag of crisps on her lap, her mind starting to liquefy from the amount of reality TV she'd just gorged on.

"Tomorrow night," Abby explained blithely. Marmite flopped on top of Ellie's feet.

"Ow, Marmite." With a grunt Ellie liberated her feet from beneath the heavy body of her dog. "What are you talking about, tomorrow night?" She turned to Abby with narrowed eyes. "What have you done?"

"I stopped by to see Dorothy," Abby explained. "And told her your dilemma."

"My what? And who? I mean, why..." Ellie shook her head, exasperated. "What does Lady Stokeley have to do with anything?"

"Why won't you call her Dorothy?" Abby asked as she flopped on the sofa next to Ellie and took the bag of crisps.

"She hasn't asked me to."

"I don't think she'd mind."

"Abby, what did you tell Lady Stokeley?" Ellie demanded. She was starting to get a little bit annoyed—and more than a little bit alarmed.

"I told her about your party. She said she'd lend you one of her dresses, and she has tons and they're fabulous. Seriously cool vintage. Plus I think you'd actually be her size. Almost."

"Are you serious—"

"And," Abby continued, "she offered to have me stay up at the manor with her while you're at the party. We're going to watch reruns of *Strictly Come Dancing.*"

"Uh-huh." Ellie shook her head slowly. She couldn't believe how thoroughly she'd been outmaneuvered. "Why did you go to all this trouble, Abby?"

"Because like I told you before, I want you to have a life. It makes my life easier." Abby dropped the light tone for a moment and regarded Ellie seriously. "Plus, I want you to be happy."

"Oh." Ellie felt a lump form in her throat. Suddenly all her protestations seemed absurdly childish. Her daughter had gone to a lot of effort to make this happen. "Well." She swallowed. "Thank you."

Abby grinned. "No problem."

Later, when Abby had gone to bed, Ellie got out her phone to text Oliver. She spent way too long considering how to phrase what was meant to be a very simple message and finally settled on *Turns out I can go to the party. See you there?*

She wavered, wondering if she should leave that question mark in, if it was too obvious, inviting a reply, practically demanding one. But then she reasoned Oliver would not be so well-versed in the intricacies of texting, and probably wouldn't even notice the punctuation. Should she dare a smiley face emoji? No, that was a step too far. Taking a deep breath, she pressed send.

Thirty seconds later a message pinged back. With a thrill Ellie saw it was from him, and a sloppy smile spread across her face as she saw the one word: *Absolutely.*

Chapter Eleven

ELLIE DIDN'T KNOW what to expect when Abby frog-marched her up to Willoughby Manor the next afternoon, but it seemed that Lady Stokeley had decided to play fairy godmother for a day... or something like that.

She met them at the door, her wrinkled face wreathed in smiles, a mangy-looking fox fur draped over her thin shoulders, and the usual Uggs on her feet. "Come in, come in," she called to Ellie, all gracious bonhomie. "I've looked through my things—dresses that haven't been worn in decades! Of course, they might be a little dusty..."

Ellie followed Lady Stokeley up the grand staircase to the first floor, eyeing the oil portraits of her neighbor's various ancestors, most of them looking suitably sober or stern. The air was so cold she could see her breath coming out in frosty puffs, and she wondered how a woman of Lady Stokeley's age survived the winter in a place like this.

"Here we are," Lady Stokeley announced grandly, and threw open the doors to a bedroom that looked like it belonged to Miss Havisham, complete with a four poster with threadbare hangings from the Tudor age or thereabouts, but fortunately, thanks to a kerosene heater, was at least warm.

"This is so kind of you," Ellie said. Abby seemed convinced that she was going to find something fantastic to wear to the party that night, but Ellie wasn't so sure. If the rest of the house was anything to go by, Lady Stokeley's belongings were more than a little moth-eaten. Ellie didn't want to offend the older lady, but she was a teeny bit concerned about showing up to a swish event wearing something that looked like it belonged in *Corpse Bride* or *The Rocky Horror Picture Show.*

"I'm glad to do it. It's been quite entertaining," Lady Stokeley replied as she walked with surprising speed to the adjoining dressing room. "Now, I got out a few things that I thought might be appropriate…"

"Do you need help?" Ellie called, for Lady Stokeley had disappeared into a room that looked to be stuffed to the rafters with various confections of lace, taffeta, silk, and satin… even from across the room Ellie saw that they looked more than a little dated and dusty. She had a jersey wrap dress she'd worn to work several times. She could pair it with heels and a chunky necklace and call it a day—or rather, a night.

"It'll be fine, Mum," Abby whispered. "Trust me."

Trust her eleven-year-old's fashion sense? Abby's idea of dressing up was wearing jeans without holes, or at least without big holes. Ellie gave her daughter a sickly smile as Abby went to help Lady Stokeley bring in the first few outfits.

A cloud of dust rose in the air as they left the dressing room carrying a froth of fabric. Lady Stokeley sank onto a stool shaped like a powder puff while Abby laid the dresses out on the bed.

"This is Chanel," she said, stroking the rust-colored velvet of one dress. "From 1970."

"Lovely," Ellie murmured. The velvet was rubbed bare in parts and the style of the dress was baggy, with a large, pointed white collar. Not exactly what she wanted to wear to the party, but Ellie wasn't sure how she was going to get out of this gracefully.

"Not that one, Abby," Lady Stokeley barked. "I never liked it. The fabric was lovely, but it looked like a velvet bin bag. Try the Balenciaga."

Ellie looked at dress after dress, admiring what she could even as her heart began to sink right down to her toes. She couldn't wear any of this stuff, and yet she didn't want to hurt Lady Stokeley's feelings.

Fortunately Lady Stokeley was a bit shrewder than she'd given her credit for.

"These all look far too shabby," she said as she struggled up from her powder puff stool. She wrinkled her nose and waved her hand in front of her face; there was still a fair amount of dust in the air. Ellie had been doing her best not to sneeze for the last ten minutes.

"I think we need to go back a bit farther."

Ellie wanted to disagree with that statement, but then Lady Stokeley emerged from the dressing room carrying a dress that looked, well, perfect.

"Oh," Ellie breathed, and Lady Stokeley shot her a smug look.

"This is more what you're looking for, isn't it?"

It was. The dress was deceptively simple, made of burgundy taffeta with a subtle lace overlay, a narrow skirt and a skinny belt in patent leather cinching the waist.

"Shall you try it on, Mum?" Abby asked, and Ellie nodded, the first fragile tendrils of hope winding around her heart. She was starting to feel like Cinderella, and no more so than when she emerged from the dressing room and Abby beamed while Lady Stokeley proclaimed,

"Ah, yes. That's what we were looking for."

Ellie did a little twirl in front of the cheval, grinning at her reflection. "It's perfect, Lady Stokeley. Thank you."

An hour later, after celebrating with crumpets and tea in the sitting room, Ellie was back at Willoughby Close with the dress hung reverently on a padded satin hanger. She quaked at the thought of spilling a glass of wine on it, or worse. It was, Lady Stokeley had told her, Chanel from the 1950s and worth a small fortune.

"And now we can do your hair and makeup," Abby said, bouncing on her bed as she hung the dress up in her wardrobe.

"You might not want to jump so much," Ellie warned. "Jace fixed your bed, not mine." She shook her head in bemusement. "And what do you mean, my hair and makeup? When have you ever been a girly girl like that?"

Abby shrugged. "It's different when it's you. Can I do your eyes?"

Ellie had serious reservations about letting her daughter near her makeup, but she couldn't pass up such a bonding opportunity, so she shrugged and smiled. "Sure."

An hour later Ellie was walking Abby up to the manor house, and discreetly checking her panda eyes in her compact. Abby had been a bit heavy-handed with the eyeliner, going for more of a Goth look than Ellie was comfortable with, but she could fix it in the car. Hopefully. Her daughter was skipping ahead, humming under her breath, and it occurred to Ellie how lighthearted Abby had seemed since befriending Lady Stokeley. Who ever would have thought her daughter would find a friend in a nearly ninety-year-old woman? And while it wasn't what Ellie would have expected, she was glad Abby seemed happy.

"Don't worry about me, Mum," Abby said as Lady Stokeley welcomed them at the front door. "I'll be fine."

"Of course she will," Lady Stokeley said with dignified affront. "She's with me. Now, don't forget to take photographs. I'm on Instagram."

"You are?" Ellie said in disbelief. The only technology

she'd seen in the house was a boxy television set that looked like it might still be in black and white.

"Yes, of course. Abby showed me."

"You did?" Ellie turned to her daughter, still disbelieving. "You don't even have an Instagram account, do you?"

"No," Abby said loftily, "but I know how to set one up. Now go, or you'll be late!"

"Okay, okay," Ellie said, smiling even though she felt the tiniest bit disconcerted that her daughter was so eager to see the back of her. "I'm going."

"Have a nice time, dear," Lady Stokeley called. She shuffled forward, staying Ellie with one claw-like hand as she dropped her voice to a whisper. "I don't know what's in fashion these days, but you might want to wear slightly less eye makeup?" Lady Stokeley's smile was both kindly and a little patronizing. "My father used to say makeup was a shallow girl's sport, but I think a little discreet touch here and there is perfectly acceptable."

"Right, thanks," Ellie muttered, blushing. She had a packet of makeup wipes in her bag and she fully intended to use them.

With her eyes mostly repaired, she had nothing to focus on but the party ahead of her. Ellie drove to the train station, her hands clenched on the wheel, a mixture of nerves and excitement stirring in her stomach. She couldn't remember the last time she'd even been to a party, a proper, grown-up party anyway. Abby's birthday party and her parents' 'do for their fortieth anniversary didn't count. The GP where she'd worked back in Manchester had had a bit of a knees-up at Christmas, if you could call a couple of boxes of wine and a few bags of crisps in the conference room after work a party. And while Ellie didn't know what to expect from the history faculty in terms of a party, she felt just about anything would be outside her realm of experience.

And what about Oliver? Her stomach started fizzing at the thought of seeing him outside of work, outside of mere friendship even. They wouldn't have the buffer of Tobias and Abby, no reason to socialize but the enjoyment of each other's company… if that was even the case. She had no idea what Oliver felt about her, if anything, and she didn't even know what she felt about him.

He was her boss—brainy, a bit nerdy, good-looking but exacting, occasionally officious, with a surprising sense of humor and a killer smile. He was, Ellie supposed, her safe crush—well enough out of her realm yet still with a dash of possibility. She didn't think anything would happen between them, especially considering how he'd reacted during that walk in the woods, but it was exciting to pretend something might.

Feeling better for having figured all that out, Ellie got on the train to Oxford with a spring in her step. By the time she reached the Eagle and the Child, she was feeling slightly less confident. It had been foolish to walk from the rail station to the pub, as her feet were now both numb and cramped and the taffeta and lace dress, even with her winter coat over it, had provided little protection against the icy wind that funneled down Oxford's streets. Plus she'd forgotten to eat dinner, and her stomach was feeling both empty and queasy.

A couple brushed by her, the woman's heels clicking smartly on the pavement, a waft of expensive perfume settling over Ellie as they moved past. They went into the pub, and the woman threw her a speculative look that to Ellie seemed smug. The door to the pub slammed in her face, leaving her quite literally out in the cold.

In that moment, despite her excitement at seeing Oliver, she was sorely tempted to slink back down the street, find some other pub that didn't have a load of posh people in it, and eat a lonely dinner by herself. Then go home and tell Abby that she'd had a fabulous time. Yes, lie to her daughter. And to Lady Stokeley for that matter.

Ellie squared her shoulders. She couldn't do that. She didn't want to do that, tempting as it might have seemed for a moment. If she turned tail now, then her fears of not fitting in, of seeming too gauche or green or simply Northern, would have defeated her. And she'd come too far, lived too long, and endured too much to let that happen. She was going to have a good time tonight no matter what.

With her head held high, her chin tilted at a defiant angle, Ellie opened the door to the pub.

OLIVER COULDN'T KEEP his gaze from veering to the front door of the pub every few minutes. It was half past seven and Ellie surely should have been there by now. He didn't know why he was feeling so jumpy about it—she'd come when she came, and that was all. What was the big deal?

The big deal was that since their dinner last weekend he'd been reliving that moment when Ellie had fallen into his arms. He'd felt her body press against his and it had been sweet, sensual, and terrifying all at once. His own body had responded with alarming alacrity, and he'd thrust her away from him before she'd felt how. He'd been embarrassed—what was he, seventeen? He'd also been unsettled. He shouldn't respond to his PA that way. He shouldn't be thinking about his PA that way. And yet now he found he was. A lot.

"You all right, Oliver?" Henry Stephenson, a colleague who had pipped him at the post for a faculty chair, raised his eyebrows, pale blue eyes narrowed. Stephenson was, Oliver knew, a notorious gossip. "You seem a bit jumpy."

"No, not at all." The smile Oliver gave was strained. He wasn't his best at these types of social occasions, and wondering and worrying about Ellie was making him feel even more wrong-footed. "How is your research going, Henry? Rebellion in the French colonies, isn't it?"

"German colonies, actually," Stephenson returned with a cool smile. Oliver hadn't meant it as a slight, but it was clear Henry had taken it as one. "It's going well. Should publish soon. And what about you? That book on Victorian children?"

"The Victorian perception of childhood, yes."

"Still aiming to have a bestseller? Be a masculine Mary Beard?" His slightly sneering tone suggested how unlikely he thought that possibility.

Oliver knew his publisher wanted to put him into some kind of BBC celebrity status, something he couldn't even fathom for himself, but he suspected Stephenson's disbelief came from envy rather than true skepticism. Although considering Oliver's social skills, maybe not. No way could he see himself on TV or something equally ridiculous.

The door to the pub opened, bringing in a gust of freezing air—and then Ellie. Oliver's gaze fastened on her, drank her in. She looked gorgeous, her cheeks pink from the cold, her body encased in—well, a puffa parka was all he could see at the moment, but still, she looked beautiful.

She'd attempted to put her hair back in some kind of French twist and fortunately it hadn't really worked; curly, golden-brown strands were falling across her shoulders, reminding Oliver of Botticelli's Venus. She looked nervous or perhaps just cold, hugging herself and shifting from foot to foot.

"Excuse me," Oliver said, not caring if he fed the faculty's rumor mill for a month. "My friend has arrived."

He strode towards her, a smile breaking out across his face like a wave on the shore. "Ellie." His voice sounded too loud, too warm, too much. It took Oliver a second to realize how he must seem, practically running towards her, hands outstretched in front of him, his voice carrying so that the people next to him fell silent, curious.

He stopped mid-stride, nearly tripping as he dropped his hands and tried to compose his features into something more sober and appropriate and employer-like.

Ellie had already caught sight of him, her eyes widening, a cautious smile lighting up her features, only for her to suddenly frown in puzzlement. Because he was acting like some schizophrenic stalker.

Oliver shoved his hands in the pockets of his trousers, attempting his own version of cool. "So. You made it."

"Yes."

They smiled at each other for another awkward moment. "Let me get you something to drink," Oliver finally said.

"I'd love a glass of red wine." She held up one finger. "Only one, though. I'm driving."

"You drove into Oxford?" Daringly he placed a hand on the small of her back to shepherd her to the bar. Well, in actuality, his hand more or less hovered by her back; he wasn't quite touching her. But still.

"No, just to the train station in Charlbury. I don't think I'm brave enough to manage all the one-way streets and things here. Plus, the parking."

"The bane of every city dweller, I fear." Oliver winced at how ridiculously pompous he sounded. Why not tuck a hand in his waistcoat while he was at it? Thankfully he was not wearing a waistcoat. A blazer and open-necked shirt were his nod to dressing up. At times like this he wished he were someone different.

"Red wine," Oliver said, and turned towards the bar.

It felt better when they both had got their drinks and had retreated to a quiet corner of the pub. Ellie was looking around in rather wary interest, her glass clutched in front of her like a shield.

"So do you know everyone here?" she asked.

Oliver gave the room a diffident glance. "Yes, more or less."

"Are they all academics?"

"And administration."

"Jeannie isn't here, though."

"No, she had a family commitment. Are you two getting along?" He was still sounding pompous, like some patronizing uncle.

"Yes, I think so. She's nice." Ellie took a gulp of wine. She was clearly nervous, which amazed him, because she was easily the most vibrant person in the room. And yet... she didn't have a PhD or even a BA. If he remembered correctly from her CV, she'd completed one-year secretarial course and that was all. He wondered why that was the case—not that there was anything wrong with that kind of course, naturally, but what dreams had Ellie had? Had having Abby—she must have been very young—derailed some of her ambition? He knew he couldn't ask; it would be presumptuous, offensive. Who was he to judge another person's choices, their ambitions or their dreams?

Ellie, he saw, had already finished her wine. "Another?" he asked.

She looked torn. "Maybe just a small one. Since it'll be a couple of hours until I'm driving."

"You could always call a taxi from the station."

"True."

She was still looking tense and Oliver wished he had the confidence, the ability, to make her smile. To cause her to laugh. Instead he went and got her the wine.

When he returned Ellie had taken a step deeper into the corner, so Oliver almost missed her in the shadows. "Are you hiding?" he asked lightly and she gave him a ruefully candid look.

"Actually, yes. Sort of, anyway. I'm feeling a bit…" She blew out a breath. "Intimidated."

Oliver handed her the glass of wine. "Why is that?"

"Because everyone here seems very important, or at least believes themselves to be important, and next to them I'm a nobody."

He smiled, appreciating her observation. "I think it's the latter, and that's a necessary distinction to make."

"Is it?"

"How many people care about what we do, Ellie?" Oliver gestured to the milling crowd. "Yes, we've all got advanced degrees and are passionate about our research, but does the world at large care about fourteenth-century attitudes towards social change, or medieval romantic poetry, or anything else?"

"Victorian perception of childhood?" she chimed in, a smile lurking in her eyes.

"Exactly. We're a bunch of pompous windbags, nothing more."

She laughed, the sound pure and crystalline, ringing through him like a bell. "At least you acknowledge it." She was almost finished her second, smaller glass of wine. "Still, I wish I was that passionate about something."

Something inside him seriously lurched at her wistful tone, and the fact that she'd said *passionate*. That she wanted to be passionate.

"What are you passionate about?" he asked.

"I don't know," Ellie said slowly. "Abby, of course, and taking care of her. Giving her opportunities."

"But for yourself?"

Ellie sighed and rested her head against a smoke-stained oak timber, looking up at him with wide, clear eyes. Her lashes were long and golden and swept her cheeks every time she blinked. It seemed absurd to notice such a detail, and yet he couldn't look away. "I don't know if I've ever thought about it," she confessed. "If I've ever had the time or the luxury."

"Perhaps you should think about it now."

"Perhaps." She held out her empty glass. "But how about you get me another drink first?"

Chapter Twelve

WHAT WAS SHE doing? Drinking too much, for a start. Three glasses of wine were really not a good idea, not if she was driving. Fine, then she'd get a cab. But as she accepted her third glass of Merlot from Oliver, Ellie knew it wasn't just the possibility of driving that made drinking a bad idea.

She was in a strange situation, with a man she liked a little bit too much, and on top of that she was feeling nervous and kind of insecure. All good reasons to stay sober and keep her wits about her. Instead she gave a mental shrug and glugged back a third glass of red. The voice of reason that had been shouting in her head was now muted to a whisper. Soon it would fall blissfully silent.

"So." Oliver had propped one shoulder against the wall, so his body was perpendicular to hers. Ellie tilted her head up, noticing the glint of golden stubble on his jaw. He had a very nice throat in addition to that lovely cleft in his chin. Very strong-looking. Funny, because she'd never really noticed throats before. Who would? She wasn't a throat sort of girl, more of a six-pack-and nice-eyes type, and Oliver had those too.

Good grief, she was drunk, and on only three glasses of wine. But then she hadn't eaten anything since lunch.

"What would your ambitions be, if you had the time to think about them?" Oliver asked.

"Hmm... well, like I said, I need to think about it first." She sounded flirtatious. Did Oliver notice? Her head felt so fuzzy she couldn't assess his reactions. She couldn't read him in the best of times, and three glasses of wine didn't help.

"Very well. Think about it, then." He propped one elbow on the beam running by her head, bringing his body even closer to hers. Had that been intentional? Her eyes were trained on the open collar of his shirt. She could see the hollow of his throat and she had the absurd urge to press her finger there and feel how warm his skin was. She should not have had that third glass of wine.

"All right..." With what felt like superhuman effort she dragged her gaze from his throat to his face. *Mistake.* His eyes were looking very warm, green glint in the gray depths, a slight smile curving that mouth that was suddenly, or not so suddenly, seeming very kissable. And she was supposed to think about her *ambitions?* Right now her only ambition was to be kissed, and she was sure Oliver didn't mean that. Although perhaps he did...

"Um..." Her mind spun emptily. All she could look at was his mouth. "I suppose..." She swallowed convulsively.

Tried to look away.

"Yes?" Oliver leaned closer. If she stood on her tiptoes, her lips would brush his jaw. *Did he realize?* She was so tempted, more than she'd been by anything in a long, long time. She swallowed again. Despite the wine she'd been putting back, her mouth felt dry.

"I suppose I once thought about getting a degree. A BA in… something." Now that sounded intelligent. *Help.*

"What subject?"

Ellie licked her lips. "Maybe… English. I didn't get a chance to decide." She'd always liked reading, and she'd got an A on her AS exam, which was amazing, really, considering she'd been eight months' pregnant at the time.

"That's something, then." Oliver leaned back, looking pleased. Ellie sagged against the wall. Now that he wasn't quite so close she could feel the oxygen returning to her brain. She felt dizzy but also rational. She'd come very close to doing something very stupid, like kissing him. That would have been a disaster. She could have ruined everything in one drunken moment.

And yet the possibility that it might not have ruined everything tantalized her. *What if…?*

But, no. She couldn't think like that. It was too dangerous. She wasn't ready to think like that, and especially not with Oliver.

"What are you doing, hiding in the corner?" A plummy, jovial voice had Ellie stiffening and then taking a needed step away from Oliver. A red-faced man in a tweed jacket with a pipe in the pocket was smiling at them both, his eyes narrowed in speculation. "Who's this, then?" he asked, his smile swinging to Ellie, who tried to smile back.

"This is my personal assistant, Ellie Matthews," Oliver said. "She's helping me with my book."

"Is she?" The man clapped a hand on Oliver's shoulder. "You can't stay in the corner all evening like an old fart," he insisted. "Come and socialize." And he drew Oliver away, while Ellie watched, helpless.

Oh-kay. Well, that had made things clear. Ellie stood there by herself for a moment, trying to keep her head high and her smile in place, as if she hadn't just been summarily dismissed. It was time for another glass of wine.

She spent the next hour drinking in the corner and covertly watching Oliver socialize—at least she hoped it was covertly. She wasn't drunk enough to be sick or fall over, but she knew she'd had way too much to accurately judge her own actions or how they were being perceived, which was a very bad thing and yet still didn't check her nervous impulse to keep at it.

It was hard not to feel rather miserable sitting there alone. A few people gave her curious smiles but no one said hello. Everyone there knew each other, and Ellie watched the air kisses and heard the great bellows of laughter and started to feel like the loneliest person on earth.

She'd missed out on so much. Parties, fun, uni, being a

part of things. All of it had passed her by as she'd struggled to be a good mum, work full time, and keep her foundering marriage afloat. She knew she was indulging in one massive self-pity party, and it would be far better to call it a night and go home. Tomorrow she'd see the funny side, maybe... Then she saw Oliver coming towards her, looking concerned, and she tried to stand up.

"Whoa." She stumbled, careening into him, and his arm came around her waist. That felt nice. That felt *very* nice. But she wasn't going to press into him the way she had on their walk last week. Oh no, she wasn't. She was just going to tell him that. The words were coming out of her mouth before Ellie could apply a filter.

"Just so you know, I am not coming onto you." Heaven help her, she was slurring. She hadn't been this drunk since... ever. Getting pregnant at seventeen put paid to any kind of social life. And as for the getting pregnant part, well, that hadn't been as much fun as it was meant to be.

"I didn't think you were," Oliver replied, sounding startled, and Ellie closed her eyes. His arm was still around her waist and now she *was* pressed up against him. She tried to extract herself, and stumbled again. Now she was making a scene.

Even worse, the mortification of the moment, as well as her inebriated state, had tears springing to her eyes. She was going to be gossiped about by the entire history faculty. She was going to get fired.

"Sorry about this," she muttered, thankfully righting herself, the tears now at bay. "I'm not used to..." She decided not to finish that sentence. "Anyway, I think I'll call it a night."

"Ellie, I don't think you're in any state to go home." Oliver sounded kind and concerned, and that made her want to cry again.

"I'm fine," she insisted. "And in any case, I'm taking the train. I'll take a cab from the station, promise."

"I would not put you on a train by yourself," Oliver said seriously.

"I need to get home." Panic clutched at her as she thought of Abby. How could she have been so irresponsible to get this drunk when she had a daughter to care for? "I have to," she said, her voice rising, and out of the corner of her eye she saw people start to turn and look.

"I know you have Abby to think of," Oliver said, his voice managing to both soothe and irritate in its unflappable calmness. "Who is she with now?"

"Lady Stokeley."

"Could she stay the night there? It's already nearly eleven—you wouldn't get back to Wychwood until well after midnight."

"So where should I go instead?" Ellie demanded. She sounded like a sulky teenager, but surely it was better than bursting into tears, which was still a distinct possibility. She couldn't believe she'd been so stupid, so *selfish,* to get drunk at a party.

"You can stay at mine," Oliver said, and shocked, she fell silent.

OLIVER SAW THE surprise flicker across Ellie's face, her eyes widening as her jaw went slack. "Yours…"

"And just so you know," he interjected dryly, "I am not coming onto you, either."

Her cheeks reddened. "I didn't mean to say that out loud."

"I realize." At least now he'd gotten the message loud and clear. She wasn't interested in him, even if he'd felt more awake, more alive, talking to her tonight than he had in years. Even if he'd spent the entire conversation aching to touch her, to twine one of those curls around his finger, draw her closer and kiss those lips he'd kept staring at.

Never mind. It wasn't happening.

"It makes sense, Ellie," he continued, because it did make sense, but also because he wanted her to come home with him, which was a little sad considering her lack of interest. "I would be acting irresponsibly to let you get on the train like you are."

"Ouch." She made a face. "Am I that bad?"

Yes, she was, but he wasn't about to tell her that. Besides, even drunk she was kind of adorable. Her hair had completely fallen out of its twisty thing and was framing her face in a curly, golden cloud. She looked like an angel. A drunken angel.

"Come on," he said, putting his arm around her waist again. She leaned into him, and he breathed in the spring rain scent of her perfume as he led her out of the pub. "My flat is only a five minute walk from here."

"What about Abby…"

"I'll call her. She has a phone?"

"Yes, but…" Ellie's face crumpled. "What is she going to think of me? And Lady Stokeley is…" She hiccupped. "Old."

"I think Abby will manage. And I'll keep it vague."

Ellie nodded, swiping at her cheeks, and handed him her phone. Something in Oliver softened at the photo on the home screen—Abby and Ellie giving huge, cheesy grins in a close-up selfie. He swiped the screen and found Abby's number, drawing Ellie to the side of the pavement as he made the call.

"Mum? How was it?" Abby's voice rushed on, loud and excited, before Oliver could utter a word. "Did you see Oliver? I *know* he's into you. Did he ask you out? Did he kiss you?" Startled into speechlessness, Oliver didn't reply, and Abby exhaled impatiently. "Mum?"

"Um." He cleared his throat, his mind spinning from everything Abby had said. "Actually, this is Oliver."

"Oh," Abby said after a long pause. "Right. All that I said before… you know I was just joking, right?"

"Of course." He still couldn't fully process what Abby

had said. Had he been that obvious? Was Ellie repulsed by him, joking with her daughter about her creepy boss? No, he definitely couldn't think about that now. "The thing is, your mum isn't feeling all that well so if it's all right by you, she's going to stay over in Oxford. I have a spare bedroom," he emphasized, just in case Abby was getting ideas. "Would you be able to sleep over at, ah, Lady Stokeley's?"

Another sizzling pause. "Sure, yeah. It's no big deal. I'll just need to sort out Marmite."

The dog, of course. "Will you be able to do that…"

"Yeah, I can manage it," Abby said loftily. She paused. "She is okay though, isn't she? I mean… she's not like, really sick or anything?"

The note of vulnerability in Abby's voice, the tremor of uncertainty, sent a pang through Oliver. He remembered himself asking a similar question at a similar age. *But he's going to get better, isn't he? He'll be all right?* His parents hadn't answered. The next time he'd been home Jamie had been gone.

"She's fine, Abby," Oliver said firmly. "Absolutely fine. And she'll be back tomorrow by lunchtime."

"Okay." Relief was audible in her voice. "Thanks."

Oliver ended the call and handed the phone back to Ellie. She looked up at him with misery-filled eyes. "I've made such a mess of this, haven't I?"

"Don't get teary on me," he ordered. "I can handle you drunk, but not sad and drunk."

She managed a smile and straightened, pushing her hair behind her ears. "All that stiff upper lip stuff, I suppose?"

"Exactly." He put his arm around her waist again, liking the feel of it there. "Now let's get you home."

By the time they got to his flat on St Aldates Ellie had stopped acting drunk and just seemed very tired. Her head lolled against Oliver's shoulder, which he didn't mind, as he fumbled for his keys and then unlocked the door to the foyer of the Edwardian building where he had a flat.

"Just a little bit longer now. I'm on the third floor." He pressed the button of the old-fashioned grill-gate lift and listened to its exhausted motor start up with a wheeze.

When he'd finally managed to get Ellie into his flat, he felt a sense of both relief and expectation. She was safe; she was there.

Ellie straightened, brushing her hair out of her eyes, as she looked around. "Nice place. Very you."

Oliver closed the door behind them and shrugged out of his coat. "Very me?"

"The books. The bike." She gestured to the book-lined walls of the narrow front hallway and then gave his bike, propped up against the radiator, a little push. Oliver quickly righted it.

"I think you could do with a large glass of water and maybe something to eat."

She pursed her lips, planting her hands on her hips. "I'm not that drunk, you know."

"Still." He moved into the small kitchen that overlooked the main eating and living area, sashed windows overlooking St Aldates. Ellie followed him, propping her elbows on the breakfast bar as she watched him.

"This really is a nice place."

"Thank you." As he took out some eggs and bread— scrambled eggs and toast was about the extent of his cooking abilities—he realized nice as she thought it, his flat was a little bit messy. In fact, a hamper of dirty clothes was in the middle of the living area because he'd been planning to put it in the washer that morning and had forgotten.

Ellie scooted onto a stool, swinging one leg in a jaunty manner, as she looked around. Oliver quickly moved around her and grabbed the hamper. He had a pair of boxers right on top. Lovely. He dumped the basket in the corner of the kitchen and draped a dish towel over the top for good measure.

"Have you lived here long?" she asked.

"About ten years. I bought it a few years after I received my professorship."

"I don't even know how old you are."

"Thirty-eight."

"Nine years older than me."

Which meant she'd had Abby when she was just eight-een. Oliver slowly stirred the eggs. Ellie sighed and rested her chin in her hands.

"I hope I didn't ruin your entire evening."

"Not at all."

"How embarrassing was I, on a scale of one to ten?"

"With ten being the most embarrassing?"

She gave an audible gulp. "Yes."

"One. Seriously, Ellie, it's fine. Everyone has too much to drink at those parties and it wasn't as if you'd grabbed a microphone and starting singing and dancing on the tables."

"True." She gave him a small, wry smile, and his heart lightened. He was making her feel better for once.

"Here are your toast and eggs. I hope they're okay. I'm afraid my repertoire is extremely limited."

"They look wonderful." She looked straight at him with a heartbreaking smile. "Thank you, Oliver."

Oliver felt himself flush and he smiled and looked away. "It's no trouble."

Which was a huge understatement. Standing in his kitchen, watching Ellie eat the food he'd made and knowing she was going to spend the night—even if it was in the spare bed—made him feel happier than he had in a long time. Made him feel as if he'd done something important, far more important than writing any dusty old book.

"I'll just go get some clean sheets for the bed," he murmured.

A short while he'd made up the bed and laid a fresh t-shirt and sweatpants of his for her to wear as pajamas. He laid out a couple of towels as well, and managed to find a toothbrush still in its wrapper.

"You're prepared," Ellie said when he showed her it all. She was standing in the door, looking lovely, as vibrant as a flame in her red dress, her hair wild and curly about her shoulders.

"It's not much, but I hope you'll be comfortable," he said, a touch stiffly because he was nervous. "Do let me know if you require anything else."

Ellie's eyes sparkled as she smiled at him. "I'm fine, Oliver. Thank you."

He said goodnight and retreated to his own room, conscious of her movements so close by as he changed into his pajamas. There was an awkward moment of brushing past each other in the narrow hall as they took turns in the bathroom; the sounds of the taps and the flush of the loo seemed very loud to him all of a sudden. He had a horrible image of him farting loudly by accident and having Ellie hear. He'd put Marmite to shame.

Fortunately nothing like that happened, and he went back to his bedroom without seeing her again. Her door was closed, the light off. The whole flat was silent, the only sound the occasional car going by outside. Oliver lay in bed, his hands braced over his head, and tried to relax. Ellie in his flat. Ellie in his spare bed, wearing his clothes, her hair spread across the pillow...

He tried to empty his mind, to think of nothing at all, but images kept popping into it like bubbles. Salacious bubbles. It was a very long time before he finally drifted off to sleep.

Chapter Thirteen

E LLIE WOKE WITH a pounding headache and a horrible taste in her mouth. She blinked in the bright, wintry sunlight coming through the sashed windows and listened to the rumble of a truck going down the street outside. For a few blissful seconds she'd forgotten everything that had happened last night, but it all came rushing back quickly enough, filling in the blanks, making her wince and cringe.

She'd got drunk. Properly drunk, nearly falling down drunk, something she couldn't remember ever doing, not even as an irresponsible teenager on a wild night out—not that there had been many, or any, of those. In fact, there had been zero. *What had she been thinking?*

The trouble was, she hadn't been. At all. She'd just been *feeling...* nervous, and then excited with Oliver, and then nervous again as well as insecure when he'd left her alone. Too much emotion and stimulation without enough food in her stomach.

Ellie rolled over in bed, squeezing her eyes shut as she brought her knees up to her chest. What on earth did he think of her now? And what about Abby?

Quickly she leaned over, her stomach lurching with the sudden movement, to look for her bag that held her phone. She breathed a sigh of relief when she saw a text from her daughter: *I'm fine, Mum. Really. And so is Marmite. x*

Good heavens, she hadn't even thought of poor Marmite last evening. What if Abby had forgotten? Her poor dog would have been in desperate need of a wee, and probably would have torn up all the paper towel and loo roll in the house. Actually, he'd probably done that anyway.

It was only a little after eight and hopefully Abby was still asleep, so Ellie didn't call. She texted back instead: *Sorry, sorry, sorry. Love you and see you soon. Xxxx*

With a groan she tossed the phone aside and braced herself to face the day. She needed to apologize to Oliver, and then hightail it back to Willoughby Close so she could check on Abby and restore her equilibrium. She felt way too unsettled, with memories of last night clinging to her like mist.

She didn't feel comfortable wearing Lady Stokeley's slinky red dress at eight in the morning, so after sneaking into the shower and giving her teeth a very good brush, Ellie put on the t-shirt and trackie bottoms that Oliver had given her last night. They were obviously his, worn to a velvety softness, and smelled like fabric softener. Stupidly, Ellie held the shirt to her face before putting it on, as if she'd catch some scent his aftershave or just *him*. The only lingering odor under the fabric softener smell was her perfume and a tangy hint of the salt and vinegar crisps she'd eaten last night.

She twisted her damp hair into a knot and then, squaring her shoulders, headed into the living area. Oliver was in the kitchen, looking as casual as Ellie had ever seen him, as well as rather sexy, in a pair of faded jeans and an Oxford University t-shirt.

"Wow." She tucked an unruly strand of hair behind one ear. "I didn't think you ever wore shirts without collars."

He turned around at the sound of her voice, his smile creasing his cheeks and lighting up his face—and making her feel warm and fizzy inside. "Only on rare occasions, such as Saturdays. Coffee?"

"Oh yes, please." She slid onto a bar stool, hooking her bare feet through the rungs. "Okay, now that I'm well and truly stone cold sober, you can tell me how bad I was last night."

"You're still going on about that?" Oliver said with a shake of his head as he handed her a mug of steaming coffee. "Really, Ellie. It wasn't nearly the big deal you are insisting on thinking it was, I promise."

"Maybe not, but…" She took a sip of coffee. "It was very out of character for me. I don't expect you to believe that, but—"

"Why wouldn't I believe it?"

She shrugged, discomfited. Who was this emo Oliver,

asking her these kinds of questions? "Because the first party I attend, I act like a lush. It stands to reason you'd assume that's normal behavior."

"Well, I don't."

"Good." She took another sip of coffee, mainly to avoid having to meet his eyes. "The truth is," she continued after a moment, still not meeting his eyes, "I haven't gone out to a party in ages. Ever, really, or just about." She managed a smile as she tried to keep her tone. "Having a baby at eighteen seriously curtails your social life."

"I can imagine." He leaned against the counter, his long, lean fingers cradling his mug of coffee as he gave her a considering look. "How did all that come about, anyway?"

"All what? You mean... *Abby?*" Startled, she nearly spilled her coffee. What exactly was he *asking...?* "The usual way," she managed. "I'm not sure there's any other."

"Sorry." A faint flush touched his cheeks. "I'm not talking about the mechanics. I am aware of those. I meant, the relationship. Your ex is Abby's dad? You married young?"

"Yes, at the end of lower sixth, before Abby was born." She willed herself to stop blushing. Of course he hadn't been talking about the *mechanics,* for heaven's sake. She twisted the mug round and round in her hands. "As you can probably guess, Abby was an accident. Not that I regret her for a minute—"

"Of course not." Oliver sounded so sure, so sincere, that Ellie sagged a little bit in relief. She hadn't been sure how she'd felt when he'd started asking these kinds of personal questions, but now that they were talking about it, she realized she didn't mind.

Actually, Ellie realized, she kind of liked it. So few people had heard her story beyond her family, who loved her and exasperated her in equal measure, and her few friends who had dropped off the radar when their lives had diverged. Partying and going to uni didn't mesh with marriage, a newborn, and nappies.

"Abby's dad was my best friend in high school," she explained. "Nothing romantic between us initially. We were just mates. He was a laugh, Nathan. Always has been. Never stuck to anything much, did terribly in school, but he was—is—funny and goofy and charming." And she'd found out what had been exasperatingly endearing as a friend was unbelievably aggravating as a husband.

"And so what happened?"

"What happened is we were stupid. I was getting stressed about my mock exams in the middle of lower sixth and Nathan gave me a hug, and then somehow, well… you know how it is when you're seventeen. Hormones took over, and I think we were actually both a bit horrified afterwards." She blushed, feeling like she shouldn't be saying this to Oliver, her boss, but he looked alert and interested, and well, it did feel nice to have someone who listened.

"And then you discovered you were pregnant?"

"I was pretty clueless, and I didn't have a lot of the usual symptoms, so I was actually past my first trimester when I realized." She shook her head. "And then we were *really* horrified, if I'm being honest. But I didn't think about a termination because I was so far gone—I just couldn't go through with it, not with a baby that I'd felt kick." She sighed. "And Nathan wanted to do the right thing. That's how he's always been—determined to do the right thing and simply incapable of doing it, properly anyway, so I end up doing it for him."

Oliver looked startled. "But you did get married?"

"Oh, yes. We got married and he promised to get a job and support me—as if he could. We ended up spending the first two years of our married life living in my parents' spare bedroom, the three of us, while Nathan bounced from dead-end job to dead-end job. It was truly awful." She shuddered just to remember those dark, difficult, and sleep-deprived years. "It didn't do my relationship with my parents any good, either. They were pretty despairing about my life choices, and as for Nathan... he kept getting fired or just walking out of a job because it was boring. And he'd always insist the next thing would be better—and it never was." She sighed. "The thing is, I knew what he was like. I'd seen it as his friend. I'd nagged him to study more, to get a couple of B techs at least, but he never listened. He was always nice about it, always promising he'd try harder, but it never happened. And things didn't change just because we were married. If anything they got worse." Days spent lazing on the sofa, telling her not to nag. Money that disappeared. Flirting with girls at the pub, stolen kisses that he swore meant nothing. And promises, so many promises, that went nowhere. And all the while Ellie had been driven quietly round the bend while her parents looked on, shaking their heads or pursing their lips at their dropout daughter and her deadbeat husband.

"That sounds tough," Oliver said quietly.

"Yes," Ellie answered slowly, "it was." She didn't like to think about those days, working and striving and always feeling like she was pushing a massive boulder uphill, afraid that one day it would roll back down and crush her... and then one day it had. "It got a bit easier when I went out to work when Abby was eighteen months old. I earned my secretarial qualification and started work in a GP's surgery. Nathan was meant to stay at home with Abby, but he wasn't particularly good at that either. He'd dump her with my parents or let her watch endless telly while he was on his phone to his mates or playing stupid online games." Belatedly Ellie realized how whingey she sounded. "He wasn't a complete waste of space. He could be good fun sometimes, which was why everyone loved him. He was really popular at school, and even with my parents, amazingly." Her parents had never seemed to be as aware of Nathan's deficiencies, as much as her own. It was a sore point that had been rubbed raw over the years. Why did her parents think she was hopeless and Nathan wasn't? She knew the answer, unfortunately. Because Nathan had always managed to charm them.

"He can be so kind," she explained, "even weirdly thoughtful considering how thoughtless his big actions are, which is why parents really liked him. They always believed he was going to do better, and they'd get annoyed with me for keeping him down." Now instead of sounding whingey, she was coming across as bitter. And she didn't want to be bitter, not after all this time. Ellie shook her head. "Sorry. I don't mean to going on about this."

"It's okay. Sometimes you just need to get it all out."

"Says a man who bottles everything up inside, as far as I can tell." Ellie kept her voice teasing. "What's your story, Oliver? You're nearly forty. Have you ever had a serious relationship? Almost popped the question?" She was amazed she had the daring to ask such a personal question, but considering how she'd just spilled her guts, surely Oliver could give her a drop or two.

"You sound so disbelieving," Oliver answered. "Yes, I've had a few serious relationships. Two, I suppose."

"You suppose?"

"I don't know how serious they were, in all honesty. I never came close to asking a woman to marry me, although perhaps the women involved thought I might have."

Ellie cocked her head. "So what happened? To these relationships?"

"They fizzled out, more or less. The first one was when I was an undergraduate—she was a PhD student and I think I was out of my league. She dumped me after a couple of months. The second was in my late twenties. We were together for a couple of years but it never seemed to be going anywhere, which was probably my fault."

"How so?"

He shrugged. "I was happy with the status quo. Dinner a couple of nights a week, a movie, sex." Ellie tried not to react to him saying the s-word. Tried also not to imagine him in bed—the muscles rippling in his back, forearms braced... really, she needed to scrub that image right out of her brain. Oliver shrugged. "I didn't really need or want more than that, to be perfectly honest."

"Ouch."

"We had a big tearful fight and she left."

"You were both tearful?"

"She was."

"Ah. That makes more sense."

He smiled wryly. "I suppose it does."

"And that's it?" Ellie asked after a moment of companionable silence. "No other relationships?"

"A few awkward dinner dates." He shrugged. "That's all I've managed. What about you? Anyone since your ex?"

Ellie grimaced. "Nope."

"How long have you been divorced?"

She ducked her head, a bit abashed. "Five years. And even before that it was a bit on-again off-again. He left, he came back, he left." She sighed. "I wanted to make a go of it for Abby's sake, and even for mine. Being a single mum, not to mention being divorced, wasn't what I wanted for my life." Stupidly she felt the sting of tears beneath her lids. The last thing she wanted was to get emotional now. Oliver had had enough of that last night. "Anyway. It came to a point where I couldn't take the uncertainty anymore, the broken promises, and I kicked him out. I think everyone still blames me."

"Abby?"

"No, I don't think so," Ellie said slowly. "But my parents. They had a soft spot for him. Still do. Seem to think his charm runs deeper than it does." Time to sound dismissive and wrap it up. She slid off the stood and placed her empty coffee mug by the sink. "I should really get going. Check on Abby. But thank you, *thank you,* from the bottom of my heart for bailing me out last night. And I promise never to drink in public like that again."

"You don't have to promise me anything, Ellie."

"I'm promising myself, then. Now let me just get back into my dress and then I'll be out of your hair."

"Why don't I drive you?"

She stilled mid-turn and stared at him in surprise. "What?"

Oliver shrugged, eyebrows raised. "Why don't I drive you? It will be quicker for you to get back to Abby and I could go check on Tobias and Jemima. I haven't seen them in a few days."

"Oh. Well." To refuse seemed ungracious in the extreme, and in any case, she didn't know why she'd want to. She needed to get home to Abby as quickly as possible, and yet...

She was still processing the rather intense and intimate conversation they'd just had. Starting to get that prickly, squirmy sensation of having said too much. And she would rather curl in a window seat of the train and ponder it all by herself, moment by moment, rather than live in the aftermath sitting next to Oliver.

"Okay," she said at last, and Oliver's sudden, beaming smile made her acquiescence worth it.

Twenty minutes later they were in Oliver's beat-up Volvo, heading east on the A40 while wintry sunlight glittered on the mud puddles in the fields on either side of the road. Ellie felt a little self-conscious wearing last night's cocktail dress, and also increasingly anxious about Abby's welfare. Her daughter had never even had a sleepover before.

"Relax," Oliver said as he shot her a sideways glance. "I'm sure she's fine. Did she text you this morning?"

"Yes," Ellie admitted. "And she is fine, I know. But I'm a mum. I'm allowed to worry. That's my job."

"Of course it is. Not that I would know," he added with a little laugh.

"No, but I'm sure your mum worried about you."

"Hmm." Oliver didn't say anything else, and curious now, emboldened by all their earlier sharing, Ellie asked,

"Didn't she?" She knew Oliver had said that stuff about

his upbringing, but all mothers cared a little bit, at least. Didn't they?

"I don't really know. I'm sure she did, in the manner of all mothers. But when I look at you and Abby, well, it's a long way off what I had with my mother, although goodness knows she had her own issues to deal with."

Ellie felt both touched and saddened by his admission. "I don't know if you ever feel you get it right as a mum. Some days I'm sure Abby will be in therapy her whole life because of me."

"You're a great mum, Ellie." *That voice.* Low, warm, buttery. It made Ellie melt inside.

"Thank you." She tried not to blush and failed. "It's very kind of you to say so." Wanting to turn the attention away from her, she asked, "If your mother wasn't worrying about you, what was she doing?"

"Playing tennis. Throwing tea parties." He laughed. "It sounds a bit shallow, but it was just the kind of life they led. My father was in law and my mother supported him socially. Children seemed like an inconvenience." He gave a little grimace. "I suppose it sounds rather archaic now."

"And what about you? And your siblings? Do you have any others besides Jemima?"

A slight yet telling pause. "No, but I did. My brother Jamie died when I was twelve."

"Oh." Ellie stared at him, appalled at how she'd inadvertently put her foot right in it. "I'm so sorry."

"Thank you. It was a long time ago. But…" He released a breath that was part shudder. "I still miss him if I'm honest. I always will."

"How did he die?" Ellie asked quietly.

"Leukemia. It came on quite suddenly. At least to me. He died within a few months of the initial diagnosis. He was only five. I think it affected all of us, even though no one ever spoke of it. We weren't that kind of family."

"No one did? Ever?" Ellie was appalled at the thought of a child going through such tragedy virtually alone.

"It simply wasn't the done thing," Oliver explained. "Sometimes it felt as if he'd disappeared, almost as if he'd never been. Strange." He gave a funny little smile, his face touched with sadness. "He was such a bright little thing, too. Always smiling. He looked up to me when it seemed like no one else did."

"Oh, Oliver." Compelled to comfort him, Ellie reached over and laid her hand on his arm. He looked startled, and she almost removed it, but then he smiled and awkwardly patted her hand with his own before returning it to the wheel.

"Thank you."

They didn't speak for a while, and when they next did it was about the lack of rest stops on the A40. Clearly they'd both had enough emoting for one day.

By the time Oliver turned into Willoughby Close, Ellie was twitching with the need to see Abby and check that she was okay. She unclicked her seatbelt before Oliver had come to a stop, and was out of the car before he'd turned off the engine.

"Abby...?" She opened the front door and then nearly fell backwards at Marmite's joyous welcome, huge paws planted on her chest.

"Hey, Mum." Abby was, of all things, sitting at the kitchen table doing her homework. Ellie sagged in relief even though she'd known all along Abby was okay.

"I'm so sorry, sweetheart—"

Abby waved her objection aside. "You don't need to be sorry. I had an amazing time at Dorothy's. I slept in a bed that Henry the Eighth was supposed to have slept in."

"Wow."

"It was a little dusty." Abby shrugged. "But that was okay."

"Well. Great." Oliver appeared behind Ellie in the doorway, and the dumbfounded expression on her daughter's face would have been funnier if it hadn't also been embarrassing.

"Hi, Abby."

"Um, hi. Oliver." Abby looked at him quizzically. "Did you drive my mum home?"

"Yes, I'm on my way to see Tobias and Jemima."

"Are you? Cool. I was just chatting with him this morning about the Middle Earth game we're playing. We're on a team going through the Desolation of Smaug."

"Chatting?" Now Ellie was the one to look dumbfounded. "Here?"

Abby rolled her eyes. "On the Internet, Mum. Honestly."

"You're welcome to come with me if you want to chat with him in person," Oliver said, and now both she and Abby looked dumbfounded. *Seriously?* "That is, if you wanted to."

"That would be fab," Abby said, rising from the table. Ellie stared at her in shock.

"Wait, what—"

"Come on, Mum." Abby gazed at her, all wide-eyed innocence. "We can bring Marmite and you guys can take him for a walk."

Was her daughter matchmaking? And none too subtly. Oliver touched her arm.

"Sorry, perhaps I shouldn't have suggested that. You're probably exhausted. You don't have to…"

His wry smile, along with the hint of vulnerability in his eyes, won her over. Ellie smiled back. "Let me just change."

Chapter Fourteen

I T WASN'T UNTIL Ellie had changed into jeans, a thick sweater, and Welly boots that she realized coming along with Oliver meant meeting Jemima. What was this woman, beset by grief and sadness and yet once a socialite, going to be like?

Soon enough they were all back in Oliver's car, driving to his sister's house, Abby and Marmite in the back seat. Marmite was hanging his head over the front seat and too late Ellie saw a wet thread of drool drip onto Oliver's shoulder. He glanced back, frowning.

"Is that what I thought it was?"

"If you thought it was a sign of Marmite's excitement and devotion, then yes."

"That's one way of putting it, I suppose." He grimaced, but Ellie didn't think he minded the drool. At least, not too much. Then Marmite licked his ear, and Oliver jerked away.

"He obviously likes you," Ellie said and hid her smile, turning to look out the window at the damp fields glittering under a golden sun. It was crisp and clear, with the tiniest hint of spring in the air, a freshness to the breeze, a promise of warmth in the winter sunlight. Her heart gave a little flutter of excitement, and she knew that she was glad to be there. Glad to be with Oliver.

A few minutes later Oliver turning into the sweeping drive of a house that nearly rivaled Willoughby Manor in terms of its size and grandeur. Ellie swallowed hard, and exchanged a look with Abby who seemed similarly awed.

"Nice place," Ellie murmured and Oliver gave a little shrug.

"It's the old rectory. A bit much considering Tobias is an only child, but Jemima…" He shrugged, sighing, and Ellie recalled him confessing that he hadn't been that close to his sister.

Oliver climbed out of the car, and feeling a bit intimidated by the huge house, Ellie let Marmite out the back, hiding behind her dog, which wasn't that hard considering his size and exuberance.

"I'm guessing Marmite shouldn't go inside," she said, and Oliver looked apologetic.

"It would probably be easier…"

"No problem. I'll tie him up for now." Jemima's lawn had the same jewel-green velvet look of Willoughby Manor's, as was. Ellie didn't want to risk messing that up either.

She spent as long as she could dealing with Marmite, which took some doing anyway because after being confined in the car for twenty minutes, and with acres of gorgeous lawn stretching in every direction, her dog did not take kindly to being tied to a gate post.

Oliver and Abby were waiting for her, so Ellie knew she couldn't stall forever. What was she worried about, anyway? She didn't care what Jemima thought of her. But everything about this situation was new and nerve-wracking, and she was going into it on little sleep.

"Are you all right?" Oliver asked, giving her a concerned smile, and Ellie nodded. She didn't even know what she was nervous about. Abby didn't seem nervous; she only looked impatient, clearly wanting to see Tobias and tackle the desolation of whatever.

Ellie fell into step next to Oliver, and felt a little tremor of surprised excitement when his hand touched her waist and stayed there, fingertips barely brushing her sweater. Still, she felt them. She felt them a lot.

He was just shepherding her inside, she told herself. He probably wasn't even aware of what he was doing. And yet… Oliver didn't seem like the kind of man who inadvertently touched people. In fact Ellie was sure he wasn't. So if he was touching her on *purpose…*

Her brain short-circuited, and suddenly she couldn't think at all. She could barely breathe. It was as if fireworks were going off in her head, a clamor of mental and sensual stimulation she couldn't begin to process. And all because his fingertips were touching her waist. Barely.

What was *wrong* with her? Why was she reacting this

way? Freaking out over nothing? The answer was all too obvious. Because, for the first time, she thought Oliver might be interested in her. It had been different when she'd been so sure it had all been in her head, when crushing on him had felt safe. Now that things had tipped, even barely, into the realm of possibility, Ellie felt as if she was about to have an anxiety attack. Not the usual reaction to a little bit of light flirting, surely.

Oliver dropped his hand from her waist as he turned to look at her, concern creasing his forehead. "Are you okay, Ellie?"

"I'm… fine," she gasped out. Oliver's look of concern deepened. Abby, standing at the front door, gave a sigh of impatience. "Really," Ellie managed, only slightly more convincingly. "I'm good."

The door opened, and Tobias stood there, a grin breaking over his face that made Ellie's own fears fade away. She was glad they'd come there, no matter what was going on in her own freaked-out psyche.

"Hey!" Tobias's gaze swiveled to Oliver. "Hey, I didn't know you were coming."

"I texted your mum…"

Tobias's smile was fading fast. "She hasn't woken up yet," he mumbled.

Not woken up? It was nearly noon. Abby gave Ellie a questioning look and Oliver's expression clouded.

"Okay. Maybe I'll just see how she'd doing."

Ellie followed Oliver into a house that was huge and immaculately decorated, but smelled stale and... lonely, if loneliness had a smell. It certainly had a feeling, and this house was it.

"Hey, Mum, is it okay if Tobias and I go into the den? His computer's in there..."

"Sure." Abby and Tobias disappeared, and with Oliver having gone upstairs, Ellie wandered into the kitchen. It was all gleaming granite and stainless steel appliances, a huge sub-zero fridge taking up most of wall, a massive Aga taking up another. It was a dream house kitchen, but it looked like it was bordering on a nightmare. Dirty dishes filled the sink and there was a smell of sour milk in the air.

With nothing else to do, Ellie rolled up her sleeves and got busy. It felt good to work, to banish those half-formed anxieties. A bit of scrubbing and she felt restored to normality. So Oliver had touched her waist. What was the big deal? She didn't have to freak out about it. And if he was interested in her...

For a few moments Ellie let herself go there. Could they date? Would it work, if they took it slowly, if she tiptoed into some kind of relationship?

It had been a long time since she'd been in a relationship, and the one she had been in hadn't turned out so well. It had involved a lot of trying and heartache and disappointment. Five years on she still wasn't sure she was ready to get back in the saddle, or even look at the horse. But maybe Oliver could convince her…

Half an hour later Oliver came downstairs, looking so tired and careworn that Ellie wanted to put her arms around him.

On the heels of her ruminations she had a sudden second's worth of bizarre and desperate fantasy that this house, this life, was hers—that *he* was hers. She could picture it all, how he'd been upstairs playing with their children, and she'd been tidying up after a lazy Saturday brunch of waffles and bacon and freshly-squeezed orange juice…

"You didn't need to clean up," Oliver said. "But thank you."

Ellie blinked, bringing the world—the real world—back into focus. She couldn't believe how quickly her mind had galloped into fantasy land. One second she'd been thinking about whether they could date and in the next she'd had them married for years. She felt as if the truth of what she'd been thinking was reflected in her face, her eyes. She turned away just in case Oliver was feeling a little more perceptive than usual.

"Is Jemima okay?"

"She's getting up, which is something."

Ellie focused on wringing out a dishtowel in the huge Belfast sink. "Is she often like this? Having trouble getting up and things, I mean?"

"I'm not exactly sure. I only come by a couple of times a week." Oliver sighed and raked a hand through his hair.

"But yes, I think so."

Ellie turned around and leaned against the sink. "It's a very tough situation." She paused, weighing the wisdom of a soul-baring confession at this point in time. She took a deep breath. "I can relate to it a bit, actually."

Oliver's eyebrows rose. "Can you?"

Ellie nodded, her heart starting to thump. She didn't like talking about that month-long black hole in her life. "The last time Nathan left, for good, I went into a bit of a spin. I'd been the one to kick him out, I know, but it had been really stressful getting to that point. Really hard. And when he was actually gone… life suddenly felt empty." She sighed, the mere memory of that time making her feel as if a dark, familiar cloud had settled over her. "It wasn't even that I missed him particularly, or that my heart was broken or anything like that. It was more… the disappointment." Although that felt like an understatement for the near-suffocating weight she'd felt settle on her. "My *life* felt broken. It was awful, the realization that my life didn't look anything like I had wanted or expected it to," she explained, "and that I'd wasted so many years, so much effort on a relationship that had never been going to go anywhere. That was a terrible thing to face." And for about a month she hadn't faced it. She'd curled up in a ball and basically stopped living.

He nodded slowly. "Yes, I can see that."

"I checked out for a little while, or as much as you can

when you have a six-year-old and a full-time job." Which, when she'd put her mind to it, had been quite a lot. "I went on sick leave for a month, and my sister Diane pretty well took over. She came over to do the washing, make sure there was milk in the fridge, and give poor Abby some normalcy. Like you're doing for Jemima. And while I could barely rouse myself to show her how much I appreciated it then, I hope she knows now. I've tried to tell her." A lump was forming in her throat and she swallowed it down. She would always be in her sister's debt for that. Diane had saved her, as well as Abby. And yet it had been hard to live in the shadow of that reality, especially when Diane, along with her parents, always seemed poised for it to happen again. "Jeez, I really thought we were done with the emoting."

He laughed and shook his head. "I thought I was the one who was uncomfortable with all that. After all, you burst into tears the second time I saw you."

"True." She still cringed at that memory. When had she not embarrassed herself in front of Oliver Venables? "Anyway, I just wanted to say hang in there with your sister. Hopefully she'll come round with time. I did." Although it had taken her sister's proverbial foot up the backside to drop-kick Ellie back into life.

"Hopefully," Oliver answered with a tired smile.

A few minutes later Jemima herself made an appearance, looking, Ellie couldn't help but notice, rather awful. Her hair had been expensively highlighted about three months ago, and two inches of dark roots were visible in the rat's nest of blonde streaks. She wore a pair of skinny designer jeans that looked more expensive than anything Ellie owned—and were covered in stains. The oversized button-down shirt was similar in both price and cleanliness, and her face was pale and lined with shadows under her eyes the color of livid bruises.

"I'm sorry I wasn't down here when you arrived," she said to Ellie, her voice strained but holding onto dignity. "Would you like a cup of tea?"

"That would be lovely," Ellie said, hoping that the power of hospitality might rouse Jemima a little bit out of her lethargy.

It did, briefly, but by the time Ellie was sipping the expensive Earl Grey Jemima had given her, she'd lapsed back into a blank, dazed state, staring off into the distance while Oliver valiantly tried to keep a conversation going.

"We were thinking of taking Ellie's dog for a walk, Jemima," he said, his voice achingly over-bright with determined enthusiasm. "Would you like to come with us? It's a beautiful day. And the fresh air might—"

"Oh, no." She shook her head, clearly not considering such an outrageous suggestion for a moment. "I'll stay here."

Oliver gave Ellie a resigned look and she tried for an encouraging smile back. Tobias and Abby were still happily immersed in Middle Earth, and so after poking her head in the den to observe them for a second, Ellie went to get her boots.

Outside sunlight was sparkling on everything and Marmite was trying to gnaw through his lead.

"Silly dog," Ellie said with genuine affection, because even though she'd been furious when Nathan had brought him home six years ago, she couldn't imagine life without him now. She turned to Oliver. "Do you know a good walk around here?"

"Across the fields gets us to Kingham and a very nice pub."

"Sounds good."

They walked in companionable silence for a few minutes, the frosty grass crunching beneath their boots, Marmite racing ahead of them. Ellie felt a weird combination of awkwardness and intimacy, the two emotions twined together so she could hardly tell one from the other.

They kept the conversation light all the way to the village pub, becoming more and more relaxed in each other's company, the companionship feeling both natural and right.

Then, settled in a comfortable booth by the open fire, over pints of shandy, Oliver said abruptly, "You could go back and get your BA if you wanted, you know. It's clear you've got a perfectly good brain, and you could make something of yourself if you wanted."

Ellie stiffened instinctively. *Make something of herself?* Because she wasn't anything now? "Why should I do that?" she asked, hearing the tension in her voice and unable to monitor it. They'd been having such a nice time, why had Oliver had to go and say something like that? Of course, the answer was because in his mind she wasn't making something of herself. She was a lowly secretary, doomed to spend her life typing and photocopying. It was as if he'd announced with a megaphone that she wasn't in his league and never would be. Or was she being paranoid? Ellie felt too tired and overwhelmed to apply any common sense to the situation.

"I thought you'd want to better your prospects, that's all," Oliver said. "You know, that ambition you talked about last night."

"Actually, you were the one talking about ambition."

Oliver frowned. "Sorry, I wasn't trying to…" He shook his head. "I've somehow managed to put my foot in it, haven't I? I didn't mean anything by it."

"I know." But the damage had been done, and Ellie couldn't recapture the lighthearted normality they'd been working towards, and neither could Oliver.

"We should get back," she said, rising from the table. "Abby has homework."

They tried to recover some of that companionable banter on the way back to Jemima's, and they almost did, but it still felt slightly strained, like a picture with a smudged fingerprint.

Ellie told herself it was better this way. She and Oliver were from different worlds. A BA, indeed. Was he playing

Henry Higgins to her Eliza Doolittle? She hated the thought. She felt ridiculous for having her heart race earlier; judging by the way Oliver walked several careful feet away from her now, there had been nothing romantic in his mind whatsoever. No, she'd just been his blasted charity project.

"What's got you in such a tizz?" Abby asked when they were back at Willoughby Close, Ellie standing at the kitchen counter sorting through the post while Abby stood by the front door, her hands on her hips. Marmite flopped down in his usual place in front of the woodstove.

"A tizz? I'm not in a tizz."

"You've been in a bad mood since you got back from your walk with Oliver." Abby walked over and slid on one of the kitchen stools. "What happened?"

"Nothing happened."

"Did he kiss you?"

"Abby." Ellie felt her cheeks warm as she glared at her daughter in exasperation. "We're just friends. Colleagues or not even that. I'm his employee."

"Uh-oh. He said something that made you mad."

"Not exactly." Since when had her daughter become so perceptive? "How were things with Tobias? You guys are friends now?"

"Yeah, but don't change the subject."

"Maybe I'd like to change the subject."

"I thought things were going so well," Abby said slowly. "I mean, you spent the night at his place…"

"Not like that," Ellie interjected, appalled. "Honestly, Abby!"

"Well, why did you stay over then?"

Ellie sighed. "The truth is I had too much to drink and couldn't be trusted to get home by myself." She bit her lip, fresh guilt assailing her. "Not a great example to you. I'm sorry."

"Jeez, Mum. You don't need to be so sorry." Abby softened the words with a smile. "You're allowed to mess up, you know? We both are. At least I am, right?"

Ellie gave a rather wobbly laugh. The love she felt for her daughter was like a giant hand squeezing her heart. Painful but so good. "Of course you are. Not that you do, very often."

"I know." Abby grinned. "Hey, you know what? Jace stopped by this morning before you got back and said someone is moving in next door."

"To Number Two? Really?" Ellie perked right up. "Do you know who it is?"

"No, but he did say it was a family, and they should be moving in over half-term."

"Wow. Cool." It was a bit lonely, being the only residents of Willoughby Close. How fantastic would it be to have a neighbor, someone who would come over for coffee and a chat, or even a glass of wine? And maybe there would be someone Abby's age... it was rainbows and unicorns all over again, but why not? She needed something positive to focus on.

Ellie spent the rest of the day sorting the house and her own head out. She needed a seriously stern talking to, and she gave it to herself as she folded laundry, spritzed kitchen counters, and paid bills.

On Monday she'd apologize to Oliver for coming over so touchy and re-establish their friendship, because that's what they were. Friends.

Clearly she couldn't handle even the hint of a relationship, judging by how her anxiety levels had sky-rocketed over the merest possibility of one, and in any case Oliver didn't have the best track record. Two serious relationships, one of which had been occasional dinners and sex. While she had to admit the sex sounded rather nice after half a decade of celibacy, she didn't want casual. She couldn't do casual, not with Abby to think of, not to mention her own battered heart.

So. That was decided. Excellent.

On Sunday afternoon Ellie walked over to Willoughby Manor to thank Lady Stokeley for taking care of Abby and return the dress. It had turned unseasonably warm, a proper spring day, or almost. Her heart lightened to hear the birdsong, and she saw the bright green shoots of the first crocuses poking up from the damp earth. Hopefully Willoughby Manor would be a bit warmer for Lady Stokeley now.

"So you had a nice time, my dear?" Lady Stokeley asked

after she'd insisted Ellie come in. Thanks to the warmth of the day, she led Ellie to a conservatory in the back of the house with views of the terraced gardens and a lot of ancient rattan furniture. "Did you take any photographs?"

Ellie made an apologetic grimace. "I'm sorry, I completely forgot." Not to mention she hadn't been in a state to do any such thing.

"Never mind." Lady Stokeley gave her a sly look. "Abby said there might be a man involved? A professor?"

"My boss, and no. We're just friends," Ellie said firmly. Here was her resolution in action.

"Pity. I could have used a little excitement in my life."

Ellie choked back a startled laugh. "I'm sorry to disappoint you."

"Abby seemed to like him as well," Lady Stokeley mused. "She was very keen. Pleased you were staying, which did seem a bit shocking, but I know times have moved on."

"It wasn't at all like that," Ellie said, blushing. She didn't want Lady Stokeley to think she was some kind of loose woman. "Anyway, Abby just wants me to get a life, so I stop obsessing about her own."

"I suppose I can see some wisdom in that." Lady Stokeley took a sip of tea. "I was never able to have children, so I'm afraid I can't relate to such concerns. But she is a charming girl."

"She's enjoyed your friendship," Ellie said. "Really, you've helped her to come out of her shell. I never would have thought it…" Too late she realized how that sounded. "Thank you," she said instead. "Thank you so much."

Lady Stokeley smiled and cocked her head in regal acceptance. "It's been my pleasure."

On the way back to Willoughby Close Ellie ran into Jace, who was loading firewood into the back of his truck.

"Shall I bring some of this over to you?"

"Yes, please. What do I owe you—"

"We're good," Jace said, shrugging her words aside. "Friends don't need to pay."

His tone was deliberately roguish and Ellie laughed. She'd gotten used to his relentlessly flirtatious charm, and knew he never meant anything by it. And it felt good to have friends. "So, I hear we're going to have neighbors next week?"

"Yep, single mum and three kids. That's what it looks like, anyway."

"Really?" Her heart leapt at that thought. Another mum battling it out in the trenches, her new best friend. *Down, girl.* "That's great. I mean, not that she's a single mum necessarily, but…"

Laughing, Jace waved her along. "I know what you mean, Ellie."

Grinning, Ellie headed back to Willoughby Close.

Chapter Fifteen

B Y MONDAY MORNING Oliver was determined to set things right with Ellie, as best as he could. He didn't know how they'd gone wrong exactly, only that they had. He'd spent the rest of the weekend working and, when he let himself, moping a little. He'd obviously offended her somehow, but he'd just been trying to be... what? Encouraging? Friendly? Something like that.

Things had been going so *well*. He'd enjoyed inviting her into his life, hearing her encouragement about Jemima. Just being with her. And then somehow it had all gone pearshaped before he'd barely been able to blink.

He fully intended to do better today, regain some ground, and then... Then he had no idea what would happen. What he wanted to happen. He was attracted to her, yes, and he liked her more than a bit. But did Ellie feel the same about him? Oliver had no idea. At times he thought she did, and other times... not. He knew he wasn't good at reading people, and Ellie made it particularly difficult. Besides, was it wise to start something with his PA? They were so different, and if it didn't work out he'd have to see her every day, not to mention deal with the faculty gossip. And he wasn't even good at relationships, anyway.

His mind was still going round and round in circles when he heard Ellie's cheerful greeting to Jeannie from the main office, and then the sound of her coming down the hallway. Was she going to walk past? She usually checked in with him first thing in the morning. He'd been counting on it. He was half out his seat to go find her when he saw her face through the glass and heard a light tap on the door. Relieved, he sat down. And then stood up again, because she was coming into the room and he had things to say. Important things.

"Ellie." His voice boomed out, and she blinked.

"Hey." She was wearing that ridiculous, rainbow-colored scarf, a fuzzy sweater and a corduroy skirt that seemed quite short. She had amazing legs. Of course, he'd noticed them before, but he found he was particularly drawn to them today. Her tights looked fuzzy too, and eminently touchable. Oliver jerked his gaze upwards.

"Look," he said, "I wanted to apologize for Sunday. If I said anything that offended you."

"You didn't, not really." The words were right but the tone was not, nor was the rather cool smile she was giving him. "So, chapter eight, right?"

"Right." Somehow that had not gone the way he'd wanted. He'd wanted more of a proper chat, a heart-to-heart even. He'd wanted to get back a little of the comfortable intimacy they'd shared over the weekend. That was clearly not happening, and hell if he knew how to go about recapturing it. He'd just completely exhausted his emotional resources for the entire day. He was sweating, for heaven's sake. "Chapter eight," he repeated, and looked down at his notes.

A few minutes later Ellie left with his notes, and Oliver sat there stewing, wishing he could have been more glib, more self-assured. He racked his brain to think of something more he could have said, something that wouldn't have sounded like he was reading from a tele-prompter, for heaven's sake. He couldn't up with anything.

By lunchtime he decided he needed a take two. He didn't have any lectures until late afternoon, and the afternoon beckoned promisingly. It was a beautiful day, a hint of spring in the air, a robin chirping outside his window, the sky a pale, fragile blue. Resolutely he grabbed his blazer and marched towards Ellie's door.

"Do you feel like grabbing a spot of lunch?" he asked while Ellie stared at him in surprise. "I know a nice pub by the river."

"Oh. Umm…"

She was going to say no. She was going to politely, kindly refuse, and suddenly Oliver couldn't take it. Not after all the deliberating he'd had about how to make things right between them again. "It's beautiful out, and I need to go over a few things with my book before my next lecture." For good measure he checked his watch, as if he had more important places to be, lots of things to do. Right.

"Oh, all right, then. It would be nice to have a change of scene." Ellie rose from her seat, her hair brushing his shoulder because the room was that small. Oliver stepped back watching as she slipped on her coat and pulled her hair out from underneath it. Small, simple gestures, but they still affected him. Still made him ache in a way he hadn't in a long, long time, if ever. He was ridiculous and he didn't care. Much.

It was lovely out, and Oliver kept the chat light, or as light as he knew how, all the way to The Head of the River, a pub with tables overlooking the Thames. It was warm enough to take one of the picnic tables outside, and Ellie sat down while he went to fetch them menus and drinks.

When they'd ordered and had their drinks in front of them, she gave him a polite smile. "So? Your book?"

Right. He could talk about his research for hours on end, boring for England, but right now his mind was completely and utterly empty. His book. What book?

"I'm rewriting chapter seven," he blurted. Was he? "It needs a lot of work."

"Okay." Her smile was still in place, but now it looked a little uncertain. Damn it, why was she acting so distant? As if they hadn't talked about their pasts, their relationships? As if he hadn't touched her waist? He still could remember the feel the perfect curve of her hip against his palm, the warmth of her skin apparent through the layers of cloth that had separated them and it made his heart race. What was this, *Age of Innocence?*

"How was the rest of your weekend?" he asked, determined not to have this just be about work. He didn't know what he'd say about his book, in any case. Chapter seven indeed needed work, but he couldn't focus on it now.

"Fine. Boring." She smiled, seeming to relax a little. "Bills, housework, walking the dog. I live a very exciting life. What about you?"

"Same, minus the dog, more or less."

And... now they were done. Oliver gazed at her in barely-concealed frustration. What had happened to their connection, damn it?

"You know I was thinking," Ellie said suddenly. She tossed her hair over her shoulders, a strangely steely glint in her eyes.

"You were?"

"Yes. I was thinking you should date."

He stared at her, caught between confusion and hope. He'd been thinking the same thing, but even so he had a feeling they weren't on quite the same page. "You do?"

"Yes, I mean, you're nearly forty, aren't you? And you said you had trouble finding women to date."

"Well, yes, but not quite like that—"

"Don't you want to settle down?"

"Eventually, I suppose, but only if I find the right woman." Who might, just might, be sitting right in front of him.

"Exactly," Ellie agreed with more enthusiasm than Oliver liked. "And how are you going to find the right woman if you're stuck in an office all day?"

"Many people face the same situation—"

"I think you should join an online dating site," Ellie proclaimed. "I'm going to join one as well."

"Oh." This was not at all how Oliver had imagined the conversation going. They were definitely not on the same page. They weren't even reading the same bloody book.

"What do you think?" Ellie asked. "We could compare dating profiles, potential dates. Give each other advice."

"Er." Oliver resisted the urge to tug at his collar. Why had Ellie come up with such an awful, asinine idea? "I hadn't thought of that. I'm not sure…"

"Of course, it's perfectly respectable these days. And there are some really good, really focused sites. I'm not talking Tinder here, obviously."

"Tinder?" As in matches and kindling? He stared at her blankly.

"I found one that's perfect for you," she continued, which gave Oliver pause. She'd been looking for an online dating site specifically for him? She wanted him safely matched up that badly? He tried to arrange his face in an expression that did not betray the level of unease he felt. "Not that I was looking," she assured him, which made him feel only marginally better. "I was looking for me, and then I saw one that seemed right up your street."

And now he was the tiniest bit curious as to what kind of dating site she thought would suit him. "Really," he said after a second's pause.

"It's called *Your Ivory Tower.* Perfect, huh?"

He wouldn't call it perfect. Arrogant and up-yourself, perhaps. "Hmm," he managed, and Ellie continued blithely, "You fill out a questionnaire and then they suggest women with similar interests, goals, all that sort of thing. You get to exchange emails and take it from there." Her smile widened. "What do you think?"

He thought it sounded atrocious, but he wasn't about to put his foot in it again. "What dating site are you looking at, then?" he asked.

"Me?" She looked startled. "Oh, um, one for single parents." Her gaze slid away and Oliver wondered if she was having him on.

"Have you made a profile?" he challenged, and she looked back at him, lifting her chin. "No, but I will. If you will."

A dare. And one he did not want to take up. Fortunately their meals came then, and Oliver hoped he could steer the conversation away from dating sites.

"What are you doing for half-term?" he asked and Ellie looked surprised.

"Working, I thought. I didn't suppose I could ask for

any holiday off quite so quickly."

"But what will Abby do?"

"She can go to the school's holiday club for a couple of days. She'll love that." Ellie rolled her eyes, looking both guilty and worried.

"I'm sure you can take some time off. I probably will, to look after Jemima and Tobias." He didn't think his sister could manage for a week on her own with Tobias off school.

"I might do that," Ellie said. "I'm sure Abby would like some time away."

"Maybe you'll have a date by then," Oliver said a touch bitterly, and then could have bitten his tongue. Why mention the stupid dating site thing again?

"Maybe," Ellie agreed, a note of steel entering her voice. "Why don't we both register now?"

"Umm…"

"You can do it on your phone." She slid her phone out of her handbag and Oliver felt he had no choice but to take his phone out as well. "Here, I'll show you." She took his phone and with a few swipes and taps had it on the dating app. Oliver blinked down at the lurid screen, taking in the picture of two up-themselves professionals giving each other smug smiles. Underneath the photo he read *Your Own Ivory Tower*. Was this how Ellie saw him?

"So." She took back his phone and started swiping the screen. "Let's start with the basics. Age, thirty-eight. Hair, golden-brown. Eye color?" She looked up, assessing. "Gray-green, I'd say. Is that a choice? Yes. Good." She continued thumbing in details while Oliver tried to keep up to speed.

"Ellie, hold on. What about your profile?"

"We'll do mine next. Now, how tall are you? Six two?"

"Something like that, but—"

"Do you work out?"

"I bike," he said stiffly. "Now, really." This was starting to get seriously out of control. "I'm not actually interested in signing up to some dating site."

Ellie put the phone down and leveled him with a direct look. "Why not? Don't you want to date?"

"I don't need an Internet site to date," Oliver said, starting to fume.

"Everyone uses them these days. There's no shame. Like I said, I'll do my profile next—"

"It's not about *shame,*" he said, his voice rising in his frustration. "Look, it's just that I…" *Like you.* The words hovered there, thankfully unspoken. He blew out an impatient breath and raked his hand through his hair. All right, even he wasn't so emotionally stunted that he couldn't understand what Ellie was doing. She was sending him a message—*I'm not interested in you.* And it had been received, loud and clear. So what was the point of protesting? He'd let her finish this pointless exercise, allow her to sign him up for the stupid dating site, and then he'd undo it all later.

He leaned back, arms folded. "Fine. What's the next question?"

OLIVER'S SUDDEN ACQUIESCENCE threw her. Ellie hesitated, trying to gauge his mood, because he'd seemed almost as if he'd been getting angry and now he looked… determined. As ridiculously determined as she'd been, and for what? Did she really want to sign Oliver up for this stupid site? Did she want to sign herself up?

She'd discovered the dating sites last night, when she'd been aimlessly surfing the Internet, feeling disconsolate. All her just-friends resolutions had started to chafe a bit, and when she'd stumbled on the Ivory Tower site, it had pushed all the buttons that didn't need another pressing. She couldn't register for the site, of course. You had to have an advanced degree—preferably an MA, definitely a BA. There were questions about what field you were in, how much money you made, whether you'd published in any academic journals or had any additional honorary degrees. It was the kind of site that was perfect for Oliver.

And still smarting from the realization that they really were from different worlds, she'd brought it up today. What on earth had she been hoping to achieve? Some clarity about her own feelings? They were as muddier as ever and now she was stuck, feeling childish for signing up the man she was more than a little interested in for a dating site.

"Okay." She swallowed and stared down at the screen. "How much money do you make?"

"Seriously? They ask that?"

"Yes—"

"Why don't I just do it?" He reached over and snatched her phone from her hand, and with pursed lips and narrowed eyes began to finish answering the questions.

Ellie was dying to have a look at his answers—she'd read through the questions last night and some of them got very personal. Like how often you liked having sex, and even what positions you preferred.

She had a feeling Oliver had reached the sex questions, because he snorted and shook his head, a faint blush touching his cheeks. Ellie sat there, inwardly squirming, wishing she hadn't brought up the whole dating site in the first place. What had she been thinking of? What had she been trying to prove?

"There." Oliver tossed her back her phone. "Sorted."

Ellie glanced down at the screen and saw the 'thank you for registering with Your Ivory Tower' message. He really had done it.

"Now you just wait for the messages to start pouring in," she said as cheerfully as she could. She felt a little sick.

"Brilliant," Oliver answered, and drained his drink. "Now it's your turn."

"Oh, well…"

"Only fair," he said sweetly, and held out his hand for her phone.

By the time Ellie had picked up Abby that evening and driven home she was in a thoroughly foul mood. Oliver had filled out her dating profile while Ellie had squirmed, resolving to delete it all as soon as she could.

Then she'd spent the afternoon berating herself being so stupid, wondering why she couldn't just admit to herself that she fancied Oliver. Because she didn't, of course. She couldn't. He was wrong for her, she was wrong for him, and in any case, she wasn't ready for a relationship. Maybe she never would be.

"Bad day at work?" Abby asked mildly as Ellie flung her bag down with a thud and then opened the door of the fridge so that it thwacked the wall.

"No. Just the usual."

"You haven't made up with Oliver, then?"

Ellie slammed the fridge door closed. "I haven't fallen out with him in the first place." Not as such. "Why does everything have to be about Oliver?"

"Whoa." Abby held her hands up. "Just asking."

"I already told you it's nothing to do with him," Ellie said crossly, and then sighed. "I'm just tired. Sorry, love." The last thing she wanted to do was take out her bad mood on her daughter. "How was school?"

Abby shrugged. "The usual."

Ellie knew better than to press. She'd learned that much self-control, at least. Besides, Abby had seemed happier these last few weeks, having made friends with Tobias and Lady Stokeley, than she had in years. Ellie definitely didn't want to mess with that.

The phone rang, surprising them both since they rarely got calls on the landline. Ellie went to answer it, shock slicing through her when she heard the all-too familiar voice on the other end of the line.

"Ellie?"

"Nathan." Ellie watched Abby's eyes widen and she strove for a neutral yet friendly tone. "Haven't heard from you in a while."

"Sorry. It's been manic." Already he had a slight Aussie twang which seemed ridiculous—he'd only been there a month—and yet was also so predictable. Nathan adapted to his surroundings. He was like water, flowing easily around everything, never able to be held or caught.

"Manic how?"

"Oh, you know." Now he went into his even more predictable evasive mode. No doubt he didn't want to give her a play-by-play of his days spent sunbathing and surfing and his nights with the surfer chick he'd picked up in a pub back in Manchester.

"No, I don't actually know, Nathan." Ellie closed her eyes. Just talking to her ex-husband made her feel even more tired and dispirited than she'd already been. "Do you want to talk to Abby?"

"Yes, but I wanted to chat with you first. How are things? How's Cambridge?"

"Oxford, Nathan. Oxfordshire, actually. And they're fine."

"Sorry. They seem like the same place to me." He laughed uneasily. "The thing is, I was just wondering if maybe you could float me a loan. Things are a lot pricier than I expected, and…"

Ellie angled her body away from Abby. "You want me to give you money?" she demanded in a low voice.

"Just a loan, Ellie. I'll pay it back, I promise."

"That's why you called?" She took a deep breath, willing the pointless anger back.

"And to talk to you and Abby," he said, all indignant, meaningless bluster. "Of course I want that. Look, forget about the money, okay? It doesn't matter." He paused, and then said quietly, "Look, I know I've been a dud." He was using a sincere, heartfelt tone that Ellie knew all too well. It was the one he used when he made promises, promises she knew he wanted to keep but rarely did. The tone that had gotten her into bed with him, once upon a long time ago. The tone that had convinced her a marriage between them could work, that he was going to get a job, take better care of her and Abby, not kiss that girl at the pub, remember to put his dirty socks in the washing machine. Oh, that tone. All those broken promises. "A dud husband and a dud dad," he said starkly, a stoic note entering his voice that made Ellie pinch the bridge of her nose. "I know that, Ellie, and I want to say sorry. I've been thinking a lot about things. I think that's what I needed, you know. The space to think."

"Talk to Abby," Ellie said abruptly and thrust the phone

at her daughter. "She'd like to tell you about our life here." She couldn't talk to Nathan anymore, not when he was taking that tack. *Space to think?* He'd had acres of space to think. Years of wasted, empty time when he could have done all this *thinking*. And what was he thinking about, anyway? How to get some money from her? The trouble with Nathan was he used and perhaps even felt enough sincerity to make Ellie start to question all her choices and feel genuinely wretched about having kicked him out all those years ago.

Not wanting to eavesdrop on Abby's conversation, Ellie opened the French windows and stepped outside onto the mini terrace. It had felt like spring yesterday but tonight it was freezing. She stood there shivering, her arms wrapped around herself, wishing that talking to Nathan didn't stir up all sorts of feelings inside her. Resentment. Regret. Sadness. Frustration. Anger too, and stupidly, a twisted kind of hope. When was she going to get over it all and move on? Maybe *she* needed to sign up to a dating site. Not *Your Ivory Tower*, though. For obvious reasons.

"Mum?"

"Hey." Ellie turned around to see Abby standing in the doorway, an uncertain look on her face. "How's your dad?"

"He's okay. He says he might come back from Australia in a while."

A while? That was specific. Not. "Okay," Ellie said, hearing the doubt in her voice.

"You don't believe him?"

Ellie sighed. "When it comes to your dad, Abby, I don't know what to believe. I want to believe the best, but I don't want you to be disappointed." Like she had been when Nathan had promised a trip to a theme park and never shown up. Or to attend her nativity play and then come in when everyone was taking their bows. Abby had frozen right there on the stage, her face a tragic mask of disappointment as she watched her dad give a sheepishly apologetic grin. That was Nathan, over and over again.

"I know he's not the best dad," Abby said quietly. "But he can be fun."

"I know." Ellie knew that all too well. Nathan was all about the fun. And when he was feeling it, when he was on form, he *was* brilliantly fun. That, in some ways, was the trouble. He wasn't a deadbeat dad a hundred percent of the time. He hadn't been a bad husband a hundred percent of the time, either. But the end result had been a lot of heartache and disappointment.

"Remember when he took me to the beach?"

"In February? Yes." It had been one of those freakishly warm days and Nathan had gone all out, shown up at their house in his swimming trunks, a swim ring around his middle and white sun cream on his nose. It was, he'd announced grandly, summer for the day.

Abby had been about eight and ecstatic. They'd spent the day at the seaside, the only ones on the beach, building sandcastles and eating ice cream. Nathan had even gone

swimming, and nearly come down with pneumonia afterwards. It had been February, after all.

"And remember when he got you all those roses?"

Ellie sighed, a reluctant smile tugging at her lips. "Yes."
He'd forgotten her birthday and so the next day he'd bought
out all the roses from the local petrol station. As if she'd
needed, or they could afford, ten sad-looking bouquets of a
dozen red roses, all of them wilting within hours. It had been
a nice thought… sort of.

"Do you miss him, Abby?" Ellie asked quietly and her
heart ached as her daughter hung her head.

"Sort of. Do you mind?"

"Mind? Why would I mind? He's your dad."

"I know, but… I know he disappoints you."

"I just don't want him disappointing *you*," Ellie returned.
She pulled Abby, her non-cuddly daughter, into a quick but
fierce hug. "But like I said, he's your dad. He loves you and
you love him, and that's great."

Abby was silent for a moment, her arms wrapped around
Ellie's middle. Ellie tried to savor it, because she didn't think
Abby had hugged her like this in years. But she felt anxious
too, because so much seemed uncertain. Nathan's phone call
felt like he'd just shaken up their life here, scattered her
fragile certainties, and she wasn't ready for that. She wasn't
strong enough yet.

"Do you think he really will come back from Australia?"
Abby asked, her voice muffled against Ellie's shoulder.

"Eventually," Ellie answered. "And when he does, I know he'll come straight to see you." At least she hoped he would. And if he didn't, he'd be hearing from her.

Chapter Sixteen

OLIVER HAD FOURTEEN messages from women who had read his profile on *Your Ivory Tower*. He hadn't figured out how to shut down his dating profile, and in the meantime, it seemed to be going crazy. Another message pinged into his inbox as he scrolled through the introductory messages, appalled and not at all interested by the photos, the gushing messages, the unabashed bragging of degrees, career prospects, even bra size. No shame, indeed.

He wished he'd never agreed to sign up; it felt like unleashing the kraken. He was now up to sixteen messages, and the last one looked to be from someone he vaguely knew. *Help.*

And then Ellie appeared in his office. "Good morning." She looked tired and strained and Oliver didn't feel he could ask why. He wanted to, though. He was just about to shut his laptop but then, damnably, she caught sight of the *Your Ivory Tower* logo, which was, unoriginally, a literal ivory tower. A wide smile stretched across her face, like an elastic band about to snap.

"You got some messages! How are they?"

"Terrible," Oliver retorted. "I'm not interested in any of them."

"Perhaps you shouldn't be so picky."

"Perhaps I shouldn't have registered for this absurd site." He gestured to the screen. "I tried to deactivate my profile last night but they make it annoyingly difficult."

She raised her eyebrows. "You want to deactivate your profile already?"

"Yes. I never wanted to go on that site in the first place." He glared at her, exasperated. "I only agreed because you were so determined." And he knew why that was. "Did you get any messages on yours?" he asked, hoping she didn't.

"I don't know." A blush touched her cheeks. "Actually, I deleted my profile."

Oliver raised his eyebrows. "That's a bit hypocritical, isn't it?" And yet he was absurdly pleased that she had.

"I know. The whole idea was stupid, really. I don't know why I thought of it." Ellie bit her lip, looking genuinely contrite. "I'd say I was trying to help, but I don't think I actually was."

Oliver sighed and leaned back in his chair. "You were annoyed with me, I think."

"Not with you. With myself." She shook her head and hurried on before Oliver could ask her to clarify. "Anyway. Do you want me to deactivate the account for you?"

"Yes, please."

She dropped her bag and came around to his side of the desk. Oliver's entire body tensed as Ellie half-crouched near him, her shoulder brushing his thigh, her body very near his and smelling of spring rain. His breathing went humiliatingly shallow.

"It's true they make it a bit fiddly. They want to keep your money, I suppose."

"You mean people actually pay for this?"

"Why else would someone create the site?" She looked up at him with laughing eyes, tormenting his libido. "But you only pay if you find an appropriate match."

Which he never would. "That's a relief, then, because I have no intention of spending a penny on this rubbish."

"Are you sure?" Ellie started to scroll down the screen, past message after message from hopeful females. "Some of these women look pretty good," she added, shooting him a curious look. "A law professor right here in Oxford? Fortysomething and with two PhDs? She's pretty." She nodded towards a photo Oliver had no interest in inspecting. "And what about this one? She speaks three languages, enjoys fine wine and foreign films and is looking for someone to share her interests."

"I don't like foreign films," he answered shortly. He was trying to keep his sense of humor about the whole thing but it was hard. "They're far too pretentious."

"What about one of the other women, then?" Ellie pressed. "No one snags your interest?"

"No." He spoke with emphatic feeling.

"Why not?"

It was so exasperating, having her ask these questions while she was practically perched in his lap and he could smell her perfume. It was making him *crazy.* "Because all these women are more or less like me," he snapped. "And I don't want to date myself. I want to date someone different, who doesn't have the hang ups I do, who can get me out of myself and make me laugh and feel normal and *fun."*

Her lips parted soundlessly as she stared at him. Oliver had the scorching sensation that he'd revealed way too much. The words had spilled from unthinkingly, and now he wished he could gobble them all back up. Ellie would undoubtedly be horrified if she realized exactly who he was thinking of. He grabbed the laptop from her. "Never mind this. I think I can figure it out myself. I do have a PhD, after all."

Ellie straightened slowly, still staring at him. Oliver kept his gaze on the screen and tapped a few random keys, wishing he could rewind the last few minutes.

"Sorry," Ellie said after a moment. "Like I said, the dating site thing was a really stupid idea."

"What did you mean," Oliver asked abruptly, still not looking at her, "when you said you were annoyed with yourself?"

Ellie was silent for a moment. "I got in a snit about your suggestion about bettering myself."

"I didn't mean it like that…"

"I know." She sighed. "But it's true, isn't it? I'm not like you. I'm not like anyone in this whole building."

"That might be considered a good thing—"

"I never had the chance to discover what I liked, what I might want to do with my life. I suppose plenty of people are the same, but…" She shrugged. "It made me realize how I've missed out, and I'm not sure I can do anything about it."

Oliver had the distinct feeling she wasn't telling him the whole story. "It's not too late, Ellie. You're not even thirty yet."

"Even so." She sounded resolute. "Anyway, I shouldn't have taken it out on you. I know you were just trying to offer me some encouragement as a—" The infinitesimal pause had him tensing. "A friend."

And there was the clarification she felt he needed. "Yes, that's right," he answered dutifully. "I'd like to think that we're friends."

"Yes, I'd say we are." She smiled, but it didn't reach her eyes. Oliver wondered if she was reassured, as he'd meant her to be. Was he completely hopeless, thinking he saw a tiny flicker of disappointment in her eyes?

"I should get to work. Chapter nine beckons." With a lopsided smile, Ellie moved from behind his desk. Oliver watched her go, wishing he hadn't clarified things quite so much.

WELL. ELLIE DIDN'T know what to make of that. Whether to be amused or appalled or interested or hopeful or... anything. She felt completely at a loss, and had for a while. About Oliver, about herself, even about Nathan. His phone call last night had left her with too many late-night doubts, staring gritty-eyed at the ceiling wondering how many mistakes she'd made in her life. Marrying Nathan? Divorcing Nathan? Moving to the Cotswolds? She could spend her life second-guessing everything and be none the wiser. For so long she'd had her head down, plowing through each day, so she hadn't been able to stop and think. Realize there was a whole world out there, and it was scary and exciting and big. Did she want to date again? Go back to university? Make something more of her life than she had already?

As for Oliver... well, that was a whole snarl of confused feelings that she couldn't begin to untangle. For a second, when he'd been talking about the kind of woman he wanted to date, it had almost seemed as if he was talking about *her*. But then in the next breath he'd agreed they were just friends. She had no idea how any of that made her feel.

Perhaps she would take a few days off next week during half-term, go away somewhere cheap—*very* cheap—with Abby. Get away from it all, if she could. The trouble was, she didn't think she could get away from her own endlessly circling thoughts.

Sighing, she pulled out her chair and started to work.

She didn't see Oliver for the rest of the day and was just

packing up to go home, when he knocked on her door.

"Do you have a minute?" he asked, and something about the wary earnestness of his expression made Ellie's heart lurch.

"Yes." She stood up, wincing at the cramp in her shoulders after spending nearly eight hours hunched over her desk. "What's up?"

"I spoke to Jemima earlier today about half-term." He gave a wry grimace. "She hadn't even realized it was half-term, so I'm glad I checked. I don't know what she would have done with Tobias home all week. Anyway." He blew out a breath. "I thought it might be a nice idea for Jemima to go somewhere new, get out of her rut, and so I rented us a cottage in Cornwall."

Ellie smiled at him, a little confused as to why he was telling her this now. "That sounds nice."

"Yes, I hope so... but I wondered, that is, if you and Abby might... well, I thought it would be nice for Tobias, and even Jemima, you know, since you had said you sort of understood what she was going through..." He trailed off, looking at her expectantly, as if waiting for an answer.

Ellie stared at him in bemusement. What was he trying to say? "I hope you have a nice time," she said when the silence had stretched on for a while.

"Oh. Yes." Oliver gave her a rueful smile. "I hope so, too. The thing is, what I'm asking is, ... do you want to go with us? You and Abby," he clarified quickly, just in case, perhaps, she thought he was asking her to run away with him.

Even so Ellie's head was spinning. A cottage in Cornwall, a week's holiday... *with Oliver.*

"I..." She tried to think of what to say, what she felt, and she realized she didn't know. "It sounds amazing," she said after a moment, and Oliver's face fell for a nanosecond before he rearranged his features in a wry expression.

"Does it? I haven't actually said much about it."

"True. But a cottage? In Cornwall? That alone amazes me. I've never been there."

"It's beautiful. We used to when I was a child." For a second his gaze turned distant. "Some of my happiest memories are from there, on the beach with... well." He snapped back to attention. "The only cottage I could rent at this late date has five bedrooms, so there will definitely be plenty of space. It's on the Lizard Peninsula, right near the beach. It would be a relaxed time—no theme parks or even the cinema, I'm afraid. Just board games and long walks, most likely."

"It sounds wonderful," Ellie said, because it did. She couldn't remember the last time she'd had a proper holiday, and the chance to truly unplug from her life for a little bit was very tempting. But it was with Oliver, not to mention Tobias and Jemima, and she didn't know how she felt about any of that. She didn't know how Abby would, either. Would they drive each other crazy all week? Would they run out of things to talk about on the first day? Would it be terribly awkward or absolutely wonderful or most likely something in between? "I need to talk to Abby first. Can I tell you tomorrow?"

"Of course."

"Thank you," she said, meaning it truly. "It's very generous of you to ask us."

"Well." Oliver gave her one of his lopsided smiles. "Hopefully it would be fun for everyone involved. Since we're all friends."

She mulled over Oliver's invitation all the way home that evening, caught between desperately wanting to go… and a little bit not. She leaned her head against the rain-streaked window of the train, wondering exactly what she was afraid of. Because it was fear that was clenching her stomach, making her heart race. Fear and a little bit of excitement.

Oliver had certainly made it clear they were only friends now, which was all they'd ever been, really. Yes, there had been a day or two where she'd wondered. A moment or two where she'd felt fluttery and hopeful and excited and scared all at once. But nothing had actually *happened* between them. This holiday could be a chance to cement their friendship, put their nebulous past behind them. What was there to be nervous about?

Still she hesitated to bring it up with Abby, even though she knew she had to. "So," she said, once the dinner dishes were cleared and Abby was about to slope upstairs to do her homework. "Half-term."

"Please don't sign me up for one those awful holiday clubs at school," Abby said. "I know you have to work but I do not want to spend eight hours a day doing rubbish crafts in some stuffy classroom. I'm too old for that, Mum."

"Abby, you're eleven." Her daughter rolled her eyes. "Okay, okay. No holiday clubs. That is…" Suddenly it seemed like a no-brainer. Why *wouldn't* she and Abby go on a fun holiday with someone she could call a friend? She was, as usual, freaking out over nothing, letting fear be her default. "Oliver has invited us to go to Cornwall for the week with him and Tobias. And Jemima, as well."

Abby's eyes rounded hugely. "Seriously?"

"Do you think I'd make a joke about this?" Ellie asked lightly. "Yes, he has. What do you think?"

"Cornwall… for a whole week? Wow." Abby's eyes suddenly narrowed to slits. "He *is* into you. I knew it—"

"No, really, he's not," Ellie cut her off. "That's been…" She cleared her throat. "Made clear. So. This is a friends-only trip. He thought Tobias might like the company—your company, that is. And I think Jemima could use some company, as well. She's been going through a difficult time."

"And what about Oliver?"

"Everybody, then." Ellie leaned back and folded her arms. "So, what do you think? Should we go?"

"Of course we should go," Abby exclaimed. "It will be *epic*. Although… I did promise to help Dorothy clean her cupboards out that week."

"I thought you'd already done that."

"Other ones. She has a lot of stuff."

"I know. And I'm sure you can help her after school," Ellie said. "I think Lady Stokeley would want you to enjoy a holiday."

Abby shook her head. "Are you ever going to call her Dorothy?"

"I'm not sure. Maybe if she tells me specifically to call her by her first name." And maybe not even then. Lady Stokeley still intimidated her, and most likely she always would.

The next morning Ellie felt fluttery with both excitement and nerves as she tapped on Oliver's door. He looked up as she came in, a cautious smile spreading across his face.

"Good morning."

"Good morning." She smiled back, feeling a lightening inside her. Why shouldn't this be easy? Why shouldn't it be *fun?* "So… that trip to Cornwall."

"Yes?" A hopeful look came into Oliver's eyes, making Ellie feel even more optimistic.

"Abby and I would love to come with you. If the invitation is still open… I mean, if you still…" She couldn't think of a gracious exit line, and so she left it at that.

"Of course it's still open. And that's brilliant. I'm so glad you both can come." He smiled and she smiled back and then they both laughed, self-consciously.

"I can pay something towards the rental…" Ellie began, although she wasn't sure she could. Not much, anyway. She'd gone on one of those self-catering cottage websites and seen how much a five bedroom place in Cornwall had been. Thousands of pounds.

"Absolutely not." Oliver held up one hand, completely firm. "I would have booked the place no matter what, so there's no need. And we might as well travel down together, to save petrol costs, don't you think? We should all fit in my estate. Even Marmite."

This was sounding cozier and cozier. "Are you sure you want to bring my dog?" Ellie asked dubiously. Although she didn't know what she would do with him otherwise.

"He can stay in the back. Less drool on me. And I'm sure he'll love it too, in Cornwall. Lots of exercise and space."

"Okay. Sounds good. Very good."

They smiled at each other again for another few seconds and then Ellie gave a little wave and got to work. She was still smiling as she sat down at her desk.

So that was that. She was going on holiday with her boss. A whole week in Cornwall. It felt surreal and scary, and also exciting, no matter that they were just friends.

She was doing this.

Chapter Seventeen

THE CAR WAS stuffed to the roof with both people and bags. And dog. Oliver eyed it all uneasily and wondered at the wisdom of taking a six-hour road trip with this motley crew. Tobias had, for reasons unknown to Oliver, descended into a sullen silence. Jemima was just as quiet, skinny arms folded tightly across her middle, her gaze distant and vacant. Ellie had stood in front of her door, an uncertain smile on her face as Oliver pulled up. He'd had a feeling she was questioning the wisdom of this trip as well.

It had all made perfect sense in his head. It had been that innate sense of rightness that had propelled him last week to suggest she and Abby come along. He'd been in her office, bumbling through an invitation, before he'd had the time to think it through properly, but he hadn't cared. It made sense... for Tobias, for Jemima, for him.

Never mind that he'd spent several sleepless nights imagining certain scenarios during their week. Certain 15-rated scenarios, or at least 12A. They were just *friends*. He knew that, but he was a fairly normal red-blooded male. Of course he was going to fantasize a little about what could happen in the evenings when everyone had gone to bed, or when they bumped into each other in a darkened hallway…

An overstuffed car filled with semi-hostile people and a farting dog, however, did not fit into any fantasy of his.

"We made it," he'd announced as cheerfully as he could as he stepped out of the car at Willoughby Close. Abby was half-hiding behind Ellie, looking apprehensive. Were they all starting to regret this trip? It felt, at that moment, as if they were no more than a handful of strangers willfully thrown together. But they could make it work, couldn't they? They *would*.

"Let me just put your bags in the roof box." Fortunately Ellie and Abby had packed light, a duffel bag each. Oliver didn't know what he would have done if they'd wheeled out one of those enormous armor-plated suitcases, as big as a steamer trunk. The kind that Jemima had brought and insisted he packed, without so much as blinking an eye.

Unfortunately, Marmite came with a lot of stuff. Dog bed, bowls, a huge sack of dog food, and, inexplicably, several rolls of paper towel.

"He likes to rip them up," Ellie explained a bit sheepishly. "Trust me, it will keep him entertained in the car."

Somehow Oliver managed to squeeze it all in, closing the boot on a panting Marmite with relief. "Do you mind sitting in the back?" he murmured to Ellie as he opened the car door for her. "Jemima…" Had insisted on the front.

"Not at all," Ellie said easily, and squeezed in next to Abby. They looked pretty cozy back there.

"And we're on our way." Oliver climbed in the driver's side and then pulled out onto Willoughby Manor's gracious drive. Their road trip had begun.

They drove in silence, save for Marmite's occasional alarmingly loud emissions, for over an hour. At one point Jemima waved her hand in front of her face, coughing theatrically.

"Good heavens, what *is* that horrible smell?"

"Sorry," Ellie said in a small voice.

Jemima half-turned in disbelief, showing more animation than she had in months. "You mean it's *you?*"

"No." Ellie's face had turned bright red. "It's Marmite, my dog."

Oliver waded into the fray, trying to placate everyone and naturally managing only to add to the tension. "Have you ever had him looked at? By a vet? Because maybe there's something they could do…"

"I have, actually," Ellie replied stiffly. "And I've also tried changing his food. I'm afraid it's just an unfortunate case of canine genetics."

Cue more silence. And unfortunately more smell. Maybe this trip had been a mistake. It didn't seem to be starting out well, at any rate, and now that he thought about it, Oliver realized he was way too much of an introvert to spend an entire week with four other people. He was going to hate everybody by the end of the week, or far more likely, everyone was going to hate him. What had possessed him to suggest such an outrageous idea?

Things didn't improve much when they stopped at a rest stop near Sedgemoor. Jemima made a beeline for the convenience shop and came back with two mini-cans of premixed gin and tonic, one already cracked open. It was ten in the morning. Abby and Tobias were, quite inexplicably, refusing to talk to each other or even make eye contact, and Ellie had taken Marmite for a walk around the car park and was now huddling in the rain, looking rather dour as Marmite crouched down to do what looked like a long and enormous poo. Perhaps that would temporarily solve the flatulence problem, at least.

"I'm sorry about this," Oliver said in a low voice as she came back to the car. Everyone else had climbed in and Ellie put her arms around Marmite's middle to heave him into the back.

"Sorry about what, exactly?"

"It just seems rather tense. Hopefully things will get better once we're there. The rain doesn't help. Bloody England, eh? Never a sunny day when you want one." He was officially babbling.

"Right." Ellie swiped a damp strand of hair away from her face. "Well, I certainly hope things get better." She glanced at the interior of the car as she lowered her voice. "Jemima's starting a bit early."

"I know." He grimaced. "I don't think she has a drinking problem, precisely…"

"But she could tone it down a bit?" Ellie finished. "Hopefully this trip will get her out of her rut in more ways than one." She smiled at him and then put her hand on his arm. "Relax, Oliver. The success of this trip is not your sole responsibility, you know."

It felt like it, though. He smiled back, wishing she'd keep her hand on his arm, that he could prolong this moment, but Jemima sighed loudly, cracking open her second can of G&T, and the drizzle had turned into a downpour. Bloody England, indeed.

IT WASN'T, AS Oliver had acknowledged, a great start to their holiday. Crammed into the backseat of the Car of Ominous Silence, with Marmite drooling on her shoulder, Ellie couldn't get to Cornwall soon enough. She'd suggested the alphabet game to Abby, who had given her a withering look.

"What are we, three?" she'd muttered, and Tobias had cracked his first smile.

"Three year olds don't actually know their alphabet that well," Ellie had shot back. She wanted this to be cheery and bonding and fun, and so far it was anything but. Abby and Tobias had, for reasons she could not fathom, decided to act as if they detested each other, both of them sitting in silence, their arms folded. Oliver was so tense his knuckles were white on the steering wheel, his shoulders nearly reaching his ears. Jemima was getting drunk, and Marmite was still farting. Plus it was cold and raining, and as they approached Exeter the traffic started to pile up. Good times.

Car trips didn't have to be fun, Ellie reminded herself. Car trips were a means to an end, and once they arrived in Cornwall, things would get better. Surely they couldn't get worse.

They stopped for lunch on the other side of Exeter, and while they were washing their hands at the sinks in the ladies' toilets Ellie took the opportunity to grill her daughter.

"What's up with you and Tobias?"

Abby stared at her, nonplussed. "What do you mean?"

"Why are you not talking to each other?"

"Because we're in a car," Abby said in the well-duh voice Ellie thought she must secretly practice.

"So?"

Abby rolled her eyes. "I don't want everyone hearing us talk, Mum. It would be so *awkward.*"

"Ah. So you're still friends?"

Abby gave her the well-duh look to go with the voice. "Of course we are."

Okay, so maybe she needed to relax a little. Abby and Tobias didn't hate each other after all, and as for Jemima… Ellie glanced at Oliver's sister as she emerged from the toilets, her face perfectly made-up and blank-looking.

"Hey, Jemima." Ellie tried for a smile but Jemima didn't

make eye contact. She walked past Ellie as if she wasn't there, washing her hands before heading back out. Hmm. A week of that was going to be fun. Ellie felt sorry for her, of course she did, but it didn't make dealing with the reality much easier. Sighing, Ellie went to join the others.

By the time they arrived on the Lizard Peninsula Ellie's mood had started to lift a little, ever in search of the bright side of things. The narrow lanes bordered by tall hedgerows suddenly gave way to stunning views of the late afternoon sunlight winking on the sea in the distance as they drove through villages worthy of a postcard or the lid of a biscuit tin, with thatched roofs and ivy climbing around doors.

And then they were finally there, as Oliver pulled up to a rambling, whitewashed farmhouse planted among verdant green fields that rolled down to a small inlet of the Helford River, a short walk from a village that looked like it belonged on the set of a BBC drama. Ellie climbed out of the car, stretching gratefully as she breathed in the fresh, damp, salt-tinged air.

She released Marmite from the boot, and with a joyful woof he was off, tearing across the fields, a picture of manic liberation.

"I think Marmite's going to like it here," Abby said with a grin.

"Yes, I think so, too." After hours of silent tension, sitting with her knees practically up to her elbows—Jemima had not seen the need to put her seat forward even the tiniest amount—Ellie was starting to recover her optimism. Marmite was going to love it here, and they were too. This was the only proper holiday they'd had in a long time, and she fully intended to enjoy it.

The next hour was spent bringing in their bags and allocating bedrooms—Jemima bagged the largest one with the ensuite without discussion, which was fine by Ellie. She didn't care where she slept, as long as she had a bed.

The farmhouse was plenty spacious, if a bit over-chintzed—the wallpapers, curtains, carpets, and soft furnishings all battled each other in their varying floral patterns. The whole place was lovably shabby, which was a relief considering they had children and a big, muddy dog to think of.

As soon as they'd unpacked, Tobias and Abby disappeared to explore outside in the last of the fading sunlight. Jemima had gone to have a rest, and so Ellie set about sorting out supper. Fortunately she'd brought a pre-made shepherd's pie for their first night. All she had to do was make a salad and open a much-needed bottle of wine.

Actually Oliver opened it, taking two glasses from the cupboard with a wry smile. "I think we deserve a drink, don't you?"

"Absolutely."

She'd spent the last six hours sitting about two feet away from him, but they hadn't talked. Now Ellie accepted a glass of wine with relief and leaned against the counter. The shepherd's pie was bubbling away in the ancient Aga, and outside she could hear Abby and Tobias's shouts of laughter. Life was good.

"I had my doubts on the way here," she said, "but this seems like it could work really well. Thank you."

"You had your doubts?" Oliver arched an eyebrow. "I was seriously considering turning around. Especially when Jemima broke out her third can of G&T."

"She's very unhappy."

"Yes." He let out a weary breath. "But you can't help someone who doesn't want to be helped, can you? At least I don't seem to be able to manage it."

"You just need to keep hanging in there," Ellie answered quietly. "My sister did, and I could never thank her enough for it."

"Were things really that bad?" Oliver braced his forearms on the counter, drawing Ellie's attention to how lean and muscular they were. He was wearing a navy-blue rugby shirt and faded jeans, and he looked scrumptious. She had to keep reminding herself that they were just friends. She had a feeling she'd be doing that a lot this week.

"For about a month, yes. I can't explain it really, except to say that my brain kind of shut down. I think, in part, I was simply exhausted. I'd poured so much effort into it. My marriage," she clarified with a sigh. "And realizing it wasn't going to work, that it really was over…" She shook her head, hating the memory. "It felt like such a waste of my life."

"I suppose that's why I haven't been tempted to tie the knot yet," Oliver said slowly. "Because it is a lot of work, isn't it? To keep things going. And you've got to make sure you're with someone who's going to work with you, who's worth it even when it's hard, even when you're doubting everything."

"Yes." Ellie swallowed, her whole body tingling from the intent look in Oliver's eyes. *He so obviously isn't talking about you, numpty.* "It is a lot of hard work, and you both need to be committed." Which was just what he said. "Right, I think the shepherd pie's ready." She swallowed the last of her wine and went to the oven. "Do you want to call the kids?" Which made it sound as if they were some kind of couple. She was going to need a lot of reminders this week.

Supper passed peaceably enough, and afterwards Abby and Tobias set up a board game while Jemima went to take a bath. Ellie had intended to curl on one of the enormous squashy sofas with a book, but Oliver had agreed to play the game and somehow he ended up co-opting her into it too.

It was surprisingly fun even though Ellie couldn't fully grasp the rules—it was another one of those complex civilization-based games that took ages and had copious amounts of cards and pieces. Still, she enjoyed trying, and more to the point, she enjoyed Oliver's gentle teasing of her own self-confessed ineptness, along with his surprising streak of competitiveness.

"You really want to win, don't you?" she remarked as he

studied a card that told him how many settlements he could build with his current resources.

He looked up, affront mixing with amusement. "Of course I do."

"I didn't think you were that competitive."

"Then I'm insulted." She laughed and threw a pillow at him, which Oliver dodged. Abby was watching her avidly, and too late Ellie realized how it might have looked. As if they were flirting. Which, of course, they were not.

But the lines continued to blur as the evening progressed, and Abby and Tobias went to bed. Ellie was about to pack it in as well but then Oliver poured them both glasses of wine from the bottle he'd opened earlier, threw another log onto the woodstove, and then settled into the sofa next to her. *Well.*

"This is nice," she murmured, mostly into her wine. She was achingly conscious of his body next to hers, his thigh inches from her own. He'd stretched one arm across the back of the sofa and if she leaned back a little she was pretty sure his fingers would brush her shoulder. Was he doing this on purpose? What did he want?

What did she?

"It is nice," Oliver agreed. "Although I wish Jemima had come down. She said she was tired, but…"

"You can't be responsible for her actions," Ellie said. "Just keep trying."

"I know." He sighed and leaned back against the sofa

cushions, and then his hand did brush her shoulder, the barest of touches that made Ellie feel as if she'd been electrocuted. She froze, so unbelievably aware of the lightest touch of his fingers. Was he aware? Could Oliver have possibly touched her by accident?

"I feel as if history is repeating itself," Oliver said after a moment. His gaze was distant and clouded, making Ellie think he didn't realize. She tried to regulate her breathing. "When my brother Jamie died, no one talked about it. We drifted around, so unhappy but not actually dealing with it—it was like the ninth circle of hell, everyone frozen in their icy lakes of silence."

Which was a literary reference she didn't get, but the gist at least was understandable. "It seems as if that's how your family operated on a regular basis."

"Yes, but I wish we could break out of it and be different. I wish Jemima could be different, but perhaps I'm not the person to confront her." He gave her a lopsided smile, shifting so his fingers were no longer touching her shoulder. "Sorry to go on about this. It must be incredibly dull."

"Not at all. I'm sorry you're going through it."

He turned to smile at her, and Ellie turned at the same time, so their faces were close. Alarmingly, awkwardly, excitingly close. Ellie's heart gave a juddering bump and she lurched upright.

"Actually, I should go to bed."

Oliver looked at her, bemused. "You haven't even finished your wine."

"I know, but…" *Why* was she so panicked? She'd been fantasizing about this kind of scenario but now that it was here, now that it wasn't all safely in her head, she went to pieces. Again. She still wasn't ready to date, to *risk,* as much as she wanted to be. "Marmite," she burst out. "I should take Marmite out."

"I'll go with you."

Ellie stared at him helplessly, caught between her longing and her fear. She wished she could act normally, let things unfurl gradually, but… she couldn't. Wordlessly she got her coat and jammed her feet into Welly boots while Oliver did the same. Marmite had been snoozing in front of the stove but he sprang up with alacrity as soon as she'd reached for her coat.

They stepped out into the dark night, a million stars glittering high above. Everything was completely still and silent, save for Marmite's excited sniffing as he ventured out into the darkness and the distant lap of the river. Ellie stood on the doorstep, trying to still her racing heart. Oliver stood next to her, hands jammed into the pockets of his waxed jacket. Neither of them spoke.

Ellie wished she could summon the courage to say something of what she felt. *I really like you, but I'm scared. I've been hurt before, and as lovely as you are your track record isn't great. And I'm not even sure what you want, anyway.*

Why couldn't she let all that spill out and see what Oliver did with it? Maybe he'd look horrified. Maybe he'd tell her he felt the same, but this felt like the real deal, and they should both jump on it. Jump on each other, for that matter. A muffled snort escaped her and she tried to disguise it as a cough.

Marmite snuffled around for a bit and then, wanting his nighttime biscuit and bed, he did a wee and then trotted back towards the house. Ellie turned to go in and collided with Oliver who had turned at the same time.

"Whoa." His hands came up to her shoulders to steady her and Ellie blinked, dazed in several different ways. Oliver's chest had been hard, and now it was very close. She tilted her head up and saw him looking down at her and the whole world seemed to hold its breath.

In the darkness she couldn't read Oliver's expression but she could feel his hands tightening on her shoulders, felt the yearning and desire flare deep in her own belly. She was terrified, but she also wanted this so very much... enough not to jerk away from him or babble something incoherent for once. She simply stood, waiting, *hoping...*

"Oliver?" Jemima's voice was high and sharp and Oliver released Ellie as if she'd suddenly become toxic and stepped away.

"Jemima." He walked quickly towards his sister who stood in the doorway, blocking the light. "I thought you'd gone to bed."

"I was about to, but then Tobias and Abby woke me

up." This was directed towards Ellie.

"I'm sorry, they're just excited to be here, I think," Oliver said. "Shall we go in?"

Fighting frustration and a deep, aching disappointment, Ellie followed them inside.

Chapter Eighteen

O LIVER COULDN'T DECIDE if a week spent in close proximity with Ellie was torture or a delight. Both, really. He was in a near-constant state of sexual frustration, which didn't improve his temper, but he also enjoyed simply being with her, whether it was playing board games tucked up by the fire or going for long walks along the Helford River.

Tobias and Abby had been getting along well, and Jemima had roused herself on occasion to join them on a walk, although her default was to simply drift about the house, as blank-eyed and vacant as she'd been back in the Cotswolds, resisting all attempts at conversation or confrontation, although admittedly Oliver had done little of the latter.

Still, halfway in, Oliver deemed the week a success. Despite the sudden, surprising moments of romantic tension between him and Ellie—he still didn't know what would have happened outside that first night if Jemima hadn't interrupted them—they'd found a nice routine of banter and good-natured teasing, the occasional deeper conversation about life or relationships or future plans. Once Ellie had shyly mentioned wanting to open a shop in a village like Wychwood-on-Lea, something that offered a bit of every-thing—tea, books, crafts, community.

"Sort of a hub," she said. "But I don't know the first thing about doing something like that."

"You could learn," Oliver had suggested. He was glad Ellie was at least thinking about doing something, making her own dreams. She nodded thoughtfully, and he left it at that.

In the middle of the week it poured rain and they decid-ed to drive to Falmouth to an indoor water park. Jemima chose to stay at home, and so the four of them piled into the estate to drive down narrow, rainy roads to an overcrowded, slightly dingy swimming pool with flume slides and a wave machine. It wasn't how Oliver would have preferred to spend a rainy day—tucked up in a cozy pub with a pint and a good book would have been far better—but he was looking forward to seeing Ellie in a swimsuit, shallow as that might have made him.

And she looked just as good in one as he'd envisioned, or actually, better. The swimsuit itself was a plain black one piece, the kind of thing a reluctant schoolgirl would wear to PE, but it still highlighted Ellie's curves admirably. Oliver tried not to stare.

As the week went on it was becoming more and more difficult to keep up this with just-friends guise. Although in truth he didn't know if it was a guise or not. At times Oliver was sure Ellie felt as he did. And at other times… not. Which left him in a particularly uncomfortable kind of limbo.

He suspected Ellie wasn't sure how she felt, and he decided the best thing to do was wait. Hopefully the moment to take things to a new level would come naturally. Oliver couldn't picture himself forcing it, in any case.

Better to live with this sweet torture, at least for now, although that solution hardly seemed satisfactory, especially when Ellie was standing in a pool, water slicking down her body, and Oliver had to dive underwater to keep from embarrassing himself. It was almost a relief when they got out of the pool while Tobias and Abby tackled the slides again, and had a coffee in the adjoining café.

The second to last night things with Jemima came to a head. Ellie had made dinner every night, sometimes with Oliver's or Abby and Tobias's help, but often not. Jemima, Oliver had noticed uncomfortably, either retreated to her room or simply sat, expecting to be waited on, which wasn't all that surprising, but he worried that Ellie might mind.

"Right." Ellie slammed her hand down on the corner, a look of steely determination Oliver recognized entering her eyes. "We're out of milk. Jemima, why don't we walk to the shop? It's not that far."

It was nearly a mile, but Oliver wisely decided this was not the time to point that out. Ellie was clearly on a mission, and he wasn't about to interfere. Perhaps this was what his sister needed.

"The shop?" Jemima blinked, an expression of mulish uncertainty on her face. "Why doesn't Oliver just drive?" She looked at him in appeal, and Oliver pretended not to notice, coward that he could be.

"Because he's had a long day and I know for a fact he hasn't read the paper yet, something he prefers to do with his morning coffee rather than with his evening pint." She'd noticed such things? He felt absurdly pleased by that notion. "Anyway," Ellie continued, "you've been in the house all day, and I think we could both use some fresh air. Come on." She was using a tone more suited for addressing a tantruming three-year-old, which wasn't, perhaps, that far off the mark. "We'll take Marmite."

ELLIE HEADED OUT into the dark, damp night with Jemima sloping behind her like a sulky teenager. She wasn't sure what had possessed her to insist Jemima accompany her; they'd been getting along all week by having as little interaction as possible.

She supposed she'd had enough of Jemima's indifference to everyone around her, even as she felt sorry for her. Although Jemima might never believe it, she did sympathize. She knew how she felt, at least a little, but she also knew Jemima wasn't going to rouse herself on her own. Ellie certainly hadn't. Sometimes you needed an emotional tow truck to get you out of that rut.

"Ugh, I really don't know why you asked me to go along with you," Jemima said in a voice stiff with affront as they headed up the narrow lane that led to the nearby village, Marmite trotting happily ahead. The night was wet and starless and very, very dark, the only sound the occasion mournful and slightly alarming bleat of a sheep.

"Actually," Ellie said, steeling her nerve, "I wanted to talk to you."

"*Talk* to me?" Jemima sounded incredulous as well as suspicious. Ellie suspected the only reason she was out here in the first place was because Oliver hadn't provided the usual escape route.

Ellie took a deep breath. "Oliver's told me something of your story. I know you've had a hard time—"

"A hard time? That's what you call it?" Jemima started walking faster, her arms wrapped around herself.

"I'm sorry," Ellie said quietly, struggling to catch up with her. Jemima had really long, really skinny legs. "You're right, it's been far more than a hard time. I'm sure it's been a completely devastating time... for both you and Tobias." Jemima's stride faltered for a second. "That's why I wanted to talk to you. Because, although you might not believe it, I've been in a similar situation."

"Oh, really? Your husband killed himself?"

Ellie winced but kept Jemima's antagonistic gaze. "No,

he didn't, but he did a lot of other things that were hard to deal with and we divorced and I ended up having a mini-breakdown. Although maybe not so mini. And I'm not trying to say my situation was as difficult or as painful as yours. Of course not."

Jemima's shoulders were still hunched, her lips trembling, her expression both panicked and hostile. "Oliver shouldn't have said anything. And the last thing I need is your advice. Who are you, anyway?" she demanded, her voice rising shrilly. "I don't even know why you came on this holiday. You're not family. You're certainly not Oliver's girlfriend." She raked her up and down with a gaze of pure contempt. "And I don't need to listen to you," she finished and then whirled around and kept walking up the road.

Ellie stood there for a few seconds, smarting from all of Jemima's comments, especially the *certainly*. Jemima didn't have to remind her how different she was from Oliver, how unsuitable. She took the deep breath and forced the hurt and outrage down. Jemima had been lashing out in her pain. Ellie understood that. Once upon a time, she'd done the same. She'd yelled at Diane to leave her alone, butt out of her miserable life. Diane had grimly stayed.

She caught up with Jemima, which was no easy task, at the top of the lane that led down to the village with its one tiny post office shop, named the Harrods of the Lizard Peninsula. They walked in silence to the shop and Ellie tied up Marmite outside and then got the milk while Jemima waited, all bristle indignation, by the door.

Once they were outside, walking back to the farmhouse, Ellie spoke. "I'm sorry," she said quietly. "I'm not trying to offend you, and I realize I don't really have the right to offer advice. I'm not family. I'm not even a friend." Not of Jemima's anyway, if this exchange was anything to go by. "But I am concerned, and I know Oliver is, as well. No one's asking you to pull yourself up by your bootstraps, Jemima, and sort yourself out on your own. Sometimes that's impossible. I know that. But what you need to do, for Tobias's sake as much as your own, is get help. A therapist, medication, whatever you need. Letting yourself fade away might seem like the preferable option at this point, but you'll regret it later, I promise." She felt her throat tighten with emotion as her own memories bombarded her. She regretted that month of checking out, a month when Abby had needed her most, her father gone, her life upended, and Ellie hadn't been there, not emotionally anyway.

Nothing she had done since could make up for that, even though she'd tried. Maybe she was too concerned with Abby's life, as her daughter had told her rather pointedly, but it was the only way she knew of making up the times when she hadn't been. She'd messed up a lot of things in her life, but she didn't want to mess up being a mother.

Jemima didn't speak, her face averted, and they walked in silence back to the farmhouse. So her big attempt at reaching Oliver's sister had been, as far as Ellie could tell, a total failure.

Then Jemima started to talk.

"He wanted to get back together." The words were whispered, barely audible. Ellie stopped.

"Eric…?" she ventured cautiously and Jemima nodded, her face still averted.

"A week before… before he killed himself. He wanted to get back together and I said no." She bowed her head, her shoulders silently shaking, and even though she never would have thought of either of them capable of it, Ellie did the only thing she could think of to do in that moment. She pulled Jemima into a hug and amazingly, Jemima went, her forehead resting on Ellie's shoulder as she sobbed.

"It's not your fault," Ellie said quietly. "You might feel like it is, like you could have prevented it, but you couldn't have. It's not your fault, Jemima." She spoke firmly even though she didn't know the situation, not fully, not really. But she did know that Jemima wasn't capable of bearing this burden alone.

"He cheated on me," Jemima gasped out. "He was never home. He had meaningless hookups in massage parlors in Thailand but I still wonder… I still think… maybe I made a mistake. Maybe if…"

Maybe if. Ellie knew the siren song of those two very damaging words. Maybe if she'd tried harder, or been more patient or loving or laidback, her marriage would have worked. Nathan would have got a job, stuck around, stayed faithful. Maybe if. *No.* Not this time, not with Jemima, not with her. She was tired of being haunted by those words, and she suspected Jemima was as well.

"There is no maybe in this situation, Jemima. There's no if. You can't second guess yourself or Eric. It keeps you stuck in the past when you need to think about your future. Tobias's future."

Jemima gave a big sniff and pushed away from Ellie, swiping her damp cheeks with her hands. "I know. But it's so hard. It's easier just to live in a… vacuum."

"Yes," Ellie agreed, "but eventually it starts to feel pretty empty. I do know that."

Jemima let out a shuddering sigh and nodded once before walking back towards the house. Ellie followed, deciding to leave it at that. She'd made some headway… she hoped. Oliver gave her a questioning look as they came into the kitchen, and Ellie smiled back with what she hoped was reassurance.

The last night of their trip they went out to dinner at a fancy pub in Helford, and Oliver insisted on paying. Ellie dressed up a little, just because she could, and also because it sort of felt like a date. A date with Oliver, two kids, and a woman who was still mostly giving Ellie the silent treatment, although it felt a little less frosty. So that was something.

She checked her reflection nervously, hoping the jersey wrap dress she'd chosen wasn't too clingy—she'd worn it to work but had always paired it with a sweater to hide her cleavage. Now those generous curves were on full display to eye-popping and possibly cringing effect… Ellie wasn't sure which one it was, maybe both. She decided to just go with it.

"Hey, Mum, can I do your makeup?" Abby asked as she barged into Ellie's bedroom and flopped on her bed.

"Not this time," Ellie answered as sweetly—and as firmly—as she could. She had no intention of rocking the Goth look for a second time.

As she came downstairs Ellie noticed that Oliver had decided to dress up too, wearing a pair of cords with a blue button-down shirt. It was his standard work uniform, and yet somehow it looked different, sexier, because they weren't at work. He'd been a bit scruffy this week, wearing jeans and going unshaven, which she'd quite liked, but seeing him freshly shaven, smelling of bay rum and wearing freshly-pressed clothes, made her insides clench and her mouth water. Almost as much as seeing him in a pair of swimming trunks had. She'd suspected Oliver was fit, but until they'd gone to the pool she hadn't realized he'd been sporting a six-pack. She'd barely been able to take her eyes off him all afternoon.

Now when Oliver turned to her, a smile lighting his features and making his eyes sparkle, she might have made a little mewling sound. He was becoming a very hard man to resist.

The pub was the most elegant restaurant Ellie had ever been in, with an open fire, squashy sofas, and flickering candlelight. The muted conversation and background classical music added to the ambiance. It was not the kind of pub where you ordered a burger.

And despite everyone else with them, it *did* feel like a date. Oliver pulled out her chair for her and insisted on ordering a bottle of very nice wine. And even as she bantered with Abby and exchanged tense smiles with Jemima, who was trying—sort of—to be part of the conversation, Ellie knew from the flutters in her belly and the fizz in her heart that this was one of the most romantic evenings she'd ever had.

It didn't end when they returned to the farmhouse, either. Ellie drifted around the kitchen, tidying up, while Jemima disappeared upstairs and Oliver chivvied Abby and Tobias up to bed.

Slowly, slowly Ellie wiped already-clean counters and wondered what she would say when Oliver came back downstairs and they were alone. What she would do. She'd been seesawing between hope and fear all week, and after so much lovely but frustrating romantic tension, she felt ready to choose hope. Almost.

"Hard to believe the week is over already." Oliver stood in the doorway of the kitchen, smiling wryly, his hair a little rumpled, making Ellie's heart go bump.

"Yes." She stared down at the counter, wiping it yet again. *What now?*

"Care for a nightcap?" Oliver asked, his voice low and—

dare she think it—full of intent.

"Okay." Her heart was juddering now, each thud almost painful in its intensity. She couldn't believe how nervous she was. Nothing might even happen, anyway, and yet…

Something might. And she wanted something to happen, despite her nerves. She did.

She watched out of the corner of her eye as Oliver took a bottle of single malt whisky from the cupboard. She hadn't even known he'd brought whisky. She didn't particularly like it either; it tasted like nasty cough medicine to her but in that moment she didn't care.

"Thanks," she murmured as he handed her a glass, shivers racing through her when his fingers brushed across hers. He took a step away, smiling as he sipped his drink.

"Cheers."

"Cheers."

The only sounds were the creak of the house settling and Marmite's snores, which were quite loud and a bit mood-killing. But whatever. They were alone, it was the end of the holiday, and after six days of ever-building sexual tension, surely now was the time for something to happen. For once Ellie didn't want to back away. Wasn't going to ruin it by panicking or saying something stupid, all because she was afraid. No, she sipped her whisky instead, and then she erupted in a fit of coughing as she remembered just how much she didn't like the stuff.

Concerned, Oliver put down his own glass and patted

her ineffectually on the back. "Are you all right? Did it go down the wrong way?"

"Yes," Ellie gasped, tears now streaming from her eyes. "Yes, I must have swallowed it wrong somehow." She willed herself to stop coughing, but it was one of those coughs that was determined to persist and turn into a deep and rather revolting hacking that had Oliver stepping away from her. Perfect. "Sorry..." she gasped out.

"Let me get you a drink of water."

Finally, after several sips of water and several more deep coughs that felt as if she might lose a lung, Ellie thought she was finished. "Sorry," she said again. Her throat felt raw and her eyes were still streaming. Not the most romantic of moments.

"Let me guess," Oliver said, his eyes glinting. "You don't actually like whisky."

"Well..." She laughed a little, not quite wanting to admit that she'd accepted the drink simply to spend time with him. "It's not my favorite," she said diplomatically.

"You didn't have to have any."

"I wanted to be polite."

He laughed softly and shook his head, and then he took a step closer to her. Ellie tensed, her body feeling like a violin with a bow about to be placed to its strings. Surely now was the time. The mood was right, despite Marmite's snores and the sudden clank and rumble of the central heating starting up. Upstairs someone closed the bathroom door with a near-slam. Still, mood. Kiss. She wanted him to kiss her *now*.

And she thought he might, as he looked down at her, a funny half-smile on his face, and she felt a tumbling sensation inside, her face tilting upwards like a flower seeking sunlight, everything in her reaching for this moment.

"Mum?"

It took Ellie a moment to register the sound. Another few stunned seconds to force herself to look away from Oliver and his sleepy smile and focus on Abby who stood on the bottom of the back stairs, looking rather miserable.

"Abby…"

"I feel sick."

Now that she was looking at her daughter Ellie noticed she looked a little green. "Oh, no," she said, coming towards her. "Was it something you ate—"

Before she could finish that sentence, Abby threw up all over herself. And Ellie.

Mood officially killed.

She spent the next eight hours taking care of Abby, who spent most of that time with her head hanging over the toilet bowl. Apparently even posh pubs could have dodgy food.

Oliver had kindly brought Abby a glass of water, and asked if there was anything he could do, and when Ellie assured him there wasn't, he'd gone to bed. So much for romance.

The next morning they loaded up in sleeting rain, the hint of spring that had teased them all week well and truly gone. Poor Abby had sat in the car with a bowl in her lap, looking pasty-faced and miserable. At least she hadn't been sick again.

As they drove up the traffic-laden M5 with all the other holiday-makers on their way home, Ellie felt a leaden sense of disappointment weighing her down at the thought of the missed opportunity last night. Of course, she'd see Oliver tomorrow when she headed back to work, but Ellie felt instinctively that it wouldn't be the same. Or rather it would be the same as it had always been. It had been Cornwall that had felt different.

"Here we are." All too soon Oliver was pulling into the courtyard of Willoughby Close and Ellie eyed her cute cottage with less enthusiasm than usual. She didn't want the holiday to end, not even after spending five hours cramped in the back seat with a dog drooling on her shoulder and a miserable daughter squeezed next to her.

"Hey, Mum, look!" Abby perked up for the first time in the entire trip. "Someone's moving in next door."

Ellie had been so swamped in her misery that she hadn't noticed the huge moving truck parked in front of Number Two. Two burly guys wearing Cotswold Removals t-shirts were unloading furniture, but Ellie couldn't see any sign of their new neighbors.

"I wonder who it is," she murmured without as much excitement as she might have had. Was this really it? Tomorrow it was back to work, same old, same old? She felt a crashing sense of disappointment, which made her realize how much she'd wanted something to happen with Oliver. How much she'd been counting on it.

Oliver parked the car and got out to wrestle their bags from the overstuffed roof box. Jemima didn't get out but she turned around in her seat and gave Ellie a half-apologetic, half-grateful smile of farewell. Ellie considered that a win.

"Thank you for everything," she said as Oliver took her bags to the door. She wrestled with the key and with a sigh of impatience Abby took it from her and unlocked the door. "It really was a fabulous week."

"Thank you for coming," Oliver answered. He took her bags inside; the house smelled musty and sour and Ellie realized she must have forgotten to empty the bin before they'd left. Junk mail and bills piled up by the door and she nudged them aside with her boot.

"Ew, Mum. You left the milk and it looks disgusting." Abby was already at the fridge, wrinkling her nose as she inspected the items within that were definitely well past their sell-by date.

"Sorry, we'll do a shop later." She turned to Oliver, giving him a smile of farewell and wishing so much that this wasn't goodbye. "So, see you tomorrow, I suppose."

"Yes, although take your time. No need to rush in. I'm sure you're tired."

"Okay. Thanks." Not that she could have a lie-in, since Abby had to get to school, but it was a nice thought.

They smiled at each other for another few seconds, and Ellie wondered if he would go in for a friendly hug. But no, Oliver wasn't a hugger. He gave a little wave instead and then turned around and headed out. Ellie closed the door, one hand resting flat on the wood, wishing she'd had the courage to be bolder. Or Oliver had.

"Do you have homework?" she asked Abby listlessly. Her daughter had managed to find a yogurt in the fridge that was still edible and was now peeling back the lid and sniffing it suspiciously.

"Nope. They didn't give any."

A sudden, loud knocking on the door had Ellie jumping back. "What on earth..." She opened the door, blinking at the sight of Oliver standing there looking rather fierce. He was practically scowling as he grabbed her by the shoulders, pulled her towards him, and kissed her hard.

Chapter Nineteen

F OR A FEW shocked seconds Ellie simply stood there, Oliver gripping her shoulders, his mouth pressed to hers. Then her brain finally caught up with what her body was feeling and she wrapped her arms around him and kissed back with everything she had... until she remembered they had an audience of two. A farting dog and a gaping daughter.

Ellie pulled away, her hands pressed to her flushed face. *Oliver had kissed her.*

"Wow," Abby said into the silence. "To think I might have missed this to go watch Netflix."

"Sorry," Oliver said without quite looking at anyone. "But I had to do that."

And then, to even more of Ellie's shock than the kiss, he turned around and walked out.

"Oliver—wait!" She wrenched open the door and hurried out, but Oliver was already getting into his car and before she could shout or flag him down, he drove down the lane and disappeared around the corner.

What?

Ellie stood there, shaking her head, her lips still buzzing. Oliver had kissed her... and then done a runner.

"Seriously?" Abby exclaimed when Ellie came back in by herself. "Where is he?"

"He's... gone." Ellie still felt dazed. "He drove off without so much as a word."

Abby goggled. "He just *left?*"

"Apparently."

Her daughter folded her arms, giving her a very smug look. "Still, he kissed you."

"Yes, but I'm not sure what it meant."

"It meant he likes you! *Duh.*"

Ellie laughed, the sound a bit high and shrill. "I don't know what it means, Abby. Maybe it just means he felt like he had to kiss me right then. Maybe it doesn't mean anything."

"Well, you can ask him tomorrow," Abby said with a philosophical shrug. As if it were that easy.

While Abby went to visit Lady Stokeley, Ellie bustled around the house, thinking about Oliver all the while. She relived the kiss over and over again—how his lips had been soft but his grip had been firm, and for a few blissful seconds she'd felt the full press of his body against hers, and it had utterly thrilled her.

She thought about him while she unpacked their bags and threw most of the clothes in the wash; she thought about it when she went to the village shop for emergency supplies; and she thought about it while she made her and Abby the simplest of comfort food—beans on toast—which they ate in front of the telly.

The hint of spring that had been in the air when they'd left had vanished, replaced by an icy, damp chill that had Ellie loading up the woodstove with the logs Jace had brought over. It was cozy and warm in the cottage, and curled up with Abby on the sofa Ellie would have felt just about perfectly content...

Except for Oliver's kiss. What *had* he meant by kissing her, and then far more aggravatingly, by driving off immediately afterwards? She toyed with sending him a text but couldn't bring herself to, not before she saw him tomorrow and assessed the situation.

After dinner she and Abby took Marmite out for a walk, both of them glancing curiously at Number Two in the close. The moving van had gone, but the house looked dark and empty and when Ellie dared to creep closer and peer in the front window she saw stacks of boxes and some furniture, but no sign of life.

"Do you think they'll move in anytime soon?" Abby asked.

"Perhaps they're coming from far away and they haven't got here yet." Already Ellie was spinning a ridiculous fantasy about another Northern family trying to make it in the tony Cotswolds, a kindred spirit each for her and Abby, someone to laugh about the Range Rovers and electronic gates and the sense of privilege most people wore like a second skin.

"Marmite." She tugged her dog along before he left a poo as a welcoming present on their doorstep.

They walked through the loop in the woods that had become comfortably familiar, dusk just starting to settle over the rolling fields in the distance as they returned to Willoughby Close. Even though it was still bone-chillingly cold, at least the evenings were a bit lighter, a small harbinger of spring.

"Mum, look." Abby tugged on her sleeve and Ellie looked up, momentarily distracted from her endlessly circling thoughts about Oliver, to see a gleaming black Land Rover Discovery parked in the courtyard next to Ellie's beat-up estate. "Who do you think it is?"

"I don't know." The sight of that pristine and expensive car made her spirits plummet a little, especially when it was parked in stark contract next to her own old banger.

"Should we knock on the door?"

Ellie glanced at Abby, her daughter's face alight with interest, and marveled at the change in her. A few weeks ago Abby would have been hanging back, shaking her head, or even beating a retreat to the safety of her own house. How had Abby grown in confidence without Ellie realizing—or even her help?

And why was Ellie now the one thinking of holding her back? The one who was afraid and insecure? She needed to take a page from her daughter's book, or even a whole chapter.

"Why not?" she said with more bravado than true courage, and she marched up to the door, Marmite trotting amenably alongside her. She knocked once and then listened to a girl's bored voice.

"*Mu-um!* Someone's here."

Ellie exchanged a questioning look with Abby and a few seconds later the door was flung open.

"Yes?" The woman who stood there was both impatient and familiar, as was the sulky-looking girl who appeared behind her, her eyes narrowing as she caught sight of Abby.

"Wait—*you* live here?" She rolled her eyes and slunk off, and Ellie watched in both anger and dismay as Abby visibly shrank, shoulders slumping, her hair swinging forward to curtain her face. From some unknown reserve of determination and strength she summoned a smile.

"Hello, Harriet. I guess we're neighbors."

Harriet Lang blinked, wrinkling her nose, still not placing Ellie which was saying something considering what a disaster the bake sale had been a couple of weeks ago.

"Ellie Matthews," Ellie supplied. "I helped with the bake sale, although I think I was more hindrance than anything else." She gave a little laugh, because damn it, she would laugh about it now. It *would* be funny.

"Oh yes, of course." Harriet gave her a distracted smile. "Sorry, I've just been manic with moving..." She trailed off, and belatedly Ellie realized how unlikely it was for Harriet Lang to be her new neighbor. It had been clear during their brief conversation back at the bake sale that she was married, and yet Jace had called her a single mum. And Ellie had assumed, from Harriet's general air of calm capability and confidence, that she owned some rambling farmhouse of Cotswold stone, with the requisite Farrow & Ball paint in every room, slate floors, and a huge Aga. Not a smallish rental, nice as it was. So what was going on? The last thing she could do was ask.

And yet she *was* curious. "So you moved from within the village?" Obviously.

"Yes…" Harriet glanced behind her, as if looking for an excuse to cut the conversation short. Ellie's fantasy that she was going to be besties with her new neighbor was laughable now. If she had to pick another mum to be a best friend, Harriet Lang was just about last on her list.

Although perhaps that wasn't entirely fair. They'd gotten off to a bit of a rocky start, but Ellie supposed Harriet seemed nice enough… to other people.

"Yes, we've moved because…" Harriet reluctantly focused her gaze back on Ellie. "We're doing some renovation on our house, and moving seemed like the easiest option. Temporarily, of course. This is a temporary measure."

Was she imagining that note of unnecessary force? Harriet's expression was a bit fixed, her arms folded across her chest. Hmm.

"Welcome, anyway," Ellie said after a tense pause. "No matter how long you're staying. We're glad to have neighbors." Even though it meant Abby now had a mean girl living next door. Great.

"Thanks." Harriet placed one hand on the door as if she was about to close it in Ellie's face. The hint was not very subtle.

"It's getting late," Ellie said, with a dutiful look at her watch. "I'll let you get on. But do tell me if you need anything…" Harriet was already nodding and, yes, shutting the door. Ellie decided not to continue with the suggestion that they all have a meal together. "Bye, then," she said, and the door clicked shut.

Abby sloped inside, kicking it closed after Ellie. "Mallory Lang next door," she said with a grimace. "Ugh."

"How much of a mean girl is she?" Not that she was judging a child she'd never actually met.

"Oh, I don't know," Abby said, blowing out a breath, suddenly exasperated with the whole conversation. Her daughter's lightning mood changes had Ellie's head spinning sometimes. "She's gotten worse but it's such an act, you know? And it doesn't work when she pretends." Which was quite an astute observation. "That's what Dorothy says, anyway," Abby continued as she went to the fridge and began to rummage through the emergency supplies Ellie had bought at the post office shop—cocktail sausages, cheese, and some yogurt. "She told me that if a girl is trying too hard it shows, and you've really got to pity her, because everyone will realize it eventually." Abby closed the fridge door. "Mum, you really need to go shopping."

"I know." And what she also knew was that Abby was growing up before her eyes, shedding her self-doubt and shyness and turning into a young woman of maturity and wisdom. More than Ellie herself exhibited at times, which was both inspiring and convicting. "You have a good attitude, Abs," she said, giving her daughter a quick one-armed hug before she squirmed away.

"Well." Abby grimaced. "I'm still not thrilled Mallory is next door, but whatever." With a gusty sigh she headed upstairs.

By the time Ellie was heading into Oxford on the train the next morning, her nerves were well and truly jangling. She had spent a sleepless night staring at the ceiling and debating the merits of pretending the kiss had never happened versus confronting Oliver head on. The trouble with confrontation was... well, confrontation. She'd never been good at it. She'd rather work hard and paint rainbows than corner somebody, which might have had something to do with the failure of her marriage. Maybe if she'd given Nathan an ultimatum instead of just trying to make up for his deficiencies, he would have grown up and they could have made a go of it. But then again, considering Nathan, maybe not.

So the other option was pretending it had never happened, which was, in some ways, preferable. Easier, certainly. But it was also cowardly and it meant trying to forget the best kiss she'd had in a decade—and, if she was being completely honest, the only kiss she'd had in five years. So not such a good plan after all.

She was still dithering between the two options as she walked into the history faculty, giving Jeannie a distracted smile as the older woman demanded details about her holiday.

"Oh, it was fabulous," Ellie said quickly, as she kept moving towards the hallway that led to her broom cupboard in the hopes of discouraging a thorough interrogation. Normally she'd love a few minutes' chat with Jeannie, but she didn't want to be grilled about Oliver... not when she feared the truth, and all its accompanying confusion, would be written on her face.

"Fabulous? Really?" Jeannie's well-plucked eyebrows rose. "Do tell all. We're all dying to know how Oliver is on holiday."

"The same, really," Ellie half-mumbled, as she started to blush. Jeannie, of course, noticed.

"The same?" She folded her arms. "First it's fabulous, now it's the same. Why do I get the feeling you're not telling me something?"

Because she wasn't. "Honestly, Jeannie, it wasn't all that exciting. We went on walks, we ate at a pub, the kids got along." She rolled her eyes. "And Oliver was Oliver, as usual.

A bit stuffy and boring but pleasant enough." As soon as the words were out of her mouth Ellie regretted them. They weren't true, and they felt like a terrible betrayal of Oliver and all he was coming to mean to her. He wasn't stuffy or boring, and he was way more than pleasant. But Jeannie was nodding, seeming satisfied, and Ellie slipped past her to her office with a silent sigh of relief.

She paused by Oliver's closed door; she could see his head bent over his desk through the frosted glass but she didn't think she was up for facing him quite yet and so she hurried past to her own desk. Soon. Soon she'd figure out what she was going to do and say.

An hour passed and Ellie couldn't concentrate on anything. She felt jumpy, as well as a little hurt that Oliver hadn't sought her out yet, which was ridiculous because *she* was avoiding *him*.

Then he knocked on her door. "May I have a word?" His expression was serious, his mouth compressed—good heavens, he looked like he had when she'd first met him, just as chilly, remote, and blatantly unimpressed. Not a good sign.

"Of course." Ellie rose, her heart starting to thump as she ran her hands nervously down her skirt. "In your office?"

"Yes."

She followed him down the corridor, feeling like a scolded schoolgirl about to be sent to the head teacher's office. Her heart was beating hard now.

"So, chapter ten." Oliver handed her a sheaf of papers which Ellie took, startled. Not what she'd been expecting. "Only two more to go and then you'll finally be free of me."

Ellie stared at him, completely nonplussed by this exchange. She'd been semi-wondering if Oliver would act like they hadn't kissed, but she had not anticipated this barely-veiled hostility. What on earth was going on?

"I'm not sure I'd phrase it like that," she murmured.

"Wouldn't you?" Oliver shrugged, all curt dismissiveness. "Never mind. It's irrelevant."

Ellie's astonishment was giving way to anger. How could he act so frosty, when *he* was the one who had burst into her house yesterday and kissed her near-senseless? "Oliver, why are you acting so cross?" she asked. "Is this something to do with yesterday?" She took a deep breath, determined not to be cowardly. "Are you regretting the fact that you kissed me?"

Chapter Twenty

OLIVER STARED AT Ellie with her aquamarine eyes wide with confusion, the pages of his manuscript clutched to her chest. He saw the pulse fluttering in her throat, and he heard the plaintive question she'd dared to ask, the elephant in the room they'd both been clambering over.

"No, of course not," he said briskly. He felt like kissing her again—that, or throttling her. Or maybe throttling himself. He was angry, yes, but even he had the emotional astuteness to know why. Because he was hurt.

Stuffy and boring but pleasant enough. She'd dismissed him so summarily, so readily, and he'd been working up his courage to tell her the truth of his own feelings.

"Oliver?" Ellie's eyes flashed. "Why are you acting this way?"

"What way?" He bristled. He felt himself doing it. "I'm simply getting on with work."

"Fine." Ellie took a deep breath. "What about that kiss, then?"

He admired her courage even if he didn't particularly like

it. They'd both been ducking their feelings for each other for a while, or at least he had. He'd thought he'd had a glimmer of how Ellie felt, but now he was afraid he'd got it completely wrong. She thought he was boring and stuffy, and she'd had to endure a week with him, as well as a kiss she undoubtedly hadn't wanted.

Yet he couldn't say any of that to her now. He didn't want to reveal that he'd overheard her talking to Jeannie—he'd popped out of his office when he'd heard her voice—or how hurt he was by her assessment. He was a man, for goodness' sake, and he was acting like a thirteen-year-old girl.

"What about that kiss?" he asked.

Ellie's cheeks were pink. "Why did you kiss me? Do you regret it?"

"I kissed you because I wanted to," Oliver said, suddenly feeling reckless. "I'd been wanting to all week. And I suppose I thought you wanted me to as well, at least a little." He drew a quick breath, determined to say it all. "I'm sorry if I was mistaken. I hope I didn't offend you too much."

"Offend…?" Ellie repeated blankly. "Oliver, what are you talking about?"

So he was going to have to spell it out. "I heard you, Ellie," he said tiredly. Suddenly it didn't matter so much anymore. He'd come to work today buoyant and yes, a little nervous, but determined to tell Ellie how he felt. He'd practiced in the bathroom mirror.

Ellie, I want to state that I harbor feelings for you. He'd sounded officious, as dry as his dreaded manuscript, and as if he was delivering a lecture to a bunch of PhD candidates. But he'd still been planning on saying something.

Until he'd heard her speak first.

"What do you mean, you heard me?" Ellie asked. She still looked genuinely confused.

"I heard you with Jeannie," he clarified. "I heard you tell her I was boring and stuffy, if pleasant enough." His mouth twisted. "Damned with the faintest of praise."

Ellie's mouth dropped open and she gaped at him soundlessly for a few seconds. "Oh. *Oh.* But..." She gulped and then licked her lips, making Oliver's libido leap at the most inopportune of moments. He looked away, simply wanting the conversation to be over. "I didn't mean for you to hear that."

"Obviously."

"No, I mean that I didn't mean it," Ellie insisted. "I just said it to Jeannie because... well, because I didn't want her to know the truth."

"The truth?" Oliver asked, although he'd meant to finish the conversation, not dig for clarification.

"That... well, the truth about us. If there even *is* an us, which it seems now as if there isn't. Not that I assumed there was, of course, but when you kissed me..." She trailed off, blushing, leaving Oliver feeling confused, hopeful, and disgruntled all at once.

"But why would you say those things?" he asked. "Why would you insult me in public if you actually felt something for me?" She bit her lip, looking wretched. "I'm sorry, but that simply doesn't make sense to me. Not if you actually…" He drew a breath. "Cared."

She stared at him helplessly for a moment and Oliver looked down at his desk, needlessly shuffling his papers, feeling like he'd already admitted too much.

"So is that it?" she asked finally, her voice choked.

He tensed, his gaze still trained on his papers. "What do you mean?"

"If you hadn't overheard me, what would you have done?" Ellie demanded. "What would you have said?"

"It's hardly relevant now."

"Humor me," Ellie insisted. "Just so I know what I missed out on."

The last thing he wanted to do was bare his heart to her *now*. He straightened, nodding towards the papers she held. "Perhaps you should get on with that."

"Seriously?" She stared at him in obvious frustration. Oliver met her gaze coolly, refusing to be moved, trying not to give in to the mute appeal sparkling in her eyes. "Fine," she bit out, and then whirled on her heel and slammed out of the office. Oliver let out a shaky breath.

A second later the door burst open, nearly rocking on its hinges and Ellie stood there, her face flushed, her eyes blazing.

"No," she said. "I don't accept that, Oliver. I know I messed up this morning, but you *kissed* me. And I haven't been kissed in over five years! So that shook me up and the fact is I didn't know how you were going to be when I arrived this morning. I wondered if you'd act like it hadn't happened—because that's what you did yesterday, driving off seconds afterwards. I mean, what was *that* about?" Oliver opened his mouth to say he knew not what but Ellie blazed onwards. "And so yes, I said that to Jeannie. I barely knew what I was saying. I just wanted her to stop asking questions I didn't know the answers to, because I didn't know whether you would be telling me you were halfway to falling in love with me or if you'd blank me out. So." She blew out a breath, his manuscript still pressed to her chest. "I don't think it's fair of you to dismiss me out of hand, but maybe that's what you intended to do all along."

Oliver gaped, struggling to find something to say. What to feel. He felt like a fish, his mouth opening and closing but no words coming out.

"Well?" Ellie demanded, tears sparkling in her eyes now. "Is that the truth?"

"No…" Oliver managed, and Ellie sniffed.

"Oh, screw it, Oliver," she said, and to his complete shock she tossed the manuscript aside, pages fluttering everywhere, and grabbed him by the shoulders. It wasn't until she was on her tiptoes, straining to meet his mouth with hers, that Oliver realized what she was doing. She was kissing him.

Thankfully his brain kicked in then, along with his libido, and he hauled her against him and kissed her back for all he was worth. She felt so right in his arms, her curvy body fitting so snugly against his, her hands driving through his hair as she kissed him back with all the passion he felt. His precious typewritten pages were scattered all over his office, crumpled under their feet as they kissed and kissed, somehow landing on top of Oliver's desk, nearly sending his laptop skittering off the edge. Even then he didn't care. He simply didn't want this moment to end, ever.

Eventually, though, they both needed to take a breath, and they broke apart, gasping and dazed as they stared at each other in shock. At least Oliver was in shock. And Ellie looked dumbstruck as well.

Several pulse-pounding seconds passed, the only sound the ragged draw of their breathing. Then there was a tap on the door and Oliver scrambled to straighten his shirt and tie, run a hand through his rumpled hair. Ellie was doing the same, tugging at her sweater before fluttering her hands about her face. They'd taken several steps apart and were now standing, rather conspicuously, on either side of his office.

"Oliver?" Jeannie poked her head in the door, her eyebrows rising at the sight of all the pages scattered about the floor, a confetti of A4 paper. "Goodness, what happened in here?"

"We had a slight mishap," Oliver said. His voice sounded strangled. "A little accident."

He saw a smile tugging at Ellie's lips and realized that, more or less, he'd just put himself in the same position that morning when he'd overheard her talking to Jeannie.

Suddenly his earlier hurt seemed ridiculous, joyously laughable—*Ellie had kissed him.* Ellie liked him. He felt like a boy in primary school, hands in pockets as he sauntered along, whistling, king of his world.

"You received a parcel," Jeannie said, handing him a package wrapped in brown paper. "I think it's the proofs for a book you're endorsing?"

"Ah, yes. Right." He couldn't care less about the book, about any book, right then. "Thank you."

Jeannie gave a deliberately lingering glance for the papers on the floor. Mischief glinted in her eyes as she murmured, "Then I'll leave you two to it." She closed the door softly, and Ellie let out a muffled laugh before clapping her hand over her mouth.

"That was awkward," she said after a moment, removing her hand and giving him a teasing smile.

"Rather." Oliver gazed at her, enjoying the way her eyes sparkled, her tousled hair tumbling over her shoulders. He could still recall the feel of her lips, her hands, her body.

"So." He smiled. "That happened."

"Yes." Ellie smiled back, and in that curving of her lips he saw all the uncertainty he felt—except he didn't feel it anymore.

"Ellie, I care about you," he said, the statement seeming to boom through his office. She blinked. "Let me take you out to dinner. A proper dinner, to start a proper relationship."

She stared at him for a moment, looking shy and, unfortunately, still uncertain. Then she smiled, and Oliver's heart felt as light as a balloon soaring up into the sky.

"Okay. That would be... great."

ELLIE WAS STILL reeling from the day's events as she drove back to Willoughby Close. The evenings were becoming lighter as spring approached, and although it was chilly outside, her heart lifted to see the pale blue sky, the evening sun gilding the fields in gold. And in all truth, her heart had already had a serious lift already. In fact, her heart was floating somewhere in the stratosphere at the moment. Oliver had said he cared about her. And he was taking her out to dinner on Friday night.

As Ellie pulled into Willoughby Close she saw Harriet Lang's gleaming black Land Rover. She'd avoided her neighbor that morning, but she didn't relish an existence of awkwardness and tension with those living closest to her.

Now, as she parked the car, she watched Harriet exit her own car, sulky children in tow. Besides Mallory, there was a sullen-looking boy of about nine and an angelic girl of around six who looked like she knew how cute she was.

Ellie had the not-so-subtle plan of waiting in her car until they were safely in their house, but she accidentally made eye contact with Harriet, who was fishing for her keys, and feeling like it would be rude not to, she reluctantly climbed out of her car and gave Harriet a wave.

"Hey there, are you settling in all right?"

"Yes, more or less, but as I said last night, it's not permanent." Harriet's voice was brittle, her expression strained. She looked down into the depths of her designer leather bag, searching for her keys.

Ellie stood there, wondering what was really going on with the Langs, because it was obvious that something was. Before she could take the leap and say something, Harriet had found her keys and lifted them triumphantly. With a last, distracted smile for Ellie, she turned to her own door. Ellie went to hers, the moment of opportunity to continue the conversation clearly over.

Inside Marmite tackled her legs as Ellie called for Abby. During half-term Abby had made a case for being allowed to go home on her own after school rather than languish in the lonely depths of after school club, and Ellie had agreed. Jace and Lady Stokeley were both around, and her daughter had shown herself to be both independent and mature. Still, she couldn't keep from feeling a prickle of alarm until Abby's voice floated down from upstairs.

With relief Ellie tossed her keys on the table and gave

Marmite a pat.

"So, how was it?" Abby asked as she clattered down the stairs.

"How was what?"

"Oliver." Abby rolled her eyes. "After that kiss…! What did he do? What did you say?"

"Nothing, for a while," Ellie said with a laugh. "We're both dunderheads when it comes to romance, I think."

"For a while?" Abby narrowed her eyes. "What does that mean exactly?"

"We avoided each other all morning, and then things came to a head this afternoon." Ellie still wasn't sure what crazy courage had possessed her to kiss Oliver the way she had, but it felt like the best thing she'd ever done.

"And?" Abby demanded when Ellie, lost in wonderful memory, forgot to keep explaining.

"And we're going on a proper date this Friday."

Abby's briefly dazzling smile faded. "But we're going to Colin's on Friday."

"Colin's…" She'd completely forgotten about Colin Heath asking her and Abby to dinner with him and his American girlfriend Anna.

"We could ask him to reschedule…"

"No, I'll ask Oliver if we can go out Saturday." She valued her new friends too much to blow them off, and she hoped that Oliver could be flexible. Plus she had another day to work up her courage for an actual, honest-to-goodness date, the first one she'd had in… well, ever.

She and Nathan had never actually dated. They'd been friends who'd had sex and then a baby. Gone and got married and then lived with regret. But dates, proper ones, not the couple of awful blind ones set up by her sister? The fizzy, sparkly feeling as you dressed up and then gazed at someone across a candlelit table? Nope. Never.

"Sounds like a busy weekend, then," Abby said cheerfully.

"Abby…" Ellie took a deep breath, knowing she needed to ask even though her daughter had only seemed excited for her to have a dating life. "You don't mind?"

Abby, on her way to do her usual perusal of the contents of the fridge, turned around. "Mind? Mind what?"

"Me and Oliver, going on a date. Dating, even, although who knows, we might have one dinner and decide to call it a day."

"I doubt it." Abby opened the fridge, stared into its chilled depths for a few seconds, and then let out a gusty sigh. "But I do mind that you never buy decent snack food."

"I'm about to make tea, anyway," Ellie said as she moved across to look in the fridge and figure out what she'd be making. "But seriously, Abby. I've never really dated before. I know I've had the odd blind date, but this is something different. At least I hope it is."

Abby gave her a kindly yet exasperated look. "It is, Mum. I'm only eleven and I know that it is."

"So, if Oliver and I did start dating properly, you wouldn't mind? Because… because of Dad?"

Abby stared at her for a moment, her eyes narrowed, her gaze assessing. Ellie had no idea what she was thinking.

"What does this have to do with Dad?" she finally asked. "I mean, I know you two aren't getting back together. He ran off to Australia with some surfer chick."

Which was information she'd tried to keep from her daughter, but Abby had obviously picked up on more than Ellie had ever realized.

"I know, but…" Ellie trailed off, unable to articulate what she meant, even to herself. *I know, but are you sure you're okay with the way our life is turning out? Because sometimes I'm still struggling.* Maybe this was a conversation she needed to have with herself rather than her daughter.

Her lovely, smart, confident daughter gave her a big grin. "Yeah, Mum," she said. "I'm totally cool with it."

Chapter Twenty-One

S O, A DATE. What exactly was she meant to wear? Abby had encouraged her to dig deep into Lady Stokeley's wardrobe again, but Ellie was reluctant. She wanted, dare she admit it, something new.

One afternoon during her lunch break she nipped out to the shops on Cornmarket Street and ended up buying a slinky black number that cost more than anything she'd ever spent on a single piece of clothing, including her wedding dress—which admittedly had been an off-the-rack maternity smock of beige polyester.

Oliver had been easygoing about changing to Saturday, although they'd both been a bit jokily uncomfortable with each other all week, trying to navigate this new normal.

On Friday night she and Abby went over to Colin's quaint cottage by the Lea River and had dinner with him and his girlfriend Anna, who was gorgeous and glamorous and obviously in love with her boyfriend. Their utter ease with one another stirred a whisper of envy in Ellie, although she was heartened by the rocky road they'd travelled to their happily-ever-after; after a holiday romance Anna had gone back to New York, too scared to try for something more permanent, and then three awful weeks later Colin had flown over and told her he was in love with her.

"And that was this Christmas?" Ellie clarified as they sat around Colin's table, his black lab Millie sprawled at their feet and ate the very messy Eton Mess that he'd made. At Anna and Colin's affirmative nods she added disbelievingly, "So you've only been dating for—"

"A month," Anna supplied, smiling. "And that was long distance."

"Wow. I never would have guessed." They acted like an old couple around each other, draping arms over shoulders and finishing each other's sentences. It would have been nauseating if it wasn't so cute. Ellie hoped she and Oliver might have the same kind of easy affection and warmth, although secretly she wondered. And then she wondered why she was thinking along those lines, when all that was happening was a single date. She did not need to race ahead and paint all those blasted rainbows, but it seemed she couldn't help herself.

Saturday came up all too soon, and now Ellie stood in front of her mirror, wondering if the little black number that had seemed so sophisticated in the dressing room was a little too slinky. Slutty, even. That was not the impression she wanted to give Oliver.

"Whoa, Mum." Abby sauntered into the room, wearing

her best jeans, her elven necklace, and a slick of sparkly lip gloss, all in preparation for her own evening spent with Tobias. Ellie was dropping her off at Jemima's before she and Oliver headed out. "Looking fine."

"Is it too much?" Ellie asked as she tugged at the neckline. She had a feeling she was showing too much cleavage. "It seemed so sedate in the dressing room…"

"I think it looks nice," Abby said, eyeing her over, and Ellie wondered at the wisdom of trusting her eleven-year-old's fashion sense. "And we're late," Abby added. "So you might as well go with it."

"Okay." Ellie grabbed a scarf just in case she decided she needed to cover up a bit more. "Let's go."

She hummed under her breath as she left the house, pausing to glance at the lighted windows of Number Two. "How are things with Mallory?" she asked Abby as they got in the car.

Abby shrugged. "We're good."

"You are?"

"We pretend neither of us exists, so that's a plus."

Ellie sighed but kept silent, determined not to nag her daughter about making friends. Abby *had* made friends, good ones, even if they weren't the kind Ellie had expected and they didn't go to her school.

She thought she was keeping calm as they drove towards Kingham, humming under her breath, when Abby gave her a rather strange look.

"Mum, are you okay?"

"Yes." Ellie pasted on a bright smile. "Fine. Why?"

"Because you're humming the Imperial March from *Star Wars*. You know, Darth Vader's theme song?"

"Am I?" Ellie let out a surprised laugh. "Well, it is catchy."

Abby's silence was eloquent.

By the time they arrived at Jemima's house, Ellie was feeling distinctly keyed up. She kept shifting her weight from foot to foot and tucking her hair behind her ears and generally fidgeting, unable to keep still for a second. When she greeted Tobias at the door, her voice came out shrill and slightly manic. Now Tobias was giving her strange looks as well.

And then Oliver was there, looking unbelievably dashing in a navy blue suit, sharply tailored with a crisp light blue shirt and a dark blue tie. She'd never seen him in anything so fancy—it put his corduroy blazer and nubby ties from work to shame.

"Hello." He smiled and pushed his glasses up with his middle finger, making her heart swell with affection. He was goofy, sexy, and charming all at once, and she was falling in love with him right there. Which was rather terrifying.

"Hello," Ellie answered, her voice coming out in a whisper.

Oliver's smile was warm, his gaze filled with admiration. "You look lovely."

Jemima came out into the hallway, giving Ellie an uncertain smile. "Good to see you again," she murmured, and Ellie answered in kind, noting the other woman's appearance—clean clothes, neat hair, and less of a vacant look. All major pluses.

"We should get going, I think," Oliver said, jangling his keys. "The reservation's at seven."

It was five minutes past. They were late, thanks to her dithering at home. After saying goodbye to an already-retreating Abby, Ellie headed outside with Oliver.

So they were really doing this. A proper date. He held the door of his car open for her, and she slid into the interior, her senses heightened in the dark, or maybe just because she was with Oliver. The car smelled of bay rum with a slight, lingering odor of Marmite, even a week after their road trip.

They drove in silence for a few minutes, darkened fields with muddy puddles that glinted under the moonlight sliding by, everything feeling hushed and expectant.

"So, where are we actually going?" Ellie asked. Her voice sounded high and strained, and too loud in the close confines of the car.

"A restaurant on the outside of Kingham. I haven't been there before but I've heard good things." He let out a little laugh. "If you want to know the truth, I haven't been on a date in quite a while."

"How long is quite a while?"

"A couple of years."

"It'll take more than that to beat me," Ellie answered. "Besides a few blind dates I'd like to forget about, I haven't been on a date since I was sixteen."

"But you've been married," Oliver pointed out. "So you've beat me there."

"Yes." But she didn't want to think about Nathan now, and she didn't want Oliver thinking about him either.

Oliver pulled into the car park of what looked like an extremely elegant restaurant housed in a rambling farmhouse of golden Cotswold stone. He hopped out and held open her door, and then they walked inside together.

As Ellie took in the sumptuous surroundings, from the candlelit tables to the crystal wine glasses and multiple forks and knives on the table, her stomach muscles clenched with nerves. Was she already out of her league? The restaurant even smelled sophisticated—a mixture of expensive perfume and exotic spices and wood smoke from the open fire. A skinny, blonde hostess in a black dress that looked nicer than Ellie's took her decidedly unglamorous puffa parka—the only coat she owned—and ushered them to a secluded table for two.

Oliver pulled out her chair as Ellie was about to sit down, making her nearly bum-plant on the floor. She let out a little shriek and clutched at the chair's arm, making other diners turn their heads and stare. What a perfect start to the evening.

"Sorry," Oliver said quickly. "I should have said what I was doing…"

"It's fine." Ellie sat down gingerly and then reached for her napkin at the same time as the hostess and they tussled over it for a few fraught seconds before she had the sense to let go and the other woman laid it in her lap. This was getting better and better.

Oliver sat down across from her and buried himself in the menu. Ellie decided to do the same. Everything looked fancy—a lot of it in French, or with ingredients that Ellie had only vaguely heard of, if at all—truffle oil, black trumpet mushrooms, samphire, bottarga. What on earth was *that?* It sounds like an unpleasant skin condition. And what was a confit, or a velouté? Ellie gulped.

Oliver looked over the top of his menu. "Do you see anything you like?"

"Oh, yes." The answer was automatic. Ellie gazed blindly down at the menu. She wished she could laugh about this, make a joke, turn a weakness into a strength, all that jazz, but at the moment she felt too uncertain and raw. She couldn't admit she'd never been to a restaurant like this one, that the words on the menu might as well be written in Sanskrit, and that she wished they'd gone to a normal pub with fish and chips and pints of ale. "I think I'll have the chicken." There was chicken on the menu, at least. She'd recognized that.

The waiter came to take their orders and their menus,

leaving Ellie with nothing to hide behind. Oliver smiled at her wryly, and in that smile she saw the acknowledgement of how strange this felt for both of them. She started to feel better.

"I wanted to thank you for whatever you said to Jemima," he said after a moment. "She's decided to meet with a therapist, and I think just making that decision has helped."

"I'm glad."

"It's been a tough road, but you know that. Anyway, I appreciate you taking the time to talk to her."

"No problem." She looked around the restaurant. "So this is a nice place. How did you find it?"

"Some colleagues mentioned it to me."

"Well, it's very nice."

Oliver inclined his head and Ellie took a sip of water. Time to think of the next conversational gambit. Fortunately their starters arrived then, so at least she could distract herself with food. Except what was on the plate was *not* what she'd ordered. At least it didn't look like what she'd ordered, which was meant to be some kind of chicken. Ellie had been hoping for the posh equivalent of a chicken pie, but this was an egg-shaped piece of meat stuffed with what looked like black pudding, and some raw-looking seafood placed on top.

She glanced at Oliver's starter, which was a reasonable-looking salad with goat's cheese and curly lettuce leaves. She could have managed that.

Cautiously she prodded her starter with her fork. Memories of eating black pudding when she was a child and being sick from it danced through her mind and she forced them away. She didn't need to think about the fact that black pudding's main ingredient was blood. She just needed to pop it in her mouth and chew. It was probably delicious.

Resolutely she did just that—and then fought not to gag. She'd forgotten how much she detested this stuff. Metallic-tasting and claggy, it coated her tongue and threatened to slide down her throat. She sat there, her mouth full, her body protesting, while Oliver gave her a curious look.

"Are you all right?"

She nodded, unable to speak, and tried to force it down. *Swallow, Ellie. Just swallow.* It wasn't happening. She could not choke it down. Admitting humiliating defeat, Ellie put the heavy damask napkin up to her mouth and spat her mouthful of blood pudding into it. She didn't dare look at Oliver's expression.

"Sorry," she managed, intending to hide the offending napkin back in her lap, but a waiter stepped forward and whisked it away, which somehow made it worse. "I didn't realize the starter had black pudding in it. My dad used to make it for Sunday fry-ups—I've never been able to stand the stuff."

"I see," Oliver said after a tiny pause. He looked startled, and Ellie cringed inwardly. This was so not how she'd wanted the evening to go.

Fortunately, as she battled her way through three courses,

things got a little better. There were no more spitting mishaps although she did fumble with the forks, but at least the dessert—a decadent chocolate mousse—was delicious. They even managed to keep the conversation on an even keel, talking about Oliver's book launch in the summer and places they'd like to travel to on holiday.

By the end of the evening Ellie was exhausted both emotionally and physically; she'd never realized how much hard work a date could be. And a date with *Oliver,* whom she found funny and charming and sexy and sweet. Why hadn't it all worked out better? Been easier?

Feeling dispirited, she headed outside with Oliver. The air was fresh and damp, stars sparkling high overhead. Oliver unlocked the car and opened the passenger door for her. Ellie slid inside, resting her head against the seat and wishing things had been different.

"Ellie." Oliver's voice was gentle as he slid into the driver's seat, turning to her with a small smile.

"I'm sorry," Ellie blurted.

"Sorry? For what?"

"For embarrassing you. I feel like you can't take me anywhere," she said in an embarrassed rush. "I spit food in a napkin."

"I'm sorry I took you to such a ridiculously posh restaurant. Even the waiter intimidated me."

Ellie gave a little laugh, starting to feel better. "He was kind of scary."

"I would have rather gone to the pub."

"Me too."

"I suppose," Oliver said slowly, "it's going to take us awhile to get used to this. To us."

"I wish it didn't. I wish I was more relaxed about everything, but I felt as tense as tightrope the whole evening."

"So did I," Oliver admitted, his wry smile widening. "We're a pair of numpties, aren't we?"

Ellie let out another soft laugh. "I suppose we are."

The moment stretched on and then Oliver was reaching for her, and Ellie went, everything in her relaxing deliciously as Oliver's mouth found hers, his hands tangling in her hair as he kissed her.

Oh, but his kisses were nice—although nice was such a mealy-mouthed word for something that was rather unbearably wonderful. She let out a breathy sigh against his lips as she sagged against the seat and Oliver continued to kiss her. His hands drifted from her hair to her shoulders and then lower, sending a shower of fireworks through her body. She hadn't been touched like this in so long she'd forgotten how it felt. How intimate and intense and perfect.

And touching him felt pretty perfect too—she let her hands roam down his chest, reveling in the feel of his well-defined pecs underneath his crisp shirt. Both their breathing was becoming ragged, the car windows steaming up. A couple walked by, their footsteps crunching on the gravel, and with a shaky laugh Oliver eased back.

"I haven't made out in a car since I was a teenager. Although I don't think I did it even then."

"No?" Ellie smoothed her hair, her heart still racing.

"I went to an all boys' boarding school. Not much opportunity." He tucked a tendril of hair behind her ear, his fingers skimming her cheek. "You looked lovely tonight. I couldn't keep my eyes off you."

"Even when I was spitting black pudding into my napkin?" Thankfully, wonderfully, she could laugh about it now. Everything felt better, easier, after that kiss.

"Yes, even then." Oliver leaned forward and brushed a whisper of a kiss across her lips. "We should head back before it gets too late and Tobias and Abby wonder what we're getting up to."

"Okay." She settled back against her seat, unable to keep a sloppy smile from spreading across her face. Never mind the black pudding, the fancy forks, the hoity-toity waiters—it had been a wonderful evening.

Chapter Twenty-Two

THE NEXT TWO weeks were some of the best of Ellie's life. In fact, she couldn't remember when she'd felt so happy, so light—maybe never. Nothing amazing happened, no rainbows, no unicorns or fantasy trips to Paris or Rome like she might have imagined, once upon a time. No, this was just normal life, but a new normal, a lovely normal.

She continued to work on Oliver's book, typing his revised chapters and taking the train to and from work. They had lunch together when they could, strolling along the river or eating outside as the weather turned surprisingly balmy for early March. They kissed—in shop doorways and under the drooping branches of a willow, wrapped up in their own wonderful world.

They hadn't managed to go on a second date—Tobias and Abby were both preparing for SATs and Jemima had started to have something of a social life, so evenings alone were a rarity indeed, but Ellie didn't mind. She liked taking things slow, needed to take them at a snail's pace for her own sanity.

Because if she stopped to think about how happy she was, how perfect Oliver seemed, she started to get scared. And that fear was poisonous. That fear kept her up at night, remembering how difficult life had been once, how long she'd tried with Nathan and had nothing to show for it. That fear told her that relationships were hard work and if one person decided to stop trying there was nothing you could do. That fear whispered that she and Oliver were too different, that he'd never had a serious, long-term relationship before, and she still didn't know what forks to use. She hated that fear.

Fortunately there were plenty of distractions from it. Work, of course, and being a good mum to Abby, who still seemed to hate school in a shrugging, philosophical sort of way. Marmite kept her busy as well, having to walk him before and after work, and keeping him off Lady Stokeley's newly restored lawn, which he sought out at every opportunity.

Friends too, had appeared in her life, sprouting like sudden flowers—Anna was moving to Wychwood-on-Lea in a month and had Skyped her several times, asking for opinions on local rental since Colin, she confided, was hopeless with that sort of thing.

Jace continued to work the low-level flirt as a matter of course, and deliver firewood to her door along with a chat. Colin's sister Emma had invited her over for coffee one Saturday.

While at the tearoom on the high street, Ellie had started chatting to the owner Olivia, who had moved to Wychwood-on-Lea from Bristol to help take care of her mum, and wasn't taking to shop management as well as she would have liked. They'd chatted about ideas, and Ellie had enjoyed a pleasant daydream of opening her own shop on the high street, with books by local authors and jam made by local farmers and all sorts of stuff. Like the nearby organic farm shop minus the hoity-toity attitude and astronomical prices.

Harriet Lang still seemed to be avoiding her, but it was more or less mutual. As much as Ellie would have liked a best friend for a neighbor, that seemed destined not to be, and they kept to polite smiles and the occasional exchange about the weather.

And then of course there was family. Her parents called to inform her that Nathan had been in touch again, making Ellie's heart sink like a stone.

"He sent the loveliest card," her mum confided. "And flowers for my birthday." The meaningful tone reminded Ellie that she'd forgotten to call, never mind flowers.

"That's very nice of him," she said dutifully, because of course it was. That was Nathan—ridiculously thoughtful in small ways while completely missing the big picture.

"Are you sure the two of you couldn't get back together?" her mother asked. "I know you had your difficulties, Ellie, but he's a nice boy and divorce…" Her mother trailed off, but Ellie knew what she meant. Her mother came from a generation that thought of divorce as a shame, a stain. One that Ellie had caused because she'd been the one to instigate said divorce.

"You do remember he cheated on me, Mum?" If kisses and a bit of groping counted as cheating, which to Ellie they did. But it wasn't even the infidelity that had bothered her the most. It was all the other stuff.

"With that girl from work? She was a jumped-up bit of fluff, if you ask me—"

"So that makes it better?"

"I'm sure he's sorry."

Ellie suppressed the swear word she very much felt like shouting. She understood, sort of, why her parents liked Nathan despite the lack of job or parenting skills. When Ellie had first found out she was pregnant, Nathan had acted like some pimply knight in shining armor, talking with her father in the sitting room, insisting that he wanted to do the right thing, that he'd take care of Ellie and their unborn child. Never mind that he'd failed on that, big time. The talk had made a deep and lasting impression on her parents, as had all of Nathan's other small, cheap gestures.

Diane had also called, no doubt at her parents' request. "This isn't about Nathan, is it?" Ellie asked tetchily as she answered her mobile at work. "Because I'm fed up about that."

"Nathan? No. He's a tosser. A nice tosser, when he wants to be, but you can do better."

"Good." Ellie breathed a sigh of relief and ignored that twinge of unease. Nathan *was* a tosser, but she still didn't particularly like her sister saying so. He was still Abby's dad. "So why are you ringing?"

"Do I have to have a reason? Can't I call my sister?"

"Yes, but you rang last week." Her sister rang her just about every week, which was starting to feel like checking in with her parole officer. "You aren't worried about me, are you?"

"I'm always worried about you," Diane said bluntly, and Ellie sighed. As much as she appreciated her sister's concern, she worried about herself enough as it was. She didn't need someone else to do it for her. "But actually," Diane continued, "Abby did mention something about a boyfriend when I emailed her…"

"Ah." Ellie leaned back in her chair. "Yes, well, I am seeing someone," she admitted with shy pride. "My boss, actually."

"Are you sure that's a good idea?"

Ellie tensed. The last thing she wanted now was one of Diane's big sister lectures to ruin her fragile happiness. "I'm quite sure."

"I just don't want to see you get hurt, Ellie."

"I don't either, Diane."

"Because this time I won't be around to pick up the pieces."

Ellie would have snapped at that but Diane sounded

genuinely worried. And remembering how useless she'd once been, and how kind Diane had been in return, made Ellie swallow down any snippy retort. "I thought you wanted me to date," she said instead. "What were all those blind dates about, then?"

"They were only three of them, and I knew none of them were serious," Diane dismissed. "I just wanted you to get out of the house and back into living."

"Well, I did, and here I am."

"It's just Abby made it sound like you were really smitten. And your boss? How is that going to work out?"

"He's only my boss for another week," Ellie protested. The book was almost finished, and Jeannie had promised her a desk in the main office, something she was looking forward to. "And why shouldn't I be smitten? Maybe I'd like another chance at happiness."

"I wouldn't mind that," Diane said quickly. "Of course I wouldn't. But I'm worried for you, Ellie. You're so far away and this bloke sounds like a real snooty type. An Oxford professor? I mean both of us barely made it through sixth form."

"I didn't make it through sixth form," Ellie reminded her tartly. "And I don't see how that matters." Even if she had to battle it mattering all the time.

"Maybe it doesn't," Diane agreed. "I can't help but worry, though. Eventually the newness wears off, and you have to make sure you're left with something that lasts."

"There's only one way to find out," Ellie answered. But like Diane, she couldn't help but worry. It was her default setting, determined optimism papering over the cracks of concern and genuine fear. What if things didn't work out between her and Oliver? What if he got tired of her, tired of trying? What if Abby got hurt along with her own broken heart?

Then, the day she'd finished the epilogue on the book and was officially no longer Oliver's PA, he asked her to accompany him home.

"Home?" She stared at him blankly.

"My parents' home," he explained. He looked nervous, shuffling papers as he sat behind his desk. "It's the anniversary of Jamie's death, and they always ask me and Jemima home for the weekend around this time. Jemima's refused, says she can't cope with it on top of everything else, but I've never not gone." He swallowed, looking down. "I know it doesn't sound like much fun, but it is rather important."

"Of course." A lump formed in Ellie's throat at the thought of so much sadness. "Of course I'll go, Oliver."

Yet it was one more thing to worry about, and a rather large one too. Oliver's parents... the distant, aristocratic father, the socialite mother. Ellie thought it entirely likely they'd both turn their noses up at her, and she wasn't sure she could blame them. Diane's words rang ominously through her mind. She and Oliver really were different. She knew that, and sometimes it didn't matter so much, and then sometimes it did.

Abby was happy to stay over at Lady Stokeley's for the weekend, and Jace had promised to take Marmite, so there was nothing to keep her from going. Nothing but her own fear.

They were both quiet as they drove from Wychwood-on-Lea to the village near Cheltenham where his parents lived.

"So what does this weekend look like?" Ellie asked when they'd been driving for a while. "What will we do?"

"We always have dinner on the Saturday night. Other than that it's pretty low key. My father might want to do some shooting."

"Shooting?"

"Clay pigeons. There's a range on the grounds."

Range. Grounds. Oliver's background was starting to seem a whole lot posher than she'd realized. "Right."

"And my mother likes to have afternoon tea... lots of fussy little cakes and cucumber sandwiches."

"Okay." She was now officially terrified.

A short while later they turned up a sweeping drive that rivaled Willoughby Manor's to a house that looked like it but on a slightly smaller scale.

"Wow." Ellie swallowed hard. "That's quite a nice pile."

"Endsleigh House." He gave her a wry grimace. "I should probably mention that my father is a baronet."

"What?" Ellie wrenched round in her seat to give him the full extent of her horrified shock. "Are you kidding me? You mean, you're like *nobility?*"

"Not nobility, no. My father is technically titled gentry."

Ellie rolled her eyes at the semantics of that statement. "But he's addressed like... like a lord?"

"You should call him Sir Archie."

"And your mother?"

"Lady Venables."

Good grief. "And you?" Ellie demanded.

He gave her a lopsided smile that made her heart turn over. "Just plain old Oliver."

"No Sir Oliver? Or Lord Venables?"

"Nope, not until my father dies and I inherit the title."

Ellie sagged against the seat, overwhelmed. "You really should have told me this earlier."

"Does it make a difference?" Oliver asked. "I'm still the same."

"Only just," Ellie muttered. She'd just gotten a whole lot more nervous. A *baronet*.

Oliver pulled up to the front of Endsleigh House while Ellie anxiously inspected her reflection in the wing mirror and tried not to throw up. What on earth were Sir Archie and Lady Venables going to think of her, with her cheap coat, Northern accent, and single mum status? And had Oliver explained that she was his PA? His parents were going to be horrified. If Ellie had been them, she probably would have been horrified.

No one came out to greet them, although a maid—in an

actual uniform, black dress, frilly apron—opened the front door. Ellie's heart was beating so hard she could feel it in her ears. She felt dizzy. Oliver slipped one arm around her waist as they walked through an impressive pair of double doors into an imposing sitting room that reminded Ellie of Willoughby Manor, except not nearly so moth-eaten. Everything looked old and yet freshly polished, clearly expensive.

"Oliver." Oliver's father turned from the fireplace, one booted foot resting on the fender. He was wearing a lot of tweed.

"Sir." Oliver called his father Sir? They didn't so much as smile at one another, never mind a hug.

Ellie tried to smile, although she was struggling with the protocol. Should she curtsey? Address Sir Archie before she was spoken to?

"And you must be… Ellie." The slight pause before her name was telling. Lady Venables rose from her chair with a smile that managed to be both gracious and fixed. Her eyes looked flinty. Oh, dear.

"It's…" Ellie cleared her throat. "A pleasure to meet you, Lady Venables. And you, Sir Archie." She aimed a smile in Sir Archie's direction; the older man was looking down his nose at her, squinting slightly, as if he couldn't quite make out who—or what—she was.

"You must call me Helen," Lady Venables said. "We don't stand on formality here."

Ha bloody ha ha. They most certainly did. "Thank you," Ellie murmured. She felt the chances of her calling Lady Venables by her first name were on par with her calling Lady Stokeley Dot.

"You had a good trip?" Lady Venables asked as she rang a little crystal bell for tea. "Where are you from, my dear? Because you certainly don't sound as if you are from around here." She smiled as she said it, but Ellie still felt the intended snub.

For the next half hour Ellie endured tense chitchat as Lady Venables asked her pointed questions and Sir Archie harrumphed and at one point blew his nose into a large handkerchief with a trumpeting sound. Ellie decided she hated them both, and then felt guilty for being so judgmental, even as she wondered how much of a hindrance this was going to be to her relationship with Oliver. Although at this point she couldn't see where their relationship could possibly go—she was hardly likely to be the next Lady Venables, was she?

After thirty minutes her phone rang, and Lady Venables jerked a little bit, her mouth pinching, as if Ellie had just burped out loud.

"Sorry, that's my daughter ringing," Ellie said with a touch of defiance. Had Oliver even told them about Abby?

"You have a daughter?" Lady Venables looked even more nonplussed.

So he hadn't told them. "Yes. She wouldn't ring, I don't

think, unless it was an emergency." Excusing herself, Ellie slipped out to the hall. "Abby? Is everything okay?"

"Why are you whispering?"

"Because I'm… oh, it doesn't matter." Ellie sagged against the wall. "What's going on?"

"It's Dorothy. She hasn't been feeling that well, and I was thinking about taking her to the doctor."

"To the doctor? How?" The doctor's was at least a mile away. "What do you think is wrong with her?" Ellie's mind buzzed with all the information. How could her eleven-year-old daughter sound so coolly competent, while she was falling apart?

"Coughing and a bit of a fever. I was just ringing for Jace's mobile number. He's not answering his home phone and Dorothy doesn't know what it is."

"Okay. Just a second." Ellie found Jace's number on her phone and read it out to Abby. "How will you get to the doctor—"

"Jace will drive us," Abby said. "Don't worry, Mum. Have a nice time."

"I can come home," Ellie said a bit desperately. At this point that seemed like a very sensible idea. "Drive you and Lady Stokeley to the doctor—"

"No way. I'm not ruining your weekend. I'll ring you when we've gone to the doctor." And then Abby hung up, leaving Ellie holding the phone and wondering if she had to go back in the drawing room.

"Was it that dire?" Oliver asked later, when they'd gone upstairs. They had separate bedrooms in separate wings of the house. Ellie couldn't help but notice that her room was a good deal more modest than Oliver's.

"Fairly," she admitted honestly. "It would have been good to know just how posh your parents were beforehand, Oliver."

He gave an apologetic grimace. "I didn't want to alarm you. And I also don't want it to matter." He looked at her seriously. "Because like I said before, I'm still the same. Same absent-minded professor that I ever was." He smiled, reaching for her, and Ellie went into his arms with a grateful sigh. It occurred to her as Oliver kissed her that they were alone in a bedroom for the first time in their fledgling relationship. Admittedly, with servants lurking about and his disapproving parents downstairs, it hardly felt like the place for an actual seduction, but still. Privacy. Soft surfaces. And Oliver's lovely, lovely kisses.

Perhaps this weekend wouldn't be so bad, after all.

Chapter Twenty-Three

I T WAS WORSE. Ellie didn't think she'd ever experienced such a dire twenty-four hours in her life. After a few blissful hours snuggling and making out in Oliver's bedroom, a maid knocked on their door and summoned them downstairs. While Oliver went shooting with his father, Ellie endured an afternoon tea with Lady Venables, whose every lift of her penciled eyebrow and twist of her thin lips made Ellie feel more and more inadequate.

When Oliver had returned from shooting he'd seemed tense and morose, offering monosyllabic answers and looking more distant and remote than Ellie had ever seen him. Her heart lurched sickeningly to imagine what Sir Archie might have been saying to him as they shot pottery birds out of the sky.

Not quite our sort is she, old boy? Fine for a roll in the hay, Oliver, but not for the real thing, what?

And in truth she couldn't even blame Sir Archie for having that attitude. She didn't belong here. She never would.

That was made abundantly clear at dinner, when she sat

at a table laden with more knives and forks than she'd ever seen before, and every conversation opener drew blood, a sword drawn and wielded. They were all polite smiles and chilly friendliness, mentions of Lady this and Lord that, and Ellie could see what was happening all too clearly. Oliver's parents were firmly nudging her out of the way, and judging from his morose silence, Oliver didn't seem to mind.

By the time she made it back to her bedroom she was thoroughly miserable. Abby rang as she was undressing, relieving at least that anxiety.

"Dorothy's got pneumonia," she announced. "But it's a pretty mild case and they think she'll make a full recovery. They're keeping her in hospital for a couple of days."

"What?" Ellie's fingers clenched on the phone. "What about you, Abby? How did you get her to the doctor? And where are you staying if Lady Stokeley is at hospital?" Already Ellie was reaching for her jeans. "I'll come back—"

"No, it's fine," Abby said, all easy nonchalance. "Jace wasn't home so Harriet ended up taking us to the doctor."

"Harriet?" Ellie repeated, gaping. "Harriet Lang?"

"Yep."

"But…" In the three weeks since Harriet had moved in, they'd had barely any interaction at all. "How was that?"

"Fine. She was really nice about it, actually."

"Wow. Okay." That was good, Ellie supposed, even if it made her feel uneasy. "But what about tonight? You can't stay alone…" And in truth, she'd rather hop back in the car and go home than endure a night at Endsleigh House.

"I'm staying at the Langs," Abby said, rendering Ellie completely speechless.

"At the Langs," she finally repeated when she felt she could string syllables together in a semi-coherent fashion. "With Mallory Lang."

"Yes."

"But I didn't think you were even friends with Mallory." Mean girl Mallory, who pointed and whispered and laughed.

"She's actually okay," Abby said. "Pretty much."

Ellie hesitated, torn between wanting to rescue Abby from an uncertain situation—as well as rescue herself. But she had the strong sense that Abby didn't want to be rescued, and swooping in at this juncture would be seriously cramping her daughter's style. Besides, she needed to see through this weekend, for Oliver's sake if nothing else.

"Okay then," she said at last. "Ring me if you need anything."

"Will do," Abby answered cheerfully, and hung up. Ellie stood there, one leg stuck in her jeans as she'd been starting to dress to go home. She yanked it out, feeling lonelier and more disconsolate than she had in a long time. She wanted Oliver, wished he would tiptoe to her bedroom and knock softly on her door. Take her in his arms and kiss her as he had this morning, and make her feel like everything was going to be okay.

But he didn't come, and Ellie had the feeling he wasn't

planning to. He hadn't even kissed her goodnight before heading off to his bedroom about a mile away from hers. She could go find him, she supposed, but she was unsure of her welcome and she didn't even know if she could find his bedroom again in this huge mausoleum. No, better to simply go to sleep, and hope things looked better in the morning.

They didn't. Ellie endured an arctic silence over breakfast, which was served in silver chafing dishes and included kippers, which Ellie thought were nearly as revolting as black pudding. Then another hour of awkward chitchat and a round of insincere nice-to-meet-yous before they were finally heading home, which would have been a good thing except Oliver seemed so dour.

He was regretting everything, Ellie was sure of it. He drove in silence, his lips pursed, a scowl settled between his brows. Ellie inwardly squirmed with misery, unwilling to break the silence and be forced to hear something she wasn't ready for.

I'm sorry, Ellie, but this has made me realize we're not suited…

She looked out the window, blinking back tears, not a rainbow in sight.

OLIVER STARED STRAIGHT ahead at the road, swamped in misery and regret. It had been such an awful weekend. He should have known better than to bring Ellie back to his parents' house, a place that held nearly nothing but bad memories for him. He should have realized it would have been tense and awful, his parents true to terrible form, all chilly politeness and raised eyebrows.

When they'd gone shooting, a sport Oliver had always found pointless and tiresome, his father had lit into him, claiming it was inappropriate to bring his 'bit of fluff' home as if she were someone proper. *A bit of fluff.* Oliver had seethed inside, struggling not to punch the man to whom he'd always shown respect.

"I'm serious about Ellie," he'd said tightly. "Sir."

Sir Archie had simply snorted and shaken his head. "Her charms will begin to pale. They always do. And then you'll find someone more of our sort."

Sometimes Oliver felt like his parents were stuck in the 1950s, although he recognized that plenty of 'their sort' would feel the same. But that wasn't him, and he didn't care, and he was falling in love with Ellie. Although after this weekend she might be wanting to call the whole thing off.

He glanced across at her, noticing how pale and unhappy she looked—about as much as he felt. He wanted to say something—to apologize or explain, but the words bottled in his throat so he couldn't get any of them out. And he was afraid it wouldn't matter anyway, because she'd had enough of him and his standoffish ways—he'd reverted to typical, awful form all weekend, stunned to miserable silence both by his parents' behavior and memories of Jamie. The anniversary of his brother's death always made him feel like a sad schoolboy inside.

So he remained silent, caught in his own web, wishing he'd never invited her home. Why *had* he? It had been an incredibly stupid idea.

He was pulling into the drive of Willoughby Manor, and then into the courtyard of Willoughby Close, before he finally worked up the courage to speak.

"Ellie," he began, despairingly, "I'm so sorry about this weekend..."

But Ellie wasn't listening. She was staring at the doorway of her cottage, transfixed, shocked. "Oh my goodness."

"What is it?" Oliver asked, and turned to see a man in dirty jeans and an old hoodie standing in the doorways, hands in his pockets, smiling sheepishly. Oliver's stomach cramped. "Who is that?"

"It's Nathan," Ellie said in little more than a whisper, and then she got out of the car.

Oliver sat there for a few seconds, unsure what the protocol was. Nathan, Ellie's ex-husband, in the Cotswolds? Hadn't Ellie said he was in Australia? Hadn't she said he was a complete tosser? So why was she hugging him then?

Oliver watched them embrace for a few more seconds and then got out of the car.

"Good morning."

"Hey." Nathan looked nonplussed to see him, and he sent a questioning glance to Ellie that might as well have screamed *who is this stupid toff?* Oliver stood up straight.

"Nathan, this is…" Oh, the pause. It was awful. It was so clearly Ellie debating how to introduce him. And then she did, most disappointingly. "Oliver. My boss."

Her boss. Not her boyfriend, or even her friend, or her date. Her boss. Which he wasn't as of tomorrow.

"Hey," Nathan said again. His eyes were telling Oliver to get lost.

"I should get back," Oliver said stiffly, trying to address Ellie alone even though she wasn't looking at him. "Things to do. Research," he added with a nod towards Nathan, even as he inwardly cringed. Was he trying to impress this loser? Every insecurity, every secret fear and failing, was coming humiliatingly to the fore in this moment. He had a horrible feeling he was going to lose Ellie, and there was nothing he could do about it.

"Okay," Ellie said after a pause. She finally looked at him, and her eyes were full of apology and recrimination. Oliver couldn't believe they might be breaking up in front of her ex-husband, while his car was still running.

"See you, then," he said, the words feeling woefully inadequate, and then he got in the car and drove away.

ELLIE WATCHED OLIVER'S car disappear around the bend, feeling as if everything that could have possibly gone wrong had. She turned back to Nathan, hardly able to believe he was here. Had his hair always been that greasy? And had he always been so short? Oliver topped him by at least three inches.

"You'd better come in," she said after a moment, and Nathan grinned. She knew by that grin that he was as cocksure as ever, sauntering into her house as if it were his own. Ellie took a deep breath, squared her shoulders, and followed him inside.

"Hey, Marmite. Hey, boy." Marmite, as ever, was thrilled to see Nathan, and as he knelt down, her traitorous dog planted paws on Nathan's shoulders and gave his face a big lick. Nathan laughed, turning to Ellie with a grin.

"Some things don't change."

"And some things do." She felt an unpleasant maelstrom of emotions at seeing Nathan here, invading her life. She still had to process everything that had happened that weekend, all the things she and Oliver hadn't said. Facing Nathan on top of all that tension felt like way too much to bear. "I thought you were in Australia?" she said as she dropped her bag by the stairs. "And have you seen Abby?"

"No, is she here?" From the suddenly alert expression in his eyes, Ellie doubted that Nathan had given Abby a thought until this moment.

"She's staying at my neighbor's."

Nathan cocked his head. "Oh? Were you out with that…" He gestured towards the door. "That stiff?"

"His name is Oliver, and yes, I was. And he's not a stiff." She took another deep breath. She was going to need a lot of them. "Actually, I've been dating him." And then she wondered why she'd used the past tense.

"Dating him? Seriously?" Nathan looked amused, which Ellie found extremely annoying.

"Yes. Seriously. Why are you here, Nathan?"

"I wanted to see you. And Abby." As an afterthought.

Ellie sank onto the sofa opposite and stared at him in weary despair. "I wish you'd phoned first."

"I wanted to surprise you."

"That you did." She sighed. "Why did you come back from Australia? Did you run out of money?"

Nathan gave her a sheepish grin. "It is expensive there."

"So is a plane ticket home."

His grin turned cocky and charming. "That's what credit cards are for."

"So what are you going to do now? Get a job, I hope?"

"Actually…" Nathan said slowly, his grin fading as he treated her to a sincere, heartfelt look. "I was hoping we might make a go of it again."

OLIVER COULDN'T CONCENTRATE on work. He couldn't concentrate on anything. He paced his flat, and then he went outside and walked along the river, revisiting in his mind every wonderful and bittersweet moment he'd had with Ellie. Their first kiss. Their second kiss. Sitting outside of the pub while she'd forced him to join that wretched dating site.

Drinking and flirting at the Eagle and Child. They'd explored a lot of the city together, and now Oliver didn't think he could ever look at it in the same way. Everywhere he looked it felt as if there was a memory of Ellie to be endured.

Because endurance was the name of game now. He'd almost called her several times, his thumb hovering over the call icon on his phone, but then he'd stopped. It wasn't fair to put pressure on Ellie now. She had Nathan and Abby to deal with, and if Oliver's gut instinct was right, some serious choices to make. She'd seen the best and worst of him, unfortunately the worst of him only that weekend. All he could do was give her some space to think... and to decide.

It hurt, though, to make that separation. It was the end of the Hilary term, students leaving the city in droves for home or further abroad. Standing in the queue of the MetroTesco Oliver overheard plans for a week of partying in Ibiza, something he'd never done. He looked at the young students with their Harry Potter-esque scarves and easy certainty and wondered if he'd ever felt that young, that hopeful. The answer came quickly, painfully—yes, with Ellie.

By the next morning Oliver's stomach felt as if it were lined with lead. Ellie hadn't sent so much as a text, and nearly twenty-four hours of silence felt unbearably ominous. With no reason to stay and every one to flee, Oliver decided it was time to book the research trip he'd been planning to Yorkshire.

ELLIE LAY IN bed and stared gritty-eyed at the ceiling. Her eyeballs ached. Everything ached. Oliver hadn't called. She'd tried to go over those surreal moments when Nathan had said hello, pulling her in for a hug she didn't want, and Oliver gone over all stiff and formal. What had happened there? What was he thinking now? What was *she* thinking?

Yesterday, without any prompting from her, Nathan had poured out his feelings. His regret at being such a lame dad. His sorrow over the numerous infidelities—some of which Ellie had never known about—over the years. He'd made the usual promises about getting a job, trying harder, insisting he meant it this time, that he was different now.

Ellie had heard it all before. She'd heard it over and over again during the six years of their marriage, and she'd heard it in earnest when she'd kicked him out five years ago, after he'd stayed over at a friend's flat, and she'd found someone's bra in his pocket.

Yet on the heels of the disastrous weekend at Endsleigh House and Oliver's awful silence, Nathan's heartfelt words started to make sense. Who was she kidding, dating an Oxford don and an heir to a baronetcy? Who did she think she *was*? She was way out of her league, and in the darkest, most despairing corner of her heart, she felt she was really in Nathan's. But she didn't like that truth, and part of her—a large part—dreaded the thought of letting him back into her life. Into Abby's life. Yes, Abby needed her dad, but did she really need Nathan? And was Ellie being selfish about not wanting to make a go of it again?

When Ellie had picked Abby up from Harriet's, her daughter had been both wary and pleased to hear her father was paying them a visit. Ellie had been too distracted to say much more than thank you to Harriet, who had looked as strained as ever, and yet softer somehow.

Nathan had been all bear hugs and tickles when he'd seen Abby, and she'd watched her daughter light up with an aching heart. By evening she was well and truly in a quandary about what to do. And Oliver still hadn't called.

Nathan took it for granted that he would spend the night, and Ellie had to clarify that he would be staying on the sofa. Lying in bed she started to picture it all too perfectly. How Nathan would make himself at home, lounging on her sofa, watching her TV, eating up her paycheck. And what would she get in return? Some fun times. A father for Abby. And a lifetime of regret, frustration, and fear.

Ellie rolled over in bed, pounding her pillow, wishing she had better answers.

Why the *hell* hadn't Oliver called?

Chapter Twenty-Four

"**H**E'S IN YORKSHIRE?"

Ellie stared at Jeannie in disbelief. It was Monday morning and after a sleepless night she'd come to work, with Nathan still snoring on her sofa. She'd pinned all her hopes, all her much-needed answers, on seeing Oliver this morning and instead she'd discovered that he'd gone to bloody Yorkshire, and might not be back until Trinity term three whole weeks away. As far as breakups went, his pretty much sucked.

Ellie had texted him twice, asking him what he was playing at, but she hadn't gotten an answer, and Jeannie had told her she didn't think there was mobile reception where he was. Ellie supposed it didn't matter much. Did she really want clarification at this point?

She spent a disgruntled day at her new desk in the main office, and all the cheerful camaraderie and gossip over the photocopying machine felt like so much noise. Her heart wasn't in it at all.

"You want to talk about it?" Jeannie asked as she brought

her a cup of tea in the afternoon, which Ellie accepted gratefully.

"Not particularly." Although they'd attempted to keep their romance quiet, Ellie knew it had got around the faculty. How could it have not? She stared glumly into her tea. "He invited me home for the weekend and it was awful."

"Weekends home usually are," Jeannie returned lightly. "Surely that doesn't mean anything?"

"It seemed to. He hasn't actually said much of anything since it happened."

"Which sounds like Oliver."

"Yes, but…" Ellie sighed. "Then he goes to Yorkshire without telling me?"

"Maybe he wanted to give you some space?"

"Then he could have bloody well said so," Ellie grumbled.

Her mood wasn't any better as she headed back to Willoughby Close, the golden stone lit up with the early evening sunlight. She opened the front door, wincing at the stale smell of beer, crisps, and unwashed male that now permeated her house. Marmite nearly knocked her over, and Nathan looked as if he hadn't moved from the sofa, except maybe to procure food and drink. And, she noticed a moment later, to have a wee, although he'd forgotten to flush the toilet. Repeatedly, by the looks of it.

"Where's Abby?"

"Abby?"

"She asked you to pick her up at school?" Abby could walk home by herself, but Ellie knew she would have been looking forward to her dad coming by. "Nathan? You did remember to pick her up, didn't you?" Even as she asked the question she knew the answer. She'd already suspected Nathan had hardly stirred from the sofa. Now she had the aggravating confirmation.

"Sorry…"

"So she hasn't come home?"

"No, I don't think so."

"You don't think so?" Ellie flung her bag on the floor, and then stared around the messy living area in utter frustration. This had been her life for six years. She didn't want to go back to it.

And then, amazingly, it clicked into place. It was as if the scales had fallen from her eyes and she could see everything with brilliant, crystalline clarity. She wasn't going to go back to this. Of course she wasn't. No matter what happened with Oliver, she didn't need Nathan in her life. She didn't want Nathan in her life, and she wouldn't allow him to waltz back in and make a mess of her and Abby's hopes. The realization was so clear and overwhelming, she almost felt like laughing with sheer joy. She didn't have to put up with this. At all.

"Nathan," she said in a steely voice. "You have half an hour to clean up this mess, gather your things, and get out of here."

Nathan looked affronted, and then hurt. "But, Ellie… I

was just messing around today. Jet lag, and all that. Give me a break…"

"No. I've given you a thousand breaks. And you're not coming back into my life just because your girlfriend kicked you out. That's what happened, isn't it?" Nathan's sulky hangdog look was confirmation enough. "I'm not going to let you break my heart again, Nathan, and more importantly, I'm not going to let you break Abby's. If you have any fatherly feeling at all, you'll clean up your act, take Abby somewhere fun, and then get yourself a damn job." With her voice and body both shaking, Ellie stomped upstairs.

Half an hour later Nathan was gone, blowing out of their house like a tornado, complete with crisp packets and empty beer bottles. Ellie felt utterly exhausted. Abby had texted her to say she was at Jace's, and so after she'd changed out of her work clothes Ellie headed up there with Marmite.

"Trouble in paradise?" Jace murmured with a smile that managed to be both sympathetic and wicked as Ellie stood in the hallway of his quaint cottage. It was an incongruous mix of bachelor's pad meets dowager's quarters.

"Paradise? I'd hardly call my life that."

"Abby told me her dad's back for a visit." Jace kept his voice low, and Ellie saw genuine concern in his eyes.

"Yes, but he's gone now. Thank goodness."

"That is a good thing, then?"

"Yes." She sniffed. "Yes, definitely." She didn't think she could talk about Oliver without breaking down.

"Mum?" Abby appeared in the doorway of the sitting room, a wary look on her face. "Is everything okay?"

"Yes. Dad's gone to stay somewhere local, but he's planning to take you out to dinner tomorrow night. I'm sorry he forgot to pick you up from school."

"It's not your fault."

"I know." And maybe she would finally stop taking responsibility for Nathan's faults and failures. Maybe she would finally start demanding more for herself and her daughter, and believing, really believing—not just clinging to some unlikely bright side—that she was going to get a happy ending. Maybe she'd damn well make her own.

The next few days passed in an unhappy blur. No word from Oliver, and Ellie decided not to text him again. Her days at work passed with agonizing slowness, and she checked her phone every few minutes, the ping of an incoming text filling her with hope before she deflated once again.

On Thursday Lady Stokeley returned to Willoughby Manor, and Ellie went to visit her after work, letting herself in since she knew she was still laid up in bed.

"Forgive my appearance," Lady Stokeley said when Ellie poked her head into the bedroom. "Pneumonia quite takes it out of one when one reaches my age."

"You look pretty good to me," Ellie said with a smile. Lady Stokeley was wearing a satin nightgown and a matching lacy bed jacket. Her skin looked pale, and there were dark smudges under her eyes that were as bright as ever. Ellie placed a plate of home-baked cookies on the bedside table. "No shop-bought macaroons," she said, and Lady Stokeley gave her a small smile.

"So," she began without preamble, "Abby has told me something of your conundrum."

"Has she?" Ellie had told Abby she didn't know where things stood with Oliver, and left it at that. "I didn't think she'd seen you since you returned from hospital."

Lady Stokeley waved a regal, beringed hand. "We've messaged on Instagram."

Ellie choked back a startled laugh. "Wow. Well. I guess Abby has an account now."

Lady Stokeley cocked her head. "So what has happened between you and your Oxford professor?" she asked.

And somehow, against all reason, Ellie found herself telling all of it—the romance, the visit to Endsleigh House, his parents' scorn, his ominous silence.

"He hasn't sent so much as a text, and I think I know why," she finished with a sniff. "It's over."

Lady Stokeley was silent for a long moment. Ellie fished a crumpled tissue from her coat pocket and dabbed at her eyes.

"I was married to my husband for thirty-one years," Lady Stokeley said after a moment. "And the whole time I had to keep reminding myself that he was still a little boy inside. All men are, but especially men from privileged backgrounds. They never get a chance to be children, you see. And so they keep it all inside."

Ellie stared at her in confusion. "What are you saying?"

"I'm saying this professor of yours brought you to the place where he felt the most vulnerable, where he had the worst memories. And you saw him at his weakest and most fearful, and he knew it. And then your ex-husband showed up—quite unfortunate timing, really—and played on all his insecurities. And so he left, because it felt easier than waiting for you to reject him to his face." Lady Stokeley sat back, her knobby, beringed hands folded over the bedcovers. "So the question you must ask yourself, my dear, is if he's worth fighting for."

IT WAS RAINING in Yorkshire. Icy, sleeting rain that reminded Ellie of her arrival in Wychwood-on-Lea. Just as before, she hunched over the steering wheel, peering through the fogged-up windscreen. She really needed to fix the defrost on her car.

She'd left Oxford right after work and driven straight through. Abby and Marmite were staying at the Langs—it seemed, improbably, that some sort of semi-friendship had sprung up between Mallory and Abby, and Ellie had had a surprising heart-to-heart with Harriet, which had provided at least part of the impetus for getting in the car and driving up here.

And so here she was, free and determined, her heart in

her mouth, navigating narrow roads, searching for Oliver. Jeannie had, with a smile and a wink, told her where he was staying, at a little country hotel near Leeds, apparently to do research on child factory workers in the area during Victorian times. Now if only she could find the place. And then think of what to say, and then work up the courage to say it.

Suddenly the hotel loomed out of the darkness-a low, rambling building of whitewashed stone. Ellie slammed on the brakes, tires squealing across wet pavement as her life and all its fragile hopes flashed through her eyes. Then she managed to right the car and with a shaky breath pulled into the hotel's car park. Now to find Oliver.

The front door opened directly into a sitting room with tartan-patterned chairs arranged around an open fire. It was cozy if a bit dated; the carpet was done in a different tartan than the chairs, and a third was on the walls. Ellie blinked, struggling not to go cross-eyed at all the competing plaid.

"May I help?" The friendly Yorkshire accent of the young woman at reception was a balm to Ellie's battered soul. It was ten o'clock on a rainy March night and she needed some help to make this happen.

"Yes, I'm looking for Oliver Venables. He checked in a few days ago, to room four?"

"Yes, of course."

"Is he here now…?"

"Yes…"

Relief poured through her. "Would you mind if I went

right up?" Ellie gave her an embarrassed smile. "I want to surprise him…"

"Of course." The woman smiled back, all innocent complicity. "I'm sure he'll be thrilled."

Let's hope so, Ellie thought as she made for the stairs.

Thirty seconds later she was standing in front of room four, her shaking hand poised to knock. Everything rested on this moment. Everything rested on the next few moments, when she saw Oliver and put her heart on the line, into his hands. What would he do with it?

There were no guarantees, Ellie knew. No promises. But she knew that if she didn't take this risk she'd regret it forever. She'd lived life safely for too long. She'd worked too hard for the wrong things, poured her energy and her emotion and her hope into something she'd known in her heart wasn't ever going to work. And even if this didn't work, even if Oliver said it was over, she knew—or at least she really, really hoped—that she'd be glad she tried.

Resolutely she knocked on the door.

"Coming," Oliver called, his voice sounding muffled, making Ellie wonder if she'd interrupted him getting out of the bath or something equally awkward. That would certainly be typical of their entire relationship.

He opened the door, still putting one arm through the sleeve of his t-shirt, revealing a glimpse of toned abs before he pulled his shirt down, gaping at her.

"Ellie…"

"Hey." Her face felt like a plateful of jelly, her smile wobbling all over the place. "So I decided to come and see where you were hiding."

He stiffened, making Ellie's heart sink. "I'm not hiding. I'm doing research."

"Without telling me where you were going? Or even saying goodbye?" The words were out of her mouth before she could stop them. This was not how she'd wanted to start this reconciliation. She was picking a fight when she wanted to be chasing rainbows.

Oliver, at least, had the grace to look abashed. "I'm sorry, I should have said something. I thought you'd be... busy."

"You mean with Nathan."

"Yes." He lifted his chin like someone about to take a punch. "Are you back together?"

"No."

"But you thought about it."

His emotional astuteness surprised her. "Yes," she admitted. "Because he's my child's father and I've always doubted myself and worried about what's best for Abby." She took a deep breath. "May I come in?"

Wordlessly Oliver stepped aside. As Ellie moved past him she inhaled the achingly familiar scent of his aftershave and nearly wept. Her knees were literally knocking and so she sat down in the only chair in the room, a plaid armchair that battled with the bedspread. Oliver perched on the edge of the bed. Ellie couldn't tell anything from his expression.

"I sent Nathan home on Monday," she said. "He slept on the sofa after making an appeal for us to get back together. And I realized I didn't want him in my life." Ellie took another deep breath; soon she'd be hyperventilating. "I want you in my life, Oliver. But maybe you don't want to be there."

Oliver didn't answer for a long moment, an endless moment, and now Ellie *was* hyperventilating. This risk taking business was *hard*.

"I do want to be there," he said quietly. "Of course I do. But I didn't think you did."

"Why would you think that?"

"Because of the horrendous weekend, and my horrendous parents, and the fact that I acted like an arse the whole time." Oliver tried to smile and let out a shuddering sigh instead. "I reverted to form. I became the worst version of myself and I hated it, and I figured you were starting to hate me too."

Ellie felt a lump starting to form in her throat. "I could never hate you, Oliver."

"I'm sorry I brought you home. I wanted you to be there for my sake, because facing my parents and the anniversary of Jamie's death are two things I dread. But I should have realized it was going to go pear-shaped. And it did."

"It doesn't matter. Well, it matters a little bit," Ellie amended. "Your parents aren't thrilled with me, I know..."

"I couldn't care less about their opinion. What matters is

you and me." He rose from the bed, coming forward to take her hands. "I know I've cocked a lot of things up, Ellie, but the truth is I love you. I should have said it before. I should have done so many things differently." He squeezed her hands. "I came here because I wanted to give you space to make a decision and yes, because I couldn't face seeing you with someone else. But I haven't stopped thinking about you, loving you, and hoping and praying that you might love me back, at least a little, dunderhead that I am."

Ellie laughed, tears of happiness stinging her eyes. "I do love you, you dunderhead."

"Those," Oliver assured her as he drew her towards him for a kiss, "are the sweetest words I've ever heard."

Epilogue

One year later

"YOU LOOK VERY dashing," Ellie said, smiling, and Oliver grinned back at her and rolled his eyes.

They were standing in front of Blackwell's, Oxford's biggest bookshop, and the newly released *The Victorian Child: Icon, Innocent, or Ignored?* was on prominent display in the shop window, along with a glossy A2 photo of Oliver.

"Very distinguished," Ellie continued teasingly, squeezing his hand. Oliver shook his head.

"I don't see BBC knocking on my door to do the next television series."

"But you wouldn't want that, anyway," Ellie answered. "Would you? Away from home for weeks or months at a time?"

They started strolling down the sun-dappled street. "No, I wouldn't. I'm happy just where I am."

And so was she. The last year had been one of incredible joys, as she and Oliver had deepened their relationship. Over the summer she'd brought him back to Manchester to meet her family, and to her gratification they'd all been impressed. Diane had even given her a discreet thumbs up, and her parents had seemed genuinely pleased.

Ellie had started to accept that her parents had her best interests at heart, even if it didn't always feel like it, and their relationship had begun to improve. Nathan had tried to step up more, and had taken Abby camping over the autumn half-term, but with Oliver in their lives, her daughter needed him less, which was a good thing since he'd been talking about moving to New Zealand.

In September Abby had started at the comp with Tobias, and the two were near inseparable. Mallory was hanging around more, too, and the miracle Ellie had been looking for—that her daughter would make friends—had happened in full, even if it hadn't been quite the way she'd expected.

Ellie had started taking some evening courses in marketing, and was toying with the idea of opening her own shop. There had been some sorrows too, of varying degrees, but they'd weathered them all and now Willoughby Close had all four cottages occupied.

And in just two months' time, Ellie and Oliver were going to get married in Wychwood-on-Lea's little parish church, and then Oliver would move into Number One, Willoughby Close with her and Abby, and Marmite of course.

They'd discussed who should move where, but really there had been no question for either of them. Willoughby

Close was where they both belonged.

Smiling, Ellie tugged on Oliver's hand. "Come on," she said. "Let's go home."

The End

The Willoughby Close series

Discover the lives and loves of the residents of Willoughby Close

The four occupants of Willoughby Close are utterly different and about to become best friends, each in search of her own happy ending as they navigate the treacherous waters of modern womanhood in the quirky yet beautiful village of Wychwood-on-Lea, nestled in the English Cotswolds...

Book 1: *A Cotswold Christmas*

Book 2: *Meet Me at Willoughby Close*

Book 3: *Find me at Willoughby Close*

Book 4: *Kiss Me at Willoughby Close*

Book 5: *Marry Me at Willoughby Close*

Available now at your favorite online retailer!

About the Author

After spending three years as a diehard New Yorker, **Kate Hewitt** now lives in a small town in Wales with her husband, their five children, and a Golden Retriever.

She writes women's fiction as well as contemporary romance under the name Kate Hewitt, and whatever the genre she enjoys delivering a compelling and intensely emotional story.

You can find out more about Kate on her website at kate-hewitt.com.

If

gre

Made in the USA
Monee, IL
16 October 2022

15987102R00204

About the Author

After spending three years as a diehard New Yorker,
Kate Hewitt now lives in a small town in Wales with her
husband, their five children, and a Golden Retriever.

She writes women's fiction as well as contemporary romance
under the name Kate Hewitt, and whatever the genre she enjoys
delivering a compelling and intensely emotional story.

You can find out more about Kate on her website
at kate-hewitt.com.

Thank you for reading

Meet Me at Willoughby Close

If you enjoyed this book, you can find more from all our great authors at TulePublishing.com, or from your favorite online retailer.

TULE
PUBLISHING